THE
GEMINI
EFFECT

CHUCK GROSSART

THE
GEMINI
EFFECT

47N⬥RTH

Published by 47North, Seattle

www.apub.com

Amazon, the Amazon logo, and 47North are trademarks of Amazon.com, Inc., or its affiliates.

ISBN-13: 9781477820452
ISBN-10: 1477820450

Cover design by Cyanotype Book Architects

Library of Congress Control Number: 2014912873

Printed in the United States of America

To Nessa

Protocol for the Prohibition of the Use in War of Asphyxiating, Poisonous or Other Gases, and of Bacteriological Methods of Warfare

(The Geneva Protocol of 1925)

The undersigned Plenipotentiaries, in the name of their respective governments: Whereas the use in war of asphyxiating, poisonous or other gases, and of all analogous liquids, materials or devices, has been justly condemned by the general opinion of the civilized world; and whereas the prohibition of such use has been declared in Treaties to which the majority of Powers of the world are Parties; and to the end that this prohibition shall be universally accepted as a part of International Law, binding alike the conscience and practice of nations . . .

Entered into Force February 8, 1928
Ratification Advised by United States Senate December 16, 1974
Proclaimed by the President of the United States April 29, 1975

Convention on the Prohibition of the Development, Production and Stockpiling of Bacteriological (Biological) and Toxin Weapons and on Their Destruction

(1972 Biological and Toxin Weapons Convention)

The States Parties to this Convention, determined to act with a view to achieving effective progress towards general and complete disarmament, including the prohibition and elimination of all types of weapons of mass destruction, and convinced that the prohibition of the development, production and stockpiling of chemical and bacteriological (biological) weapons and their elimination, through effective measures, will facilitate the achievement of general and complete disarmament under strict and effective international control . . .

United States
Signed April 10, 1972
Ratified March 26, 1975

Soviet Union
Signed April 10, 1972
Ratified March 26, 1975

Entered into Force March 26, 1975

THE FIRST NIGHT

CHAPTER 1

The extermination of the human race began in a salvage yard.

Under the left rear fender of what remained of a 1962 Chevrolet Nova, to be exact. A rusted shell of what was once called a Chevy II—a "Deuce" to those who loved them—built at the old Kansas City GM Leeds assembly plant during the last week of November 1961. *Wagon Train* was America's favorite TV show in the winter of '61. On the radio, Jimmy Dean's "Big Bad John" replaced Dion's "Runaround Sue" at the top of the Hit Parade. Roger Maris, Mickey Mantle, and the rest of the New York Yankees had won their nineteenth World Series by beating the Cincinnati Reds 13–5 in game five.

The world turned, counting down.

In the weeks and months before Chevy's newest grocery getter rolled off the assembly line, the world witnessed Berlin split in two by concrete barricades and concertina wire, and heard news of a 58-megaton Soviet nuclear device—Царь-бомба, the Tsar

Bomb—detonated over the Novaya Zemlya archipelago in the Arctic Ocean. Eleven months later, grainy reconnaissance photos of Soviet missile sites in Cuba would take the world to the brink of nuclear annihilation.

Dallas crowds stood dumbstruck less than two years after the Deuce left the showroom floor, as American innocence slipped away in the back of a '61 Lincoln Continental. A big-eared Texas politician, standing next to a woman in a bloodstained pink Chanel suit, put his hand on a Bible, took the helm of history in his well-washed hands, and slithered full speed ahead toward Southeast Asia to keep all the dominoes from falling.

The Nova was built in a time of war—a cold war. The fear was real then, under the skin, every moment of every day. Like two bullies on the block vying for dominance, a brawl between the opposing forces was a foregone conclusion; it would happen, eventually. Maybe tomorrow. Or even today.

It was an era of calculated risks and strategic brinkmanship by two great powers, each holding a uranium-edged blade to the other's throat. Missiles sat at the ready in buried coffins and silos, armed bombers lined the ramps, and alert crews awaited the Klaxon's scream.

MAD was the acronym of the times: mutually assured destruction, the ultimate catch-22 of the twentieth century. They kill us, we kill them. When the missiles launched and the bombers flew, even the most steadfast warriors on either side knew there'd be no victory parades.

Scientists designed the city-killing bombs, but they'd also built smaller weapons, engineered to be just as deadly, and in some ways, even more destructive. *Virulence* and *infectivity* supplanted *blast* and *radiation* in the killing lexicon. Careful planning and controlled employment of these tiny weapons would render the MAD game obsolete. There'd be a winner, *and* a loser.

The research had been promising—and productive—until it escaped from a clean room.

In a '62 Deuce.

CHAPTER 2

The Nova's trunk, shut for years as the car silently rusted away in the salvage yard, had sprung open when another wrecked car was dropped on its roof. The old Chevy had leaned toward the passenger side for nearly two decades, and now the driver's side drooped down. Just a few degrees of movement, but it was enough.

It'd been raining steadily since that day, now a week past.

The rain, each drop carrying tiny particles of toxic garbage continuously pumped into the atmosphere, pooled in the low areas of the trunk. In short order, the corrosive filth—a stew of many ingredients—slowly began to eat through the exposed steel.

One particular ingredient, however, made the crucial difference. By itself, the man-made agent was simply horrid. Combined with just the right amount of other things, mixed for just the right amount of time, it became incomprehensively hellish.

Mother Nature was funny that way. Complex. Unpredictable.

And unforgiving as hell if you fucked around with her.

• • •

The events of this night had been set in motion years before, with an escape, a bullet, and a mistake. On the Nova's last trip, its driver had been murdered, his killers following the voices in their heads screaming at them to kill, to run, instead of following their specific instructions to find the car, secure the passenger, and return with him where he could be quarantined . . . and, of course, studied, for as long as he remained alive.

Contact, and resulting exposure, soon changed their plans.

Their protective suits had been mistakenly equipped with the incorrect filter, allowing the aggressive contagion to enter their bloodstreams and instantly ravage their sanity.

After killing the frenzied driver with a single bullet to the head, and six or seven more to his neck, chest, and legs as their own diseased frenzy began to build, they stuffed the driver's bullet-riddled body in the Nova's trunk and left the infected corpse to bake in the New Mexico summer heat. They drove west, escaping whatever threats their fevered minds had fabricated in their quickly twisting consciousnesses, only to meet an abrupt end against a bridge abutment fifteen miles away. Luck—in the form of an exploding gas tank—had been on mankind's side that day.

Over the next three days, the inside of the abandoned Nova's trunk became a sauna of stinking rot and bile as dead flesh swelled and burst in the intense heat, the ruined body spilling its macabre contents to congeal on the floor.

A frantic search, now involving nearly a hundred people flushed from classified agencies to cover an expanded four-state area, ended suddenly with an intercepted radio transmission over the police net. An abandoned car had been found, sitting two hundred yards off Interstate 40 near tiny Manuelito, New Mexico. With a body in the trunk.

In less than an hour, the state police became onlookers as others arrived to take over their crime scene. People in white suits and masks.

They were there to hide an unfortunate mistake, to erase the evidence.

To keep a secret, a secret.

The car was quickly taken to a salvage yard in another state—ironically, the same state where it'd been built—and the paper trail of its history thoroughly expunged. The Chevy would meet its fate in a glowing smelter of molten steel, the last bit of evidence turned into a shiny set of stainless flatware.

But the car wasn't immediately destroyed as planned. A '63 Nova had taken its place in the smelter, similar enough in appearance to the '62 it just happened to be sitting next to that the crane operator selected it instead, an honest mistake, which condemned his two grandchildren—not yet born—to a horrific death at the hands of something he couldn't even begin to comprehend.

. . .

For twenty years, the Nova sat in a far corner of the yard, useable parts stripped away occasionally until only a shell remained. But within the shell, within the empty trunk, an echo of the body it once held still lingered. It was an echo of the damned, hiding in the crevices, between plates of rusty steel. Waiting. Living. And now, with the rain adding a special twist to the mix, mutating.

Nature had been fucked with. And Mother was pissed.

CHAPTER 3

Rats prowled the salvage yard, scurrying from junk heap to junk heap, searching for anything to quell their endless hunger or add to their nests of assorted garbage. Underneath the Chevy, a single rat crept toward the left rear wheel, having spied a shiny piece of foil sticking out of the mud. For the rat, the piece of trash was a treasure; for humanity, however, it represented an end of things, for at the same instant, the Nova's trunk began to leak, the pool of muck inside having finally eaten a hole in the rusted steel large enough to pass through. Just one drop at a time.

The rat sat on its haunches, holding the silvery gum wrapper in its forepaws, small, beady eyes examining the find. A moment before it scurried away with its booty, a single drop from the trunk landed on its back. Just one drop. The effect was nearly instantaneous. The other rats scattered, spooked by the sudden commotion.

A large Rottweiler tied to a fencepost at the far end of the salvage yard pricked its ears up and growled, but only for a second. The sound, the terrible screeching, caused the dog to cower against the yard's security fence and whimper like a scared pup.

Beneath the car, the rat lay on its back, legs kicking furiously, clawing at the air, a high-pitched squeal escaping its open maw, much too loud to be produced by its tiny lungs. Its head lolled from side to side and its tongue flapped about like a meaty whip. Beneath the rat's coarse hair, bones were snapping, rearranging, fusing. Muscles were flexing, ripping, building. Cells ruptured and then re-formed. DNA strands resequenced, and resequenced again. Something was being born, at the same time something else was dying.

The rodent's violent struggles suddenly ceased, and it lay deathly still.

All that could be heard in the salvage yard was the staccato tap-tapping of the rain against rusty steel, the broken snare drum thuds of water droplets hitting the mud.

Quiet. For a time.

Just the sound of rain.

Other rats crept from their hiding places, sure that whatever had startled them was gone, and it was safe to forage once again. Moving slowly, a rat crept toward its fallen comrade, which would make a fine meal for it and a few others. Sniffing the air, it sensed no danger and drew closer. Perching itself against the soft underbelly of its meal, it lowered its head for the first bite.

In a ravenous flurry of newly formed claws and teeth, the unsuspecting rat was torn to shreds, pieces of its body powerfully flung from underneath the Chevy and splashing into the mud, small crimson pools gathering around the shredded strands of brownish-red meat.

The other rats scattered, startled, but only for a moment. The smell of blood drew them closer.

A pair of bright yellow eyes peered out from under the old car. It could see them gathering, creeping nearer. Thick blood dripped from its new set of oversized fangs. Its rippling musculature quivered in anticipation, the restructured body tensed to strike.

Fifteen feet away, one of the rats gulped down a strand of bloody muscle from its shredded comrade, still warm and twitching in the mud.

At once, more unearthly screeching shattered the night.

And then, there were two. The pair moved quickly, biting, tearing, eating. Infecting.

Soon, there were six.

Then, fifty.

The wailing of the changeling rats filled the air with an eerie sound, a shrill screeching building in intensity with each new addition to the fold.

And then, all at once, as if triggered by an internal clock, each of the infected creatures began to convulse violently, snarling and wailing as they were seized by the next stage of their evolution.

Hides split. New legs burst forth from where there'd been none just moments before. Single heads became two.

The first furious doubling—one of many to occur in the next hour—had begun.

• • •

The Rottweiler clawed at the chain-link security fence, trying to scratch his way through the metal, as hundreds of pairs of glowing yellow eyes moved closer, bouncing across the darkness toward him.

The dog's whining abruptly ceased as the things covered him, tearing him to shreds with hundreds of razor-sharp fangs and claws, slicing and cutting in a feeding frenzy as quick and violent as a school of piranhas devouring a careless river animal.

The new things quickly escaped the confines of the salvage yard and began to spread, the killing sound building in intensity. Neighborhood dogs slung their tails between their legs and cowered in the corners of their yards, instinctively aware that something they couldn't possibly escape was coming.

Yard by yard, the frantic yelping of terrified pets was replaced with the muffled thunder of hundreds of tiny, powerful legs, and then by the sickening sound of flesh being ripped and torn. Outside the houses and inside.

The creatures moved as an unstoppable wave, killing and feeding, but in some cases simply biting, an infectious, vampire-like bite ensuring the growth of their new species, adding others to their numbers, both animal and human.

The killing wave grew in intensity as the things continued to double, again and again. Their numbers increased exponentially as they spread in a circular pattern from their point of origin in the salvage yard . . . five miles, ten, then fifteen, leaving nothing but death and an eerie silence in their wake.

The onslaught slowed as a blush to the east heralded the rising sun. The creatures flooded into the sewers, into Dumpsters, basements, into the dark places—any place to hide from the coming light of day.

As the first blazing arc of the sun broke the horizon, all grew quiet. In a nearly thirty-mile radius from the salvage yard in Kansas City, life had virtually been extinguished. But there was other life, *new* life, cowering silently in the shadows.

At the beginning of this night, thousands of people had crawled into their warm, snug beds, having no inkling whatsoever that by morning, they'd have fallen from being the ruling species of the planet to a step lower on the food chain. Some of them never woke up. Some did and realized, painfully, new kings of the jungle were on the prowl.

And the new kings were hungry.

DAY ONE

CHAPTER 4

Piercing screams, unnaturally loud, echoed through abandoned streets.

She was hurt. Badly.

In the course of his duties as a police officer, Officer Bob Knowlton had dealt with severely injured people before; he'd pulled mangled bodies—some dead, some not—from twisted and torn cages of steel on the highway more times than he could count, but he'd never seen anything quite like the screaming, bloody woman he now struggled to hold in his arms.

"Calm down, lady!" the officer pleaded. "Stay still! Stay *still*!" He fought to hold the woman steady as she thrashed against his grasp, trying with all her might to break free and get farther away from the building from which she'd stumbled seconds before, away from whatever had ravaged her body so savagely. From the look of her injuries, Knowlton thought the woman had been attacked by an animal, a big one at that, and it'd nearly torn her to pieces.

But, that's impossible . . . right?

Sheer horror was flowing from the woman's body like a pungent, acidic mist, seeping from every single pore. Knowlton could smell it, almost taste it, as if he'd popped a triple-A battery into his mouth and bitten through the casing.

The woman's eyes were wild, crazed, shining like two bright lamps of absolute terror. Blood gushed from a deep gash on her forehead and flowed freely down her face, soaking the neckline of her dress and cementing strands of her long blonde hair to her shoulders in pinkish, sticky swirls. Her dress was torn from shoulder to midsection, long parallel tears running down the fabric, crimson edged. A shredded stocking hung from her left leg, revealing hideous slashes running from thigh to calf, torn skin, and muscle dripping blood on the asphalt.

Stinging, bitter bile filled Knowlton's throat as he watched ropes of pinkish bowel begin to erupt from a yawning gash glimpsed beneath the torn remnants of the woman's dress, pushed from her belly with each terrified scream, with each struggle. *Oh Jesus and Mary I don't want to be seeing that . . . Quit moving! Oh God please quit moving.*

Her piercing screams suddenly became throaty, a low and mournful moaning, as she instinctively reached down to retrieve what was spooling from her body. As she did, Knowlton noticed part of her hand was missing. The thumb and index finger were all that remained above a thin gold watch circling her delicate wrist. The rest of her hand was gone . . . No, not just gone, it had been bitten off. *Bitten clean off!*

Swallowing a sudden mouthful of vomit, Knowlton took the woman's face in his hands and forced her to look up at him. "Tell me what did this to you!" he shouted, hoping to get some sort of information from her before she succumbed. Her eyes were sightless, rolling back in their sockets like two small ships starting to capsize. Her skin, slippery with blood, felt icy cold, shock and blood loss having taken their final toll. Knowlton looked up at his partner and exchanged a knowing glance. They both knew she was a goner.

As the woman mercifully went limp in his arms, he gently lowered her body to the pavement, trying to provide some sort of comfort to her as she died. There would be no EMTs arriving at the scene in time to save her. Not this morning, anyway. And even if there were, they wouldn't have been able to do anything. Knowlton was amazed she'd lived as long as she had.

After the woman's last breath escaped her lungs in a long, wheezing sigh, the street grew quiet again. Unnaturally so. All the normal noises of the city were absent. The air seemed flat, dead. All Knowlton heard was his own breathing, and the sound of his heart pounding away furiously in his chest. Knowlton suddenly felt very alone and vulnerable in the abandoned center of the city, with only his partner—and gun—for company.

The two officers looked into each other's eyes; both saw apprehension, both saw fear. The radio calls they'd heard all morning had been choppy, undisciplined. Frantic calls for help, for backup, had raced across the net. They'd heard reports of abandoned vehicles, empty streets, and shattered buildings . . . along with other things, similar to what they'd just experienced. Whatever was happening, it seemed to encompass the entire downtown area.

Knowlton stared at the smashed doors of the building from which the woman had emerged. Something was in there, he knew. Something terrible.

As he wiped the sticky blood from his hands onto his uniform trousers, Knowlton wanted nothing more than to run away, to get back into his cruiser and drive as far away from this place as he could, as fast as he could. His instincts were screaming at him to do just that, but he couldn't. He was a cop. No matter how scared he and his partner were, no matter how unbelievable this all seemed, one fact remained: they still had a job to do. To serve and protect.

Drawing his weapon with a trembling hand, Knowlton motioned toward the building and whispered to his partner, "Let's go take a look."

Both officers sprinted to the lobby entrance, taking positions on either side of the smashed doors. Broken glass crunched underfoot as they pressed themselves against the burnished brass door frame.

Peeking inside, Knowlton saw most of the lobby was illuminated by sunlight pouring in through huge plate glass windows, which formed the building's facade, but the rest of the interior was cloaked in shadows. The interior looked like a hurricane had swept through. Overturned furniture was scattered about and papers littered the marble floor, but what shocked him most was the stench. It was an animal smell, a dirty stink of something unclean, wafting through the shattered entrance. He'd grown up on a farm and had spent countless hours cleaning horse stalls, replacing dirty straw with fresh. Mice loved to nest in the hay, leaving intricate tunnels through the soiled straw, which he uncovered with his pitchfork. The stench coming from the building reminded him of the smell of mouse droppings in dirty hay, but this was stronger, much stronger. Glancing toward the rear of the lobby, he saw that the main hallway, extending toward the back of the building, was dark. The power was still on, as evidenced by the low hum of the ventilation system, but all the light fixtures had been smashed. Every single one of them. Knowlton tried to ignore what his gut was telling him. The lights had been smashed on purpose, by something—or some *things*— aware of what they were doing.

The main hallway looked like a darkened throat leading far back into the belly of the building, swallowing the light. For a few seconds, both officers stood still and listened. Nothing. No motion inside that they could hear. No motion they could see. They could hear themselves breathing.

From the south, a string of gunshots echoed. From a fellow officer? A citizen? Then, silence again.

With a nod of his head, Knowlton signaled his partner to enter the building, he himself following just a few steps behind. Both officers walked slowly across the lobby, sweeping their eyes, and weapons, from side to side.

They walked farther into the building, following the trail of blood on the marble floor left by the woman now lying dead in the street. Something was wrong—the air was wrong, the sounds were wrong. Something evil was here, hiding in the shadows, lurking menacingly at the back of the building's throat. The hair on the nape of Knowlton's neck stiffened, and tiny pinpricks of trepidation rippled up and down his spine. Knowlton couldn't shake the sudden feeling that he was being watched.

He stopped, crouched, and stared down the darkened hallway, trying to discern any detail. The focus of his right eye alternated between the three white dots on his 9mm's sights and the broken light fixtures hanging from the ceiling. Broken glass covered the hallway floor.

On the left side of the hallway, at the boundary of sunlight and shadow, he could see a bloody smear on the wall—a handprint leaving a long red trail to the floor below, like a painting of an outstretched arm, a hand reaching for help as its body is dragged back into the blackness.

Someone had died there. And it hadn't been pretty.

His mind was racing: *An animal did it, big animal no that's impossible but her wounds looked like a tiger had torn her apart but that can't happen . . .*

In unison, both officers flicked on their flashlights, pointing them in line with their weapons, illuminating where they'd shoot.

The dual beams of light flashed down the hallway, the small glass shards on the floor sparkling like diamonds.

The light revealed carnage.

Shoes. A couple of purses. A briefcase. What looked like a janitor's mop bucket? Items were strewn along the hallway, each lying near—or in—a pool of dark, thick redness. Many people had died here. Right where they stood. But there were no bodies.

"Jesus Christ!" Knowlton whispered, just loud enough for his partner to hear. A drop of ice-cold sweat trickled down his neck.

A whisper back. "I don't think Jesus had anything to do with this."

Suddenly, his instincts screamed at him—it was an odd feeling, coming out of nowhere, but incredibly strong. A feeling of impending danger. Turning toward his partner, Knowlton said simply, "I think we need to get out of here."

Before his partner could answer, the air was filled with an odd chattering sound, a clicking noise coming from the darkened hallway. Both officers immediately pointed their flashlights toward the far end of the hall, where it branched off into two perpendicular hallways, both out of view. There was nothing at the end of the hall. Nothing but the strange sounds.

"Do you hear that?" Knowlton asked. "What the hell?"

For a moment, as they faced each other, both officers lowered their flashlights, returning the hallway to darkness.

And then, they came.

The hallway erupted in an earsplitting roar, a bizarre chattering, a clicking, so sudden and intense that it slammed into the stunned police officers like a thunderclap, nearly knocking them off their feet. Knowlton grimaced with pain as needles of sound stabbed at his ears, the noise so indescribably loud that he could feel it reverberating deep within his chest.

As he stared down the hall through squinting, terrified eyes, all the inexplicable events he'd seen and heard that morning—the deserted city streets, the panicky radio calls, and the dead woman's horrific wounds—suddenly made perfect sense.

For a second, he didn't move. He didn't blink. Didn't breathe. Recoiling from the vision before him, Knowlton took a step backward as hundreds of yellow eyes, shining brightly like pinpoint flames, bounded toward them down the length of the darkened hallway, covering every inch of the floor, the walls, and the ceiling as they came, moving at an astonishing rate of speed. At that moment, he knew he was a dead man, just as dead as the woman outside on the street. These things had killed her. And they would kill him, too.

Adrenaline pumped wildly into his bloodstream. Everything began to move in slow motion.

As he reached for his pistol, Knowlton heard a sharp popping sound to his left as his partner began to fire, spent 9mm brass spinning through the air as he quickly emptied his clip.

Closer.

Fifteen yards.

The second hand on Knowlton's watch clicked forward another second, an eternity passing in a single mechanical action of delicately machined steel springs and interlocking gears.

Ten yards.

He wanted to shut his eyes, to avoid looking into the hurtling death that would slam into him in a matter of moments, but at the last instant he regained his senses. He aimed his own pistol and began to squeeze the trigger. Again. Again. And again. Aiming at the glowing eyes. There were so many of them!

His partner suddenly turned and ran toward the shattered entrance, a full clip of ammunition—never inserted into his weapon—bouncing on the floor, dropped when he'd made the snap decision to abandon his partner and run for his life.

As the things began to emerge from the shadows, Knowlton noticed the wave began to slow. He could see his targets more clearly and was shocked at what he saw—they were *rats*! Hundreds of them! But they weren't rats, were they? They couldn't be! They were huge! Clawed and fanged, muscles rippling under coarse hides covered with wire-like hair—no, these definitely weren't normal rats. They were an abomination.

Three of the things slid into the sunlight, their claws squeaking as they skidded across the marble floor, desperately trying to halt their momentum. Their mouths opened wide, revealing rows of knife-edged teeth framed by stiletto fangs.

Bathed by the sunlight now, they began to shriek.

They contorted their muscular bodies, squirming on the floor like animals crushed under the wheels of a truck, enduring a few seconds of absolute misery on the asphalt before life mercifully slipped away.

The rest of the things piled upon one another, just at the boundary of light and shadow. They formed a living, screeching wall, each vicious yellow-eyed beast tossing long strings of saliva from a snarling mouth, each bright eye fixed on the prey that stood just feet away. So close. But they would come no farther.

Two of the creatures slowly clawed their way back toward the pack. They were pulled into the undulating wall in a flurry of claws and fangs, and torn to shreds. The weak providing sustenance for the strong.

The third one was stronger. The incredible hunger was too great for this one. In spite of the pain, it continued. It had to. It knew nothing else.

With a last burst of strength, it pounced.

Knowlton screamed and fell to his knees as the creature's fangs entered his left thigh, cutting through nearly to the bone. He instinctively reached down with his free hand to grab at his attacker, but it was attached to his leg like a vise. Panicky, he swatted at the thing, trying desperately to break its grip on his thigh, but it was too strong.

Knowlton remembered his gun. He aimed carefully, but found it hard to focus. His eyes—there was something wrong with his eyes! He tried to pull the trigger, but stared in disbelief as his weapon dropped from his right hand, which to his horror was contorted into a clawed club of swollen joints and crooked bones, perched at the end of what was now an oddly curved forearm. He grabbed the gun from the floor with his left hand and squeezed the trigger. A single shot tore into the thing's head, splattering gore across the floor. It dropped from his thigh and thudded to the floor, a foamy ring of blood covering its snout. His blood. He tried to kick his legs to scoot away, but suddenly realized they weren't working. His arms weren't working, either! His limbs felt like they were on fire!

He watched helplessly as his arms and legs kicked and flailed about wildly, as if he were a marionette being danced about the stage by a crazed puppeteer. He heard the loud snap of bones breaking as his legs zigzagged in the air like a child's crude drawing of a lightning bolt.

The changeling fury moved up his body toward his head, turning his lower torso into a quivering mass of vibrating muscle and greasy, twisting viscera. His entire body was racked by unimaginable pain, a sledgehammer of flame searing every fiber of his being. He tried to scream, but his lungs were no longer functioning.

In his last few moments of sentient thought, he felt as if he were being torn apart from the inside out, exploding in a million different directions at once. A big, bloody Fourth of July firework at the end of the show. Burning out. Ceasing to exist. And then, there was blackness.

An end of things.

Transformation.

Then, a beginning of things.

When the eyes opened again, they burned like two small super-novae in the vile brightness, the hellish face contorted into a grimace of extreme pain. What had been a police officer a few minutes earlier quickly hobbled on newly restructured legs into the shadows of the hallway, long clawed hands shielding its yellow eyes from the light. The ratlike killing machines parted as it walked among them, like an army breaking ranks for a passing general. With the others, it waited in the darkness. Soon, night would fall . . . the time to hunt. To run. To feed.

CHAPTER 5

A little over a thousand miles to the east of Kansas City, the day had begun as countless others before it, the events unfolding in the Show-Me State not yet realized by those scurrying through the halls of government in Washington, DC, as the nation's bureaucracy began to churn through another day of obliquely serving the citizenry.

For one man, it was the start of another seemingly interminable day in the Big Chair.

He tossed his morning briefing papers to the corner of the Resolute Desk and turned his chair to face the thick windows that framed the back of his office, taking a brief moment to turn his mind away from the heavy load he was already feeling. Outside, a shifting patchwork of moisture-laden clouds hung low in the sky, the heavy slabs of mist quickly gathering together to conceal what little blue sky had been visible earlier, teasing him with the chance of a bright, sunny day. Sighing, he peered through the trees as a lone ray of sunlight faded away from behind the top of the distant Washington Monument, the slate-gray sky now completely matching his mood.

All the great men who'd sat in this office—made decisions that changed the course of history, sent thousands of people to their deaths, or provided a helping hand to those in need during times of strife—always seemed larger than life to him. And yet, here he was, sitting in their office.

His office, now.

Andrew Smith had never viewed politics as a worthwhile profession, but after his retirement from the United States Navy, he found he wanted—no, needed—to serve his country in another capacity. After all, old habits die hard. His name was familiar enough; the pictures in *Time* magazine of a bloodstained admiral dragging the dead and injured from a burning building after a massive terrorist attack, himself badly injured from burns and shrapnel, had made him an instant hero in the eyes of most Americans.

Hero—a word he hated having associated with his name, but it hadn't hurt at all on the campaign trail. People knew who he was, and more importantly, knew *what* he was. He had character. He was brave. On top of that, although he'd never admit it himself, he had the looks for it; he struck a commanding pose, standing a little over six foot four, his broad shoulders and lean waist indicative of a steadfast attention to physical fitness during his years in the naval service. He was never one to succumb to the excessive vanity suffered by most politicians, and his silver-gray hair celebrated his age, which created an almost grandfatherly persona, making him a wise, comforting figure the American people could trust. Most notable, however, were his intense steel-blue eyes, full of clear purpose and sincerity. A majority of voters had decided he was the right man for a wrong time, and they'd placed him here in the White House to make a difference. To save the Republic from the ash heap of history.

To win a war.

For years, Andrew Smith had watched thousands of his fellow citizens slaughtered around the globe, for no other reason than they were Americans. The economy had faltered horribly, struck here and there by well-planned terrorist strikes that'd had more effect than a stadium full of economic experts could've possibly predicted in their worst business school nightmares. The nation had been struck overseas, struck at home, on American soil, in big cities and small towns. Recession and inflation were once again household terms, spoken more often than anyone cared to hear, and unemployment was at near-record levels. The big *D* word—*depression*—was lurking just around the corner. All this now sat squarely in his lap.

At first, he'd been elected a state governor. Then, after time, appointed secretary of state. And now, after what seemed like a wild roller coaster ride of campaigns, fund-raising, and heartache, Andrew Smith was president of the United States.

During the normal course of his day, he rarely had moments to himself. Government agencies needed him; foreign dignitaries, lobbyists, representatives, and senators needed him; state governors, local county governments, and the party needed him; the people needed him. Sometimes, it felt as if hundreds of steel cables were hooked into his skin, each pulling in a different direction, with no way for him to know which cables were pulling toward something worthwhile, and which cables would just tear out and leave nasty scars if their pull was resisted long enough.

In ten minutes, his first meeting of the day was scheduled to start. Ten short minutes to savor, to watch the first drops of rain begin to fall, and to be alone with his thoughts. Time to ponder where he'd been, where he wanted to go—where he wanted the nation to go—and time to wish that somehow things had turned out differently so he didn't have to do it alone.

His moment of peace was shattered as Jessica Hruska, the national security advisor, and Marshall Stone, the secretary of defense, rushed into the Oval Office, with the secretary of Homeland Security, Hugo McIntyre, in tow. This was far from normal protocol for Andrew Smith's Oval Office. No one ever burst in unannounced, and if they did, they'd better have a damned good reason.

When Jessie Hruska spoke, her voice steeled with purpose and her eyes shining with immediacy, Andrew knew her reason would be more than sufficient.

"Mr. President," she said, "we have a situation. It's Kansas City."

• • •

Ten minutes later, alone again in the Oval Office, Andrew tried to digest what he'd just been told. It wasn't easy.

He'd given the necessary orders his advisors needed to get the ball rolling: investigate . . . find out exactly what was happening, control public panic, mobilize whatever elements of state and federal forces needed to be activated to bring him options in the next hour for the best manner to proceed. At this point, he knew that's all he could do. Although it was frustrating, he had to sit back and let the massive apparatus that was the United Sates government spin up to handle the situation, let other people do the jobs they were trained to do. In another hour, he hoped the situation would have enough clarity for action. Correct action. And then, he would do *his* job. Set a course of action and lead.

As he stared across the office at a favorite portrait of Harry Truman, the situation he'd been presented with continued to tumble through his mind: a whole city, with possibly hundreds, if not thousands dead and missing! How could it possibly be true? Could it be some sort of terrorist attack? Could someone have been able to dream up a weapon that would do this? Was it a weapon, or something else?

Give 'Em Hell Harry just stared right back. *Make the right call, Mr. President,* Truman seemed to say from the canvas. *And don't ever forget the buck stops with you.*

24

• • •

The directors of the Central Intelligence Agency, the National Security Agency, the Federal Bureau of Investigation, the National Guard Bureau, and the Red Cross all received calls within fifteen minutes.

A well-greased wheel began to turn, driven by the necessity of quick reaction to any unknown, rapidly unfolding situation. The nation had learned the hard way that a delayed reaction to a crisis could spell disaster. Every minute wasted meant more dead citizens. It was a simple equation.

As each of the directors hung up their secure phones, they all turned their thoughts to Kansas City and immediately issued orders through their chains.

Analyze—get people on the ground as soon as possible. Figure out exactly what the hell was going on.

Listen—grab every electron in the air and thoroughly wash it for information. If anyone's talking, open up the big ears and listen.

Activate—contact the governors. Start at the top of the recall rosters and get the guardsmen moving. Get ready to federalize.

Prepare—check the blood supplies. Get medical personnel and relief supplies ready to roll.

Move!

The wheel was turning. It was a well-practiced procedure, refined over time and surprisingly effective. This was no longer the America of Norman Rockwell—this was an America that had been sucker punched a few too many times, learned to react, to bob and weave, and to hit back with one hell of a right cross.

Each of the directors took a moment to reflect on exactly what they'd heard just minutes before. It sounded incredible! How could an American city be nearly wiped clean of hundreds, if not thousands of people? Who was responsible for such a heinous act? How was it done? Was it over, or was it just beginning?

As they mulled over these unanswerable questions, a single, chilling statement from the national security advisor stuck in their minds . . .

"There's something in the city," she'd said. "Some *things*."

CHAPTER 6

At that same moment, eleven hundred miles to the west of Kansas City, Carolyn Ridenour stared intently at her computer screen, engrossed by a stream of numbers parading across her flat panel display.

To the untrained eye, the data stream was just a jumbled mess of figures, but to Carolyn, the numbers were speaking to her in a language only a few could understand, telling her the results of the tests she'd been running on the contents of a single business-sized envelope whose recipient had discovered, much to their horror, was filled with a white powdery substance and a poorly spelled note predicting the "End of amrican Imperlism!" It'd arrived at her facility at about 5:00 a.m., after a supersonic trip from Washington, DC, on board an Air Force fighter jet, and she'd been working on it ever since. "That's it," she whispered. "Come on, baby, show me . . ."

Lieutenant Josh Ewing, sitting next to Carolyn in front of a matching set of screens, turned his head to face her, a mischievous glint in his eyes. "Carolyn," he said, "I don't mind being called 'baby' . . . I kinda like it, actually . . . but show you? Right now? In here? Might be a little tough, but if you insist, I can make it happen."

Carolyn grinned, but never took her eyes off the screen. "In your dreams, Josh. I definitely don't want to see *that*."

"Okay, fine. I can dream, though, can't I?"

"Sure, you can dream," she said, shaking her head. "Just keep me out of them, okay?"

He let five whole seconds pass. "It won't bite."

"Josh!" she said, laughing. "I'm trying to concentrate here!"

"I can't help it, Carolyn!" he said, his voice full of feigned exasperation. "You have no idea what it's like for a horny young stud like me to find some action in Salt Lake City, of all places."

Carolyn was pretty sure Josh's dream woman was more of a blond, busty ex-NFL cheerleader than a self-described brainiac like herself, but in another time, in another place, she knew she could be attracted to a man like Josh. He was young, smart, and good-looking, but she wasn't about to jeopardize her work by allowing herself to become involved in some sort of silly office romance. She, and Josh, too, for that matter, needed to stay focused. Lives depended on the work they were doing. Many lives. But she wasn't so cold as to avoid some innocent flirting. In fact, she quite enjoyed it, because it provided a break from the constant pressure.

"You're right, Josh," Carolyn said, with the smokiest voice she could muster. She turned toward him, smiled, and lightly placed her hand on his thigh. She also let five whole seconds pass, watching the confusion build in his eyes until she couldn't keep a straight face any longer. She patted his leg and giggled. "I have no idea what it's like to be a horny young stud." Turning back to her screen, she added, "You need to get out more, LT. Sow some of your wild oats."

Before Josh could respond, Carolyn's screen announced the results of the tests she'd been running with a muted beep. "Hah!" she exclaimed. "I knew it!"

Josh leaned over from his station to take a look. "So, is it ricin? Anthrax? Or something really horrible . . . Lead-based paint chips from a baby crib, maybe?"

Carolyn tore the readout from the printer, a little disgusted with the amount of time it had taken to get the results she expected all along. In the old days she could've analyzed the envelope's contents in a matter of minutes, but ever since some of the bad guys had ingeniously learned to mask substances like ricin and anthrax with harmless, nonhazardous compounds, or sometimes even with illegal drugs, she now had to go through a much more painstaking process that could take hours to complete. The obvious answer, reached after a quick initial analysis, could be completely wrong, and the results deadly. The battery of tests was necessary, but in this case, a wasted effort. "Well, you're close, Josh," she answered, handing him the printout. "It's a mixture of some pretty horrible stuff."

"Cocaine?" Josh said, reading the computer's analysis.

"Yep. High quality, at that. Cut with powdered sugar."

"So," Josh said, tossing the readout onto the counter, "not only do we have an idiot who tries to scare the hell out of someone with an envelope full of fake anthrax, we have an idiot drug dealer?"

Carolyn nodded. "Or a druggie who ran short of powdered sugar and used what else he had around the house." She held up a plastic baggie containing the suspect anthrax letter and wiggled it in front of Josh's faceplate. "This, Lieutenant Joshua K. Ewing, fellow Dugway Proving Ground Federal Penitentiary inmate, can get back on a plane and head to FBI headquarters. Hopefully they can lift some prints and get this asshole. He ruined my morning." She tossed the baggie to Josh. "I'm going to head upstairs. I didn't have a chance to grab any coffee when I got called in this morning, and I have a splitting headache."

"Caffeine's highly addictive," Josh said, dropping the baggie into a transport pouch, which would soon be on its way to the J. Edgar Hoover Building for the fibbies to play with. "Need your fix, huh?"

Carolyn huffed into her helmet microphone. "Yes, I need my *fix*. Maybe I'll just grab a needle and shoot some java right into my bloodstream." The booties of her protective biohazard suit made scuffing noises as she walked across the stark white floor toward the sealed chamber's exit portal.

As Josh watched her leave, he imagined he could peer beyond Carolyn's biosuit and spy the gorgeous form within, her hips swaying with each stride of her deeply tanned legs, brunette hair bouncing about her bare shoulders, and her—

Carolyn mashed the chamber's exit button. A high-decibel buzzer screamed a warning that the clean room was no longer secure. From the ceiling, a series of rotating beacons splashed red light across unnaturally white walls. Every computer screen in the facility instantly blinked off, concealing their secrets. Hundreds of tiny clicks resounded through the room as automatic locks slid into place, sealing each drawer and container. The alarm's blare, lasting but a few seconds, was replaced with a muffled roar as banks of hidden fans rapidly adjusted the room's airflow to keep airborne particles from taking a trip out the exit portal as well, the air pressure abruptly fluctuating, then stabilizing.

His mind's eye slammed shut during the sudden commotion and, sadly, Josh saw Carolyn's protective suit was back, covering her from head to toe.

Josh enjoyed working with Carolyn but found it difficult to keep his mind from wandering—like now—imagining how nice it would be to peel her out of that biosuit, one little zipper at a time. She was his supervisor, but she wasn't Army. She was a government civilian, which meant there were no "superior officer" barriers to contend with if he chose to, well, get at those zippers. To make matters worse—or better?—Carolyn was hands-down one of the most beautiful women he'd ever met. But there was work to do, important work that required absolute, intense focus. As a member of Vanguard, making a mistake was simply not an option. His fantasy, he knew, would remain just that.

"I'll still be here when you get back," Josh said through the tiny microphone in his protective helmet. "Like always."

Carolyn momentarily turned to face him, her brown eyes twinkling with amusement at the tone of his voice. "Hopefully you'll have that strain figured out by then, Eeyore." She winked at him through her faceplate, and then entered the first of four airlock sections on her way topside, beginning the meticulous process of keeping all the bad stuff down in their deep classified hole where it belonged, and away from all the good stuff that lived above.

The six-inch-thick portal door slid closed behind her, heavy locks sliding into place with a dull thud. Hundreds of container locks clicked open again. The environmental control system brought the room back to its normal operating environment—optimum temperature, optimum air pressure, optimum airflow.

Back to work.

Just another day at Vanguard, a highly classified government biosafety level 4 complex.

Two hundred feet underground.

Josh turned to his bank of computer screens—alive with data once again—and tapped a fresh sequence of commands on his keyboard; there was a new, mutated strain of the Ebola virus he had to figure out how to kill.

In case it fell into the wrong hands.

CHAPTER 7

Conversation halted as President Andrew Smith entered the briefing room; he immediately sensed the tension in the air, a subtle static that indicated events were moving rapidly, maybe a little too rapidly for informed, decisive action. Andrew drew a deep, long breath, mentally steeling himself to receive the platter of tangled, squirming vipers he knew his advisors were about to toss in his lap, a platter emblazoned with the Seal of the President of the United States.

The assembled members quickly took their seats as Andrew took his.

With a quick glance around the table, he took stock of his advisors; luckily, all the primaries had either been in Washington or in close proximity when the call to convene had sounded. The experts Andrew needed nearest during a crisis—his war cabinet—were now staring back at him, waiting for the word to begin the meeting.

To the president's left sat the hulking form of his SECDEF, Marshall "Tank" Stone, nicknamed not only for his imposing size, but also for his prior life as an M1A Abrams jockey during the first Gulf War. To his right sat the secretary of state, Adam Williamson, former ambassador to the People's Republic of China and career diplomat. Around the remainder of the table sat Hugo

McIntyre, secretary of Homeland Security; Harold Ahrens, director of the Federal Bureau of Investigation; Jake Kesting, director of the Central Intelligence Agency; and General Rayburn "Scythe" Smythe, chairman of the Joint Chiefs of Staff. Three chairs down from the president sat Jessie Hruska, his national security advisor.

As per standard procedure during an unfolding, unpredictable crisis such as this, the vice president and some key deputy directors were on their way to alternate command centers at different points around the country, serving as a secondary source of command and control if something unthinkable were to happen in Washington. This was continuity of government, a concept born during the Cold War, when Soviet ballistic missile submarines prowled the oceans off the coasts of the United States, positioned to launch a debilitating strike from beneath the waves with little or no warning, severing the head of the Yankee snake before it could coil and strike back. Continuity of government had presented the Soviet planners with a many-headed snake, a hydra they couldn't hope to subdue entirely. And they never tried.

Now, it was a drill Andrew's administration practiced often, refining the swift movement of subordinate decision makers to safe—or, at least safer—locations away from DC. This morning, prudence dictated he put the program into motion. And he had.

As if on cue, a plasma screen on the wall opposite the president winked on, revealing the face of Allison Perez, vice president of the United States, who at that moment was aboard an aircraft heading to what the press liked to call an "undisclosed location." Her jet-black hair was tied tightly in a bun, and her piercing, dark eyes communicated nothing but serious intent, a steely readiness to act. "Good morning, Mr. President," she said, staring at her own screen showing the members assembled in the conference room.

"Good morning, Allison," Andrew answered.

Of all the people Andrew could've chosen as his running mate, Allison Perez was the best. A former Coast Guard chopper pilot, Allison had entered politics reluctantly as well, encouraged by those around her to make the jump to a different sort of public service after she'd made the front page of the papers by saving uncounted lives during the Houston port attacks. To Andrew, she was a kindred spirit of sorts: disciplined, smart, humble, and, most of all, fearless. He knew Allison could *be* president of the United States, and if he were to fall, the country would be in good hands. It was a comforting thought.

"All right, people," Andrew said, signaling the start of the meeting. "What do we have so far?"

Hugo McIntyre, Homeland Security, spoke first. "Mr. President, this morning at approximately 0530 hours central time, Kansas City police and fire departments started receiving a flood of emergency calls on the 911 system. As you know, sir, our field offices are automatically alerted if a certain number of 911 calls are received over a specified period of time. Our field office in Kansas City received the automatic alert notification at approximately 0550 hours. At that time, the system had received over three hundred 911 calls. The information we have is preliminary at best, but the majority of callers were frantic about some sort of animal attacks."

For a second, Andrew wasn't sure he'd heard his secretary correctly. "Animal attacks?"

"Yes, sir." Hugo paused for a moment and cleared his throat. A nervous tic. "What we've been able to screen from the calls so far involved what could best be described as a multitude of large rodents attacking people throughout the city." He directed the president's attention to a briefing slide projected on one of the large wall screens. A red, roughly circular line cut across a map of the Kansas City metro area, stretching nearly thirty miles across at its widest point. "This graphic represents the affected area, Mr. President, based on the reports we've been able to sort through."

Andrew silently stared at the graphic, trying to wrap his mind around what he was seeing.

"This spread," Hugo continued, "occurred before sunrise. As soon as the sun came up, the animals seemed to concentrate themselves in houses and other buildings, away from the light." Hugo cleared his throat again, clearly shaken by the incredible information he was providing. "The spread has stopped, but whatever these things are, they're still active. Some first responders have been attacked after entering darkened structures. They've reported smashed light fixtures in the infested buildings. It seems the animals have an aversion to light."

Animals? A slight chill shot down Andrew's spine. *No, not animals.* Smashing light fixtures indicated intelligence. "How many of these 'large rodents' are we talking about, Hugo?"

"Impossible to ascertain at this point, Mr. President. General Smythe will brief you in a moment on the actions we've taken to find out. For now, we know a large number of these creatures have completely devastated the population in a large portion of the Kansas City metro area. Inside the red-bordered area, sir, we estimate deaths could number in the hundreds of thousands."

"You're telling me that everyone inside that red circle has been killed?" Andrew asked.

Hugo cleared his throat once more, struggling to force the words from his throat. "The things aren't just killing, sir. They're eating. Feeding. It's a massacre, Mr. President."

A massacre. The room was silent for a moment as a flash of disbelief crossed the president's face. None of this seemed real! A major American city, eaten alive? How could it be? "Okay, by the numbers," Andrew said. "Let me hear it."

Adam Williamson spoke next. "Mr. President, our embassies and consulates have been informed, worldwide. Chiefs of station in high-interest areas have their ears open and are listening hard." He momentarily shifted his glance to Jake Kesting, silently communicating to the president that State and CIA were working hand in hand. "No information has been released to any foreign governments, nor have we received any inquiries. However, the press is starting to report on the situation, and we should be getting some questions soon."

"Brief the Brits, Adam. Let them know what we've got so far. Don't hold anything back." To the room, the president added, "I'll be addressing the nation at noon our time. Inform the networks and get started on a rough draft of my speech once we adjourn. For now, get a statement out that we're taking immediate action to control the situation and to help the citizens of Kansas City. If this is out on the wires for too long without a word from us, we could be asking for public panic. We don't need that again." Every person at the table remembered the Cleveland attack, and how events had quickly spiraled out of control. So many innocent citizens had died, most because of a panicked rush to get away from the city. They all had clear memories of that day, a day that saw the United States suffer a severe radiological attack in the middle of a major American city. A city that was still uninhabitable in some areas, and would be for years to come. None of the memories were pleasant. But, as an administration, they'd learned from it, and sworn *never again*.

"And," Andrew added, "those who wish us ill need to know now is *not* the time to decide to start screwing with Uncle Sam. I'll make that clear as well." The president turned toward his SECDEF. "Tank, what have you got?"

Tank leaned forward and adjusted his glasses. "Mr. President, activation orders have been issued to Guard units in Missouri, Kansas, Nebraska, Colorado, Iowa, Illinois, Arkansas, and Oklahoma. The first Kansas and Missouri units should be in position to enter the city within the next couple of hours. A Civil Support Team from Fort Leonard Wood is on its way as well. They're one of our specialized Army Guard units outfitted for detecting NBC—nuclear, biological, and chemical agents. All active duty units in CONUS have assumed DEFCON 3. Combat air patrols have been initiated over all major cities, no-fly protocols have been initiated with the FAA, and anti-air batteries are on alert around DC, New York, Philadelphia, Boston, San Francisco, and Los Angeles. NBC detection teams are on the streets in our major cities. The threat boards are blank. No indication this attack is connected to any foreign troop movements or hostile action. If this is the first shoe to drop, Mr. President, we'll be ready for the second one." Tank turned and looked at General Rayburn "Scythe" Smythe, United States Marine Corps, chairman of the Joint Chiefs of Staff, who spoke next.

The general sat ramrod straight in his chair, always the Marine officer. His gray crew cut, jutting chin, and impeccable olive drab uniform made General Smythe look just right for the role—a perfect choice by a Hollywood casting director. The right sleeve pinned to his shoulder, however, removed any illusion of the sort. This man was a combat veteran, and he'd paid dearly for his service—an unspoken bond that he happened to share with his commander in chief. His booming, gravelly voice resounded around the room.

"Mr. President, none of the fixed NBC detectors in Kansas City were triggered prior to, nor have any activated since, the start of this situation. This suggests there are no known radiological, chemical, or biological agents present in the city. It does not, however, rule out the possibility that there may have been something else released that our current suite of detection devices cannot pick up. As Mr. Stone mentioned, I have deployed a sniffer unit to the city, and they'll be taking readings shortly." General Smythe looked down at his watch, strapped to his one remaining wrist. "They should be making their first report within the hour. If there's something in the air that caused this, they'll find it."

The president swung his chair toward the general. "Are you telling me you believe these animal attacks were caused by a release of some kind of chemical or biological agent we don't know about?"

The general shook his head. "No, sir, I am not. Right now, we're faced with a situation that has no readily available explanation. I want to cover this particular base as soon as possible."

"I agree, General. Continue."

"We've established a cordon approximately forty miles from the center of the Kansas City metro area. Guard units have taken up positions on the major highways and are prohibiting entry to anyone other than official personnel. Other routes of ground transit will be covered as soon as we get more troops activated and on the move. The local police are covering until we get in place. The Guard units will also be available to handle any civilian personnel evacuations, if you deem it necessary, sir."

"Good work, Ray," Andrew said. "I don't know if this is some sort of terrorist attack yet, but we're going to treat it like it is until we know otherwise." Terrorists managing to release a rampaging horde of killer super-rats in a major city was . . . well, unlikely, but then again, flying hijacked airliners into the Twin Towers and the Pentagon seemed unlikely on September 10, 2001, too. The shaggy, one-eyed mullahs crawling around in caves on the other side of the world could be quite creative at times, especially when it came to killing innocent people.

Andrew wasn't willing to exclude that possibility. Not just yet.

He turned to his national security advisor. "Jessie, what's your read on this?"

At first glance, Jessie Hruska didn't appear as one might envision a senior presidential advisor. She was forty-three years old, much younger than the majority of her counterparts at the table.

Her shoulder-length red hair, emerald eyes, and athletic figure were more fitting for a model gracing the cover of a fashion magazine than for the fiery, hard-as-nails political pit bull that sat three chairs down from the president of the United States. Many had underestimated her because of her youth and appearance, and they'd paid dearly.

Glancing at her notes, Jessie summed up the facts. "We have thousands of citizens dead and missing. There's evidence of animal attacks—rodents—that have wiped out a major American city. There's no overt indication of chemical, biological, or radiological agents as the cause, at least not yet. No evidence of foreign government involvement, no evidence of terrorist organization involvement, no evidence of any nation making a move in another part of the world while we're dealing with this situation, no evidence of *anything*." She met the eyes of the other principals before continuing. "We don't know a whole lot right now, and that's not good. We're going to be in front of the American people in an hour and forty-three minutes, and we don't have any facts." She shifted in her chair, turning slightly to face the president directly. "You said it yourself, sir. Public panic is a possibility we need to act to prevent immediately. We saw what happened in Cleveland. We waited to act, and we lost citizens because of it. We need to evacuate whoever is left in the city, and in the surrounding rural areas as well. Until we're absolutely sure what we're dealing with, we need to get our citizens out of there."

Hugo spoke up. "Ms. Hruska is right, sir. It would be prudent to isolate this region as best we can, to get our people out. People will start moving out of the area of their own volition as soon as the news starts to spread, and it *is* spreading. We need to manage it."

The president turned his attention to the screen on the wall. His vice president had been silent so far, listening and, he knew, analyzing every bit of information.

"Allison, your thoughts?"

"Sir, I agree with the actions that have been taken so far. I also agree with Ms. Hruska that we first need to figure out exactly what message we'll be sending to the American people, and second, get our people clear of the Kansas City area. When you address the nation, sir, people are going to want to hear the facts. They'll need assurances their government is in complete control of the situation. They're going to want to hear what actions we're taking, and they're going to want to know what they'll need to do. Instructions, sir, where to go and how to get there. I suggest Mr. McIntyre provide that information immediately after you finish your comments."

As always, he and Allison Perez were on the exact same page. "I agree, Allison," Andrew said. "I'm going to tell them what we know. Kansas City, and the nation, has suffered a terrible tragedy. If we have evidence that shows this is not a biological or chemical attack by the time I go live, I'll tell them that, too. If we don't have evidence of what this is, I'll tell them we're doing everything possible to find it." Andrew pushed his chair away from the table, signaling that the meeting was nearly concluded. "Hugo, you'll follow my comments with instructions for our citizens still in the area. We need to get them out of there in an orderly fashion. The Guard troops moving into the area, along with local police, will handle that task." He turned to his SECDEF. "Tank, as soon as we can, we need to get boots on the ground in there. I don't know what has caused these . . . *animals* to start a massacre like this, but we need to make sure they're contained. As soon as our citizens are out, I want these things *dead*. Bring me options as soon as you can."

"Roger that, Mr. President."

Andrew stood. "We're facing an unknown here. Each one of you has to keep your ears open and your agencies moving. I'm not sure where this situation will lead. You'll need to be ready to execute when I call on you, but be flexible. In twenty-four hours, we may be facing a completely different landscape of challenges. We'll convene again following my remarks to the nation. I'll expect more clarity on this situation by then." He smiled, ever so slightly. "You've all done good work. Keep pressing."

With that, the president left the room.

CHAPTER 8

It took Carolyn fifteen minutes to travel to the surface from her subterranean work area, the normal time it took to travel through the decontamination chambers, the guard stations, the series of airlocks, and a long elevator ride two hundred feet up to the desert floor of the Dugway Proving Ground.

Dugway was the US Army's chemical and biological warfare proving ground; that part of its mission was public knowledge. The sprawling facility belowground, however, was another matter. Carolyn's job was hidden from the view of most of the personnel working on the secure facility, some of whom held pretty hefty security clearances. Not everyone had a need to know, regardless of how high their clearance was. So, they didn't.

She and her coworkers were at the cutting edge of radiological, biological, and chemical warfare research. After the threat of America being attacked with these types of weapons became a very real possibility—and after the Cleveland attack, a sobering event—the government brought the best of the best from academia, from the scientific world, and from the military to the deserts of Utah and handed them a large chunk of the classified black world budget to build the organization that now existed two hundred feet underground. Their mission was not to develop these weapons for use by the United States, a course of action the nation had abandoned decades earlier, but rather to do everything possible to prevent their use through improved detection capabilities, negate their use through intensive study of foreign capabilities, and control the situation if they were used against the United States or allies by providing immediate expertise to an on-scene commander.

Chemical weapons were once called the poor man's nuclear weapon. They still were, but these days the poor man could also get his hands on some exquisitely nasty little viruses and quantities of deadly radioactive waste materials that served the same function rather well. They were the weapons of terror. And some were damned frightening.

She sat near her favorite window of the dining facility, which offered a wide view of the desert landscape, while slowly sipping a cup of coffee generously sugared and creamed to her liking. As the caffeine entered her bloodstream, the throbbing in her head began to subside. Few people would admit it, but the guy with the donkey from Colombia was probably the most successful drug dealer on the planet.

Having been born and raised in the green environs of Kentucky, Carolyn found the desert landscape surrounding Dugway quite difficult to warm to. It wasn't lush like home, but in its own way, it was just as wondrous. Out on the desert at night when the sky was clear, she felt as if she were staring directly into the far reaches of the universe. It was the most beautiful nighttime sky she'd ever seen.

After a while, she'd begun to look forward to making the eighty-five-mile trip from Salt Lake City, where she and most of her coworkers lived on the weekends, to the nearly 800,000-acre Dugway complex. The work was tough and demanding, and it required a meticulous focus, but the reward was more than enough to make it all worthwhile. She and the other members of the ultra-classified Vanguard organization were making a real difference.

Through their hard work, they could save innocent lives. Nothing was more rewarding than that.

As she took another sip of her beloved light brown fluid of life, she saw her reflection in the window staring back at her. Here she was, thirty-two years old, single, and by her own estimation very attractive, sitting in the middle of the Utah desert doing a job she couldn't talk about. Not what she'd expected to be doing at this point in her life.

She'd graduated near the top of her class at Bowling Green University, taken a job at a pharmaceutical research company, and even tinkered with the idea of buying her own house. Life was definitely good. But then came September 11, and the horror unfolded before her eyes on the television screen, as it did for millions upon millions of people across the globe. She watched as the second plane slammed into the doomed tower, watched as valiant firefighters and police ran headlong toward their deaths, watched as people made the unimaginable decision to leap to their deaths hundreds of feet below rather than be burned alive inside the upper floors of the towers.

She saw the Pentagon in flames.

She saw the crater in a Pennsylvania field.

And when the towers fell, she knew the world had changed.

Her world had changed.

All of a sudden, her personal comfort didn't seem quite as important. Her country had been attacked by people for whom life held no apparent value—and chances were, they were going to do it again. She wanted to do something but didn't know how she could help.

The day Carolyn received the phone call, however, was the day she knew she *would* be able to help. One month later, she was in Utah.

She was startled by a hand on her shoulder.

"Carolyn, you need to report to General Rammes's office." It was her branch supervisor, and he had a deadly serious look on his face. "Now."

"What's wrong?"

"You'll be briefed when you see him. And get ready to travel."

She set her cup down, sloshing a little coffee onto the table. "Travel? Where to?"

"Missouri. You're the team lead. Get moving!"

CHAPTER 9

The modified Bradley fighting vehicles were the first military vehicles to enter the city on the ground, their diesel engines thrumming
loudly through the dead streets. These were the "sniffers," equipped
to sift through every single molecule of air for something recognizable as a chemical, biological, or radiological agent. Buttoned up
within their armored vehicles, the specialized crews slowly made
their way through the abandoned city, scrubbing the air for the
reason why thousands of people had been slaughtered.

Speakers mounted below police choppers and Army Blackhawks
blared instructions to people still on the ground: *Stay away from the
buildings, stay calm, stay on the main thoroughfares, stay calm, head
toward Interstate 29, head north, help is on the way . . .*

A trickle of people on foot, and a few in cars, were slowly snak-
ing their way out of the city, for the most part following the directions they'd been given. Those who'd followed other routes were
being held at different points around the exclusion zone—a rough
circle measuring forty miles from the center of the city—and were
given whatever food, water, and medical attention they required.
After being tested, screened, and interviewed, they could be taken to
more prepared evacuation centers, which were at that very moment
being set up at five areas ringing the city. Just within the forty-mile

exclusion zone, lumbering dual-rotor Chinook troop carrier heli-copters began to line the ramp at Kansas City International, which was in the process of being transformed into the main evacuation point. When complete, it would be configured to handle a large number of people. There weren't that many coming out of the city, though. Not at all.

Inside one of the modified Bradleys, a Missouri Army National Guard major pressed his mic button. "Brooklyn, this is Brooklyn One. Status. Over."

The ten other Bradleys under his command radioed back in numbered order:

"Two, all sectors covered. Negative results."

"Three, all sectors covered. Negative results."

"Four, negative results all sectors."

"Five, neg. All sectors complete."

The other five Bradley crews reported the same thing. Nothing. The air was clear.

"Roger, Brooklyn," the major radioed back. "Copy negative results. Good work. Rally at Bravo. Out." The major switched his comm gear to his command net frequency. "Jersey, this is Brooklyn One."

"Brooklyn One, this is Jersey. Go."

"Brooklyn reports negative results all sectors. I repeat, negative results all sectors. Brooklyn rallying at Bravo. Out."

Within minutes, the information went up the command chain, and soon thereafter orders were sent back down. In the next few hours, boots would be on the ground, and hunting season would be officially opened.

Sundown was in seven hours.

CHAPTER 10

Andrew Smith sat behind his desk in the Oval Office, a prepared copy of his speech at his fingertips. The teleprompter on the camera in front of him slowly began to roll. He was live in three, two, one . . .

"Good afternoon," he began, staring straight into the camera lens and directly into the eyes of tens of millions of Americans looking for guidance, hoping for answers. "Over the course of the past decade, this nation has suffered severe tragedies, and it is my sad duty to report to you that today, we have suffered yet another.

"Early this morning in Kansas City, there was a wave of attacks against our fellow citizens. Sadly, many people have been lost or are missing. The exact cause of these attacks is still being determined, but I have been informed they were caused by . . . animals."

The president looked down from the camera, momentarily losing his famous on-camera persona. That last word—*animals*—hung in the air like a line from a bad science fiction movie. Suddenly, Andrew knew reading a prepared speech wasn't what the American people would want from him. He looked up from his desk, slid the paper copy of the speech away, and spoke from his heart instead of the teleprompter.

"This is not easy, but I'm going to be straight with each and every one of you. This is what we know. An approximately thirty-mile radius of Kansas City has been . . . Everyone within a thirty-mile radius has been killed or is currently unaccounted for. The death toll . . . There's not an exact number I can give you, but if I could, it would be too terrible to comprehend.

"We don't know how, or why, this has happened. I can assure you that I will do everything in my power to ascertain why as quickly as I can, take immediate action to destroy this threat, and take care of the people who have been affected. These animals, described as some sort of large rodent, are still in the city. As of now, they've stopped their spread and are remaining stationary. We believe they have an aversion to light.

"I have directed the secretary of Homeland Security, along with the secretary of defense, to take any and all actions necessary to respond to this catastrophe. Kansas City is off-limits except for military and civil defense personnel.

"I have ordered a complete evacuation of every person within a forty-mile radius of Kansas City. If you're within this zone, please follow the directions of the military and civil authorities. I need you *out* of the immediate area. Most of all, I need you to stay calm. The military forces of the United States are being mobilized as we speak to enter the city and eliminate these things. For your safety, and the safety of those I'm ordering into the Kansas City area, I need the exclusion zone cleared."

• • •

A little over sixteen hundred miles to the west of DC, near Colorado Springs, Vice President Allison Perez watched the president's speech from deep within the Cheyenne Mountain complex. She'd known Andrew for a number of years and wasn't the least bit surprised he'd gone off script. It was a habit that drove his speechwriters batty, especially on the campaign trail, where a carefully crafted message meant votes in November, but it was simply who he was. They'd won anyway.

She turned to Admiral Keaton Grierson, commander, United States Northern Command—USNORTHCOM. "What are the numbers from KCI, Admiral?"

Admiral Grierson shook his head. "Not good. There's a few hundred, but nowhere near what we prepared for."

"Jesus, Keats. A whole city."

"Yes, ma'am." There was nothing more he could say.

Allison looked back up at the screen. The man delivering a message to the nation was, she knew, the right man for the job. As a leader, Andrew Smith had no equal. But as with any president, the constant pressures of the job were starting to take their toll. And after the loss of his wife . . .

Allison didn't want to admit it, but Andrew seemed different now. The entire nation had mourned alongside him, but when he buried his beloved Kate, part of him went into the ground with her. His flame had grown dimmer. She'd noticed, but his staff had not. At least not yet. If—or more likely, when—they did, Allison would protect him as best she could. She hoped he could hold it together well enough to keep the American people from noticing. Or, for that matter, others around the globe. A weak president invited disaster—a cold, hard fact they'd all lived through with Andrew's predecessor. They'd be watching him closely, especially now, and if they sensed weakness . . .

"The threat boards, Admiral."

"Clear, Madam Vice President. Nothing outside of the norm."

Allison nodded. "Keep both eyes open, Keats. The wolves at the gate can get a little frisky as soon as we hit a crisis like this." Foreign policy was one of Andrew's strengths, Allison knew. *Talk to them, Andrew, wave the torch. Warn 'em off.*

The president continued.

"In closing, I realize this may not seem real to some of you outside of the Kansas City area. When I was first informed of this situation earlier this morning, I honestly felt like I was trapped in a bad movie. I wish that's all it was, but this is real. I promise each and every one of you that your government will take all steps necessary to control what has happened and to help all of you who have suffered, and are suffering, great loss." A pause. A deep breath. "In my free moments this morning, I've prayed. I urge all of you to do the same, whatever your beliefs may be."

His gut told him things were going to get worse. Now it was time for the president to speak to the rest of the world.

Andrew leaned forward, his piercing blue eyes peering straight through the camera lens to the millions of people watching this broadcast around the globe, both friend and foe.

"To those nations and people who wish us ill, I issue a simple warning. The United States has been wounded this morning. That is a fact. *This* is also a fact: although wounded, we are not weakened. You may delight in the news that we've suffered a terrible loss, but do not let our misfortune provide you the sudden courage to decide that now is the time to move against us. We are a peaceful people, a peaceful nation, but our sword is out of the sheath this day, and can be swung in many directions with an unforgiving, fearful vengeance. Stand fast."

No president had ever been so direct, especially on live TV to a worldwide audience. His message was simple and clear: *Don't fuck with me right now, because I won't think twice about ripping your heart out with my free hand.*

Andrew's gaze softened as he returned to addressing the American people. "My fellow Americans, we will persevere. The strength of the American spirit can overcome anything. We've shown our incredible fortitude in times of crisis, and I ask each of you to display that same courage now. Together, as a nation, we will get through this, and we will prevail. May God bless each of you, and may God continue to bless the United States of America."

• • •

"We're clear, Mr. President." The camera was off.

The first person to approach Andrew was his national security advisor. He looked up at Jessie as she walked around the corner of his desk.

"Mr. President . . ." She wasn't sure what to say.

Andrew stood and buttoned his suit coat. "Well, that wasn't what we'd written, but I couldn't read a prepared speech. I had to be straight with them."

"Sir, you did just fine." Jessie smiled, trying to give her president some assurance that the speech he'd delivered was probably the most heartfelt, direct message that'd ever gone out from the Oval Office. She put her hand on his shoulder, a gentle touch—definitely a break from the professionalism Andrew demanded from his people, but right now, it seemed appropriate.

He welcomed it.

"Thanks, Jessie," Andrew whispered. "Now let's go figure out how to kill these goddamn things."

CHAPTER 11

The big choppers' dual rotors sliced through the air with a reverberating, chest-rattling *thwacka thwacka thwacka* as the helicopters settled on the tarmac at Kansas City International, now devoid of any airliners or other civilian activity. KCI was now a military base of operations, the central evacuation point. For hours, the CH-47 Chinook crews had repeated a steady pattern of arriving, unloading, and departing, the evacuation of everyone within the forty-mile exclusion zone surrounding Kansas City now nearing completion.

Shouting to be heard over the choppers' roar, Colonel Garrett Hoffman, United States Army, grabbed his sergeant major by the arm. "Sergeant Major! What's the count?"

The senior enlisted soldier glanced at his clipboard. "We've got three birds on the ground in the city, Colonel, three more outbound, and four more on the way in. Once those four are loaded up and out of there, helo ops are complete. There's five trucks on the way out of the city on I-70 West, and another six trucks going east." He made a few quick mental calculations and added, "The city should be clear in another hour, ninety minutes tops."

"Okay, pass the word," Garrett ordered. "The city will open in ninety minutes." He looked to the sky when he heard the multi-engine rumble of a C-130 Hercules approaching the field. There were already a number of Air Force cargo haulers on the ramp, mostly C-17 Globemasters and a few other C-130s, including three of the deadly AC-130 gunships. The cargo haulers were being used to fly people in and out of the airport, and the big gunships were arming up for possible use against whatever was in the city. Garrett had heard the president's address to the nation, and afterward he was definitely in a hunting mood. He'd seen what the AC-130s could do—up close and personal—and he couldn't wait to see their firepower unleashed on whatever had taken the lives of so many of his fellow citizens.

He quickly noticed the Herc that just landed didn't have USAF markings. As a matter of fact, it had no markings whatsoever. He turned again to his sergeant major, who, from the look in his eyes, obviously knew what he was about to be asked. In a low voice, Garrett asked anyway. "Sergeant Major, who the *fuck* is that, and what the *fuck* is he doing landing on my fucking strip?"

"I don't know, sir. I'll get on it." With that, the sergeant major double-timed toward the terminal.

From experience, Garrett knew unannounced C-130s—sans markings—were almost always a portent of additional ass pain, something he definitely didn't need at the moment. It was probably carrying CIA, DIA, or some unnamed black agency muckety-mucks who were "here to help." Garrett had a well-tuned operational ballet going on right now, and the last thing he needed was a bunch of black ops bastards—or worse, sport-coated bureaucrats—crapping in his sandbox.

Garrett scowled as the lumbering whale of an aircraft pulled to a stop, shut down its two inboard engines, and opened its back ramp. Garrett walked toward it, lighting a cigar as he went, and when he noticed the first person to exit the back of the Herc was a civilian woman—in a skirt, of all things—he muttered two simple words. "Fuck. Me."

To make Garrett's moment even more special, he watched four additional people in various combinations of civilian attire come plodding down the Herc's ramp.

The sergeant major came running up from behind, matching his commander's stride as Garrett made a beeline toward the skirt-clad sandbox crapper. "Sir, we received instructions to let this bird land and give the people on board whatever support they require," the sergeant major said, huffing, short of breath.

Garrett wheeled on his sergeant major. "Instructions from whom?"

"Direct call from General Worthington. From the Pentagon. A few minutes ago. Sir."

"Worthington. Great." Hoffman took a long draw on his cigar, and cursed when he realized it had already gone out. He tucked it into his ACU blouse pocket. "Did General Worthington happen to mention who these people are?"

"No, sir."

Garrett spat a piece of tobacco as he watched the civilian woman inventory her gear as it was unloaded from the back of the C-130. She was having a hard time keeping her hair from blowing in her face from the rotor wash of a Chinook landing nearby, and she was desperately trying to keep her skirt from ending up around her neck. For a second, Garrett thought she looked like a brunette Marilyn Monroe standing over a steam vent . . . and he couldn't help but register the fact that this lady had one hell of a set of legs. "All right, Sergeant Major," Garrett growled. "Let's go find out what kind of fucking support they need."

• • •

Carolyn's team's gear was offloaded quickly, and the unmarked C-130 immediately closed its ramp and taxied toward the active runway. The small group of civilians huddled around their equipment and sheltered their eyes from the propeller wash as the big Herc pulled away.

Carolyn fumbled in her jacket for the orders she'd been told to provide to whoever was in charge at the airport. From the urgent manner of the two men walking toward her in Army camouflage uniforms, she figured they must be the ones.

"Ma'am, I'm Colonel Hoffman. This is Sergeant Major Wallace."

Carolyn stuck out her hand and was a little surprised that it wasn't taken immediately. After what seemed like an eternity, the tall one with the silver eagle insignia on his hat—a full-bird colonel, she knew—took her hand and shook it. Very firmly. "Colonel, I'm Carolyn Ridenour," she said.

"Good," Garrett barked. "Now that the pleasantries are out of the way, you can tell me why you're here."

Well, he's a direct bastard, isn't he, Carolyn thought to herself. She handed him a copy of her orders. "I'm here under orders from General Derek Rammes."

Behind them, the unmarked C-130 thundered back into the air.

Garrett scanned the orders and handed them back, disgust crossing his face.

Carolyn waited a few seconds for the colonel to say something. He didn't. "Is there something wrong?" she asked. "I was told the vice chief of staff of the Army was going to call directly to explain my team's arrival. General Worthington?"

"Worthington called," Garrett said, shaking his head. "You're a little late, Ms. Ridenour. The city is clear."

"The city is clear?" Carolyn was shocked. Her stomach sank as she watched the C-130 bank to the southwest, climbing away.

"Yes, the city is *clear*. No chemical, biological, or radiological agents found." Garrett looked up at the speck in the sky that had been the unmarked C-130, clearly frustrated that he now had to deal with a bunch of stranded civilians. "And there went your ride."

Carolyn's first assignment as a team leader wasn't supposed to pan out this way. She could feel her team members staring at her, waiting for her to do something. Problem was, she wasn't sure what to do. "Well, Colonel," she said defiantly, "it looks like you're stuck with us for the time being."

"No, ma'am, I'm not," Garrett said. "We'll have a truck for you and your team available within the hour. Sergeant Major, take these people to the terminal and have their gear—"

"The gear stays with us, Colonel," she interrupted. *If you're going to be an ass*, Carolyn thought, *then I'll return the favor.*

Garrett narrowed his eyes at her. "Like I was *saying*, Sergeant Major, have their gear taken with them to the terminal."

"Yes, sir."

"Ms. Ridenour, it's been a pleasure. But I have work to do. Good day." With that, Garrett strode off to take care of more pressing matters. Carolyn's gaze burned dual holes into his back.

"Ma'am, if you'll follow me, I'll take you to the terminal and get you and your team settled until we can schedule transportation for you out of here. I'll have your gear brought up to you."

"Thank you, Sergeant Major." In a small way, Carolyn was glad she wouldn't have to work with Colonel Garrett Hoffman after all. *What an asshole.*

CHAPTER 12

An hour and fifteen minutes after Carolyn and her team were stranded at the airport, the first troops entered the city. On foot, they moved from house to house, building to building, slowly moving toward the center. AH-64 Apache gunships prowled overhead, looking for targets. Higher in the early evening sky, an AC-130U Spooky gunship slowly circled, awaiting a call for fire support.

Structure by structure the troopers went. Looking in the corners. Looking in the basements. They found more evidence of the night's terror. Pools of congealed blood. Torn clothing. Small bits of what used to be people.

But nothing more.

This was going to take some time.

In the western sky, the bright orange orb of the sun kissed the horizon, signaling the end of one of the worst days in American history.

• • •

Carolyn stared at the TV, wondering when she'd be able to get her team on the road back to Dugway. The televisions in the KCI terminal had been left on, and every single news channel was replaying the president's address from earlier in the day.

" . . . and take care of the people who have been affected. These animals, described as some sort of large rodent, are still in the city. As of now, they've stopped their spread and are remaining stationary. We believe they have an aversion to light . . ."

Carolyn hadn't learned all the facts of what had happened in Kansas City until she'd seen the president's speech and watched the news. When she and her team had left Dugway, they were briefed that there might've been a biological or chemical attack in Kansas City—she was prepared for that. She'd been a team member in Cleveland and had a good idea of what her team was going to have to do once they landed. During the flight from Las Vegas, they'd been given no additional information and apparently hadn't been pulled off the assignment once the city had been declared clear. Frustrating, but understandable. Communications in a situation like this—with thousands of different messages flying to and from a hundred different places . . . Well, sometimes the ball gets dropped. Obviously, someone dropped hers.

As Carolyn watched the president's address for the third time, something suddenly dawned on her. *He said the attacks were from some sort of animals, and they hid in the buildings when the sun came out. No, not just animals . . . Large rodents. A mutation? And they're afraid of light?* She whispered to herself, "The spread stopped . . . when the sun came up?"

Carolyn looked out the window as the last fiery rim of the sun sank below the horizon, and a chill snaked up her spine. It was a hunch at best, but she suddenly knew what might have caused this. And if she was right . . .

The glass windowpanes in the airport terminal started to vibrate, ever so slightly. From outside, there was a muted clicking sound, a strange chattering noise. Coming from the southeast. From the city. Even inside the terminal, it could be heard.

She could feel it.

The darkness had come.

Like millions of bats pouring out of an underground cavern to rule the night, they came.

THE SECOND NIGHT

CHAPTER 13

"Movement! We have movement! Pilot! Target target target!"

As the AC-130 slowly circled above the darkened city, its infrared night-vision targeting sensors suddenly lit up with hundreds—no, thousands—of targets, each glowing with demonic intensity, moving fast from hundreds of different locations, all at the same instant.

The pilot had been intently watching the oil pressure on engine three, and the call from his infrared detection set operator had startled him. "Say again?"

"Jesus Christ! They're all over the place!"

He definitely heard him that time. The pilot dipped the wing of his gunship and looked through his targeting sight to his left. What he saw chilled him. "Holy mother of God."

The ground below him was alive with the bright green infrared signatures of thousands of small targets flowing outward from the darkened buildings slowly rotating clockwise below his orbiting gunship. It was an almost liquid wave of targets, each abandoned building erupting like a miniature volcano spilling bright green lava out of every crack, flowing fast toward the troops on the ground.

The combat-proven gunships were designed to deliver truly fearsome firepower. They carried a single 105mm M102 howitzer, capable of firing anywhere from six to ten rounds per minute, an L60 Bofors 40mm cannon capable of delivering either single precision shots or a hellish volley of 120 rounds per minute, and a GAU-12 25mm Gatling gun capable of spitting out 1,800 rounds per minute. During the last ten years of conflict, the deadly AC-130s had drawn enemy blood hundreds of times. The misguided mullahs hated seeing these things circling their safe little caves. It was usually the last thing they saw before they were cut to pieces by a hail of good old American steel. The AC-130s could deliver surgical firepower or, if the situation called for it, area saturation. In layman's terms, that meant *Fuck it. Kill everything.*

This was one of those situations.

"Call 'em!" the pilot screamed into his headset, ordering the radio operator to inform the ground units that his aircraft was about to engage. "Spooky's going hot!" *All right, you little bastards, let's party.*

At the same instant the ground troops received the frantic warning call from the gunship's radio operator, the AC-130's 25mm Gatling gun belched a long tongue of flame toward the ground below. The *WRAAAAAAAAHH* from the screaming minigun could be heard from inside the cockpit, even over the gunship's four thundering Allison turboprops. The rate of fire was so intense that the hundreds of white-hot shells etched a blinding line through the air from the gun's spinning barrels directly to the ground below. The flaming laser beam of 25mm shells danced across the ground like a death wand wielded by an evil god, an aerial meat grinder shredding everything it touched.

Hundreds of the creatures vaporized in clouds of blood and gore, but hundreds more took their place. Moving fast.

The 40mm Bofors started pumping out rounds as well, each a glowing streak of death screaming down from the orbiting gunship and impacting the ground with a shower of sparks. *Bam bam bam bam bam*—the 40mm shells slid rapidly through the feeder as the weapon hammered away. The smell of burning cordite filled the inner spaces of the gunship.

A shudder shook the plane as the mighty 105mm Howitzer fired, sending high-explosive anti-personnel shells toward the swarm of targets, shredding hundreds with each powerful explosion. *Kra-BAM!* A six-second delay. *Kra-BAM!*

The gunship was firing fast and furious.

But still, the things came.

Unstoppable.

To the east and west of their position, two other orbiting gunships opened up on different parts of the city. The night sky suddenly brightened with the fury of the gunships' coordinated wrath. The abandoned city was bathed in an unnatural, hellish glow.

The pilot watched as the wave of targets sped outward, still spilling by the thousands from the darkened buildings, from the sewers, from the hiding places. He knew his crew was killing them by the hundreds, but still they came. There were too many of the goddamned things!

He saw tracer fire below to the south of his position.

The ground troops had made contact.

He swallowed. Hard.

CHAPTER 14

Captain Pfortmiller's soldiers had been sitting atop their line-abreast formation of Bradleys, waiting for the order to saddle up and move into the city, when the strange clicking noise, the earsplitting chattering, shattered the dead-quiet countryside like a rolling thunderclap.

"What in the holy hell is that?" Pfortmiller asked no one in particular.

The command net erupted all at once. The radioman, Specialist Gorhau, cupped one earphone with his hand, pressing it against his ear. "Cap, there's movement in the city . . ."

The *WRAAAAAAAAHH* of the AC-130's Gatling gun could barely be heard over the muffled thunder of thousands of clawed, muscular legs tearing across the paved streets, concrete walkways, and grassy areas of the city. The ground was vibrating. Through the vehicle's steel tracks. Through the ceramic armor. Through the hard rubber soles of their combat boots. Like a mild electric shock.

"Jesus, there goes the gunship," Pfortmiller said. "What the hell are they shooting at?"

The orderly chatter across the command net was suddenly replaced by frantic calls of contact by the forward units, from the east, from the west. Calls for fire support. And then, screams.

Pfortmiller sat atop his Bradley fighting vehicle, watching the fire rain down from the gunships, listening to the unnerving chattering sound coming from the city in front of him and the electronic disarray on the radio net. Whatever was happening, it was happening way too damned fast. They were supposed to move into the city in less than twenty minutes. *So much for that plan*, he thought.

He could hear the sound of automatic weapons fire, forward from their position. Tracers arced low across the sky, bright streaks across his night vision goggles' field of view. "Here they come! Positions! Now now now!" he yelled, trying desperately to be heard. His troopers reacted instantly, racing to whatever fighting positions they could find.

He tried to break through on the command net: "Empire, this is Saginaw. Empire, this is Saginaw! We have contact to our front! Please advise, over!" Nothing. The net was a complete jumble of uncoordinated, unintelligible radio calls. Except for the screaming. He'd been in combat before, but it was never like this.

The chattering was incredibly loud, getting closer.

He watched as tracers from the forward firing positions suddenly ceased. One by one, they went silent.

We're getting overrun. The realization made his blood run cold.

If he'd had more time, he could've gotten his troops back inside their Bradleys, but he knew it was too late. As he slid inside the armored troop carrier and started to pull the upper hatch closed, he saw them. Thousands of pairs of pinpoint lights—glowing eyes—racing toward his position. The ground was covered with them.

He slammed the hatch closed and screamed his orders into his helmet microphone: "Saginaw, fire at will! Fire at will! Fire at will!" He knew with a sickening certainty that there were no friendlies remaining to their front. Their field of fire was clear.

He ripped off his night-vision goggles and peered through his infrared viewer. They were less than fifty yards away, tiny yellow orbs glowing like the eyes of the devil himself. Running among the horde were other things, on two legs, leaping like gazelles with each step. He'd never seen a real monster before.

The Bradley's gunner opened up with his 25mm Bushmaster cannon, the loud *bam bam bam bam bam bam* of the rapid-fire gun shaking the interior of the armored vehicle. Pfortmiller's viewer flashed as hundreds of bright tracer rounds slammed into the onrushing wave of things. His troops were firing.

He watched helplessly as the rampaging horde slammed into his position. His troops fell where they stood, covered by the squirming mass, pieces of their bodies torn and thrown into the air by the monstrous frenzy.

He could hear the muffled thunder as they covered his Bradley and feel the vibration as they ran past his position.

The things were still coming, filling his viewer's field of view.

Captain Pfortmiller knew he was a dead man.

With a terrible screeching noise, the upper hatch of the Bradley was ripped off its hinges, the steel wrenching and splitting as it was torn free.

Pfortmiller looked up into the face of evil. Two yellow eyes buried in the face of something that just couldn't be real burned bright as they stared back at him. Rows of black, razor-sharp teeth filled its grinning mouth.

A long, clawed hand gripped him by the top of the head, his skull cracking loudly as the powerful claws found purchase. It wrenched his body out of the Bradley with a single pull and threw it to the ground. It was eaten in a matter of seconds by an undulating black mass of claws and teeth.

Next came the gunner.

And then the rest of the crew.

The thing standing atop the empty Bradley licked its bloody claws with a long, leathery tongue, savoring every drop. A low moaning escaped its lungs. It leapt to the ground, running toward the *others*, covering large distances with each long stride. Moving fast.

It could smell them.

CHAPTER 15

Transfixed by the strange vibration of the terminal windows, Carolyn suddenly noticed that the activity outside had intensified—people were running around the tarmac like ants whose hill had been kicked by a mischievous kid.

One of her team members leaned close and asked, "Carolyn, what do you think is going on?"

"I don't know, Matt." But she did. They could all see the bright flashes of fire streaking to the ground from the gunships in the distance. Her team had all heard the president's speech. They knew what the gunships were firing at, but none of them wanted to acknowledge it.

A door opened twenty yards down the concourse, allowing the outside sounds to enter, and an armed trooper ran inside, turning toward their position. The shrill clicking and chattering was deafening. It abruptly ceased as the door slammed shut.

"Ms. Ridenour?"

Carolyn stepped forward. "I'm Ms. Ridenour."

"Ma'am, you and your team have to follow me."

"What's going on, Sergeant?" Carolyn's throat suddenly felt tight, constricted, as adrenaline pumped into her bloodstream. She could see a twinge of fear in the sergeant's eyes.

"You're being air-evaced out of here." He quickly glanced at the tarmac, and then back to Carolyn. It was going to be close.

"Why?" Carolyn asked, surprised at how shaky her own voice was. "What's happening? What is that noise?"

In no mood for further questions, the sergeant spoke clearly and forcefully, like a father telling his daughter to quit playing in the road because there's a car coming. "Ma'am, you need to get out of here. You need to follow me *now*."

Carolyn and her team turned toward their gear, which was neatly stacked ten feet away.

"The gear stays. Y'all don't have a whole lot of time." The sergeant, tired of explaining himself, turned and headed back toward the tarmac door at a slow run.

"Jesus, Carolyn," Matt said. His eyes were wide with fright.

"I know, I know." Carolyn was scared too, but this was her team, and it was time to be the team leader and take charge. "All right, people, you heard him. Let's go! Quickly, before our ride leaves without us."

Carolyn and her team ran after the sergeant, who'd already propped open the door and was waving them through. The unnatural sound was even louder now, and Carolyn knew whatever was making it was getting closer.

As she stepped through the door, automatic weapons fire rattled from the far southern edge of the airport. She could see the tracer fire. The air smelled hot, electric. For a second, one of her team members stopped on the metal stairway, frozen stiff by what he was seeing. The sergeant grabbed him by the jacket and literally dragged him down the stairs, sending him sprawling onto the tarmac.

The sergeant screamed to be heard. "Follow me!" He pointed to a helicopter in the distance, its dual rotor blades beginning to rotate.

There was more weapons fire. From the eastern part of the airport. Closer than from the south.

Good God, they're all around us! Carolyn realized. Her stomach sank. She'd never been so scared in her entire life. It was happening too fast! They were nearly forty miles from the center of the exclusion zone, ten miles from the edge of where the things had stopped at daybreak—how could the things have moved so far, so fast? Her heart was beating so hard she felt as if it would burst from her chest and go bouncing toward the helicopter without her.

As she ran toward the chopper, she saw them. Small yellow dots shining in the dark just beyond the hail of tracer rounds, which were now flying from the entire southeastern edge of the airport. The sight was indescribable—there were thousands of them! The huge rodents the president had spoken of . . . They were real. God in heaven, they were real!

The sound of weapons fire was nearly continuous. She'd never been a soldier, and had never been anywhere close to a war zone. She found the intensity of the firefight spreading around her almost too much to take in all at once. The earsplitting crack of automatic weapons fire, the flashing lights from the tracer rounds—it looked like what she'd seen on the news, but this wasn't on a television screen in her comfy living room. She was in it. And whatever the enemy was, it was almost on top of them.

A thunderous roar suddenly rolled over the airfield as a fighter jet swooped in low, dropping a pair of cluster bombs at the far southern edge of the airport, each one splitting apart at a predetermined height and releasing hundreds of small bomblets on the thousands of yellow dots below.

As the fighter climbed, its afterburner throwing a long tail of blue flame behind it, the bomblets exploded all at once, like the finale of a fireworks display. The sound followed a second later, knocking two members of Carolyn's team to their knees as they covered their ears with their hands.

"Up up up! Let's go!" The sergeant was screaming, still waving his arm to follow. Carolyn saw him nervously shifting his glance back and forth from them to the firefight now just a few hundred yards away. She got the impression he really didn't want to stay here any longer than he had to, or at least wanted to get the damned civilians off his hands so he could help his buddies.

As they neared their ride, Carolyn noticed the other choppers on the ramp had also started their engines, and people were rapidly trying to get on board. Around them on the tarmac groups of soldiers rapidly set up fighting positions, placing heavy weapons on their stands, slamming belts of ammunition into the feeders.

These soldiers were staying to fight. No matter what.

Carolyn knew she was seeing real bravery.

A loud explosion erupted to her left—one of the helicopters at the far southern edge of the tarmac had exploded, pieces of the spinning rotor blades flying through the air. Next to it, another chopper was trying to lift off—but it was covered by something, things jumping from the ground, the things with the yellow eyes. Hundreds of them!

They were on the tarmac!

She watched the big Chinook rock side to side, unbalanced by the weight of the creatures—a black wave of the things!—leaping onto it from the tarmac. As the chopper slowly rotated, Carolyn could see the back ramp was still open, and the creatures were all over the inside. She looked away as the chopper abruptly tilted forward, the front rotor blades striking the cement in a shower of sparks, tossing long, ragged shards of metal into the air. A second later, the Chinook slammed back down onto the tarmac, exploding in a bright flash as the fuel tanks ruptured and the spilled fuel ignited.

She and her team were now sprinting as fast as they could toward their chopper. The crew chief was at the rear of the Chinook, waving them in. Their escort suddenly stopped, dropped to one knee, and started firing his weapon. Carolyn turned and looked behind for just a second and saw a black wave of the things speeding across the tarmac toward them. She saw people running, trying to get away, but they were overtaken, disappearing in the wave of fiery yellow eyes.

So close.

They weren't going to make it, she knew.

They were all going to die.

She instinctively ducked her head as she ran below the rotor blades, even though the spinning disk was high above her head. The crew chief pointed his sidearm over her head and started firing.

This time, she didn't turn around.

Carolyn willed herself to stop and wait as the members of her team entered the rear of the Chinook. She was, after all, the leader, and she should enter last.

She counted three of them. Three of four.

She spun around and saw the fourth member, Matt, running toward them. *He must have fallen!* she thought. Behind him was something she'd never seen before—and hoped never to see again. Something right out of the depths of hell. A creature on long legs, jointed like a Hollywood special effects monster. She screamed helplessly as the thing reached out with a long, clawed hand and grabbed Matt by the head.

"Matt! No!"

The beast effortlessly tore Matt's head from his shoulders, a fountain of blood shooting into the air from severed arteries. The lifeless body fell to the cement.

The creature threw the wide-eyed head to the side as the crew chief's bullets slammed into its chest. It was still heading toward them, but the impacts were slowing it down. With each shot, it threw its head back and screamed a horrible wailing sound, its mouth open wide, revealing rows of obsidian knives.

The engines spun up and the Chinook began to rise. The pilot wasn't willing to wait one second more.

Carolyn tumbled into the back of the chopper, immediately followed by the crew chief, still firing as fast as he could.

Carolyn crawled on all fours toward the front of the chopper, trying desperately to put as much distance as she could between her and the wide-open rear ramp.

As the chopper lifted off, she watched in horror as a clawed hand grasped the crew chief by the ankle and yanked him out.

His piercing scream was cut short. And his eyes . . . For a second, Carolyn had seen the terror in his eyes as he was pulled from the chopper, yanked away from safety to certain death. She knew she'd never forget those eyes. She looked away and covered her mouth with her hand, sickened, her body starting to shake as the reality of the situation hit her. The crew chief had saved her life by standing and fighting, delaying the creature's advance, and if he hadn't . . .

Over the scream of the engines and the *thwap thwap thwap* of the rotor blades slicing into the black sky, clawing at the air to gain altitude, she could hear the chattering, the clicking, so intense that she covered her ears to muffle the terrible noise.

From what she'd seen, she knew everyone left on the ground was as good as dead. None of them had a chance.

• • •

As the big Chinook sped northward, the automatic weapons fire on the tarmac behind them slowly diminished. And then ceased. The earsplitting chattering stopped as well, replaced with the sickening sound of flesh being torn and ripped, the sound of screams from dying lips, as the things systematically exterminated every human being left on the ground at KCI.

And then, the things ate their own dead.

In an hour, they were moving again. Toward the *others*. They could smell them in the distance. And the night was still young.

CHAPTER 16

Just ten minutes after arriving on station, his matte-black U-2 Dragon Lady soaring through the thin upper atmosphere above Kansas City, the pilot—wearing much the same gear an astronaut would—recorded the rapid advance of the mutated creatures using his array of sophisticated sensors. The information was transmitted to the National Military Command Center—the NMCC—in the bowels of the Pentagon.

It was one of many reports streaming in, all grave in nature.

Positions were overrun. Contact was lost with almost all the military units preparing to enter the city. Survivors—of which there weren't many—described waves of hideous things tearing through their positions, decimating the troops, killing every person in their path.

Thousands, if not millions, of the creatures. And they were moving fast.

Kansas City was now empty. There was no life there. The things had streamed out of the city, overtaken every single military unit in their way, wiped out the evacuation centers that had received the survivors from the previous night. Unstoppable. And worse, they were showing signs of intelligence. They were moving with a purpose, demonstrating intent. They weren't spreading out at random.

The combined readings from the quickly growing armada of airborne infrared sensors chillingly showed the things had split into six distinct groups, spreading from the dead city like a gelatinous sea creature stretching its stinging appendages toward other cities.

Topeka.

Wichita.

Springfield.

St. Louis.

Des Moines.

Omaha.

Cities full of people who hadn't been evacuated. Not to mention all the small towns that lay in the paths between these six cities and Kansas City. There had been no need to evacuate any of them. Until now.

Andrew Smith sat in the White House situation room, completely dumbfounded by what he'd heard from his SECDEF and secretary of Homeland Security. "How many did we lose?" he asked.

"Mr. President," Hugo began, "we're still trying to figure that out. We had roughly two thousand troops deployed around the city, and about a hundred within the city itself. We've had about fifty survivors accounted for so far. The numbers for the civilians . . ." He paused. "The evacuation centers have all been hit. We don't have contact with any of them. We have to assume, sir, based on the reports we've received from the survivors, there probably aren't—"

"You're telling me they're all dead?"

"Yes, Mr. President," Hugo answered softly. "They're all dead."

Andrew cupped his face in his hands. *This can't possibly be happening,* he thought. *A whole city is dead, hundreds of troops are gone, and six more cities . . . Six cities . . . are in danger.*

"Sir?" It was Marshall Stone.

Andrew looked up, his eyes weary.

"Mr. President, I suggest we deploy troops to those cities as quickly as we can. There's not enough time to get everyone out before those things reach them."

Not enough time. "Which city will they reach first?"

Hugo answered. "Topeka, sir. It's closest. We've already started initial evacuation actions, but like Tank said, there's not going to be enough time. At the speed they're moving, they could be in Topeka within the hour. We've already lost contact with Lawrence."

The president knew Lawrence, Kansas, was the home of KU, the University of Kansas. A college town. Full of kids. The thought sickened him. "How fast are these things moving?"

"We estimate roughly forty-five to fifty miles per hour, Mr. President," Hugo said.

"What?" Once again, Andrew felt a chill crawl up his spine. The creatures had enough intelligence to smash light fixtures to get out of the light, and they could move at incredible speed. "These are *animals*, right? You told me they were some kind of rodents, for Christ's sake! Nothing can run that fast!"

"These can. Sir." Hugo couldn't think of anything else to say.

"How do we stop them?"

The SECDEF and secretary of Homeland Security looked at each other, apparently hoping the other had an answer. Neither did.

Andrew wasn't willing to live with silence from his advisors. He fixed his gaze on his SECDEF. "Come on, Tank, I need some goddamned answers here."

"Mr. President," Tank said, "we've killed thousands of the damned things. But there's hundreds of thousands of them, possibly more. We've had AC-130s pounding them as hard as they can, but they're not making much of a dent. We're trying to get forces in the area as quickly as possible. A-10s, F/A-18s, other strike aircraft . . ."

"Do you mean to tell me Kansas City had hundreds of thousands of coordinated, bloodthirsty rats? Where the hell are they all coming from?"

"We haven't been able to explain the large numbers yet. Sir."

"Have we caught any of them?"

"Sir?"

"Have we caught any of them!" Andrew immediately regretted his outburst. He knew he couldn't let the frustration he was feeling get the better of him.

Tank shook his head. "Not to my knowledge, Mr. President."

"Tank, Hugo, we need to know what the hell they're made of. These may have started out as normal rats, but they're certainly not normal now. We need to take one apart and see what makes the goddamned thing tick. See what the living hell turned them into some sort of superbeasts."

Hugo cleared his throat. "It's not just rats, sir. We've received reports of other things. Two legs. Standing upright."

"People?" The realization hit Andrew like a hammer blow between the shoulder blades. Whatever had turned the animals into ferocious killers had also affected people.

"What used to be people, sir."

"How many?"

"We've seen a few," Tank said. "Mostly, it's four-legged animals, but it appears some people have been . . . mutated, too."

"All right. I want those cities evacuated. I want us to get as many people out of there as we can. Even if we save the lives of a few thousand . . ."

"The orders will go out immediately, Mr. President," Hugo said. "We'll save as many as we can."

"Get on it, Hugo. Tank, I want you to start killing those things by the hundreds of thousands. They need to be stopped. Right here, right now. If you need any authorizations for special weapons . . ."

"Understood, Mr. President." Tank noted the word *nuclear* had not been spoken. For now, it would not be considered.

"And," Andrew continued, "I want to grab one. Catch one of the little bastards and tear it apart for info. I want to know how I can kill them without blowing our own country to bits in the process."

"Roger that, boss."

"Before the both of you leave, I want to make something perfectly clear." The president's eyes were burning bright, no longer showing any signs of weariness. "I will not let this situation spiral out of control. We were caught completely off guard tonight, and we've lost a large amount of blood and treasure because of it. We will get our people out of the way. Save who we can. That is priority number one. Priority number two is killing those things. Stop them before they decimate more of our cities." He paused, thinking about how to word his next statement.

With the number of people lost in less than twenty-four hours combined with the speed at which the things were moving, Andrew knew he was facing an inconceivable loss of American life in a very short amount of time, and he had to take drastic measures to stop it before it was too late. In his gut, he knew he might be witnessing the opening stages of a battle that, if lost, could spell the end of the United States. His gut instinct, which had guided his decisions for years, was almost always correct.

"We will accomplish both priorities simultaneously, gentlemen. If we can't stop them outside of the cities, we may have to kill them wherever they are at the moment we have forces available. This means there may be civilian casualties. Some of our citizens may have to be sacrificed in order to save the lives of millions of others. This blood, gentlemen, will be on my hands. *My hands*, and no others. Is that clear?"

"Yes, Mr. President."

"Yes, sir."

As both advisors turned to leave the situation room, the president opened his comm channel to the vice president. He needed to touch base with Allison Perez.

• • •

"Madame Vice President, the president is on button one."

"Thank you, Major." Allison Perez was still at NORTHCOM, keeping abreast of the fast-moving situation as best she could. "Yes, Mr. President. This is Perez. You're on speaker. Admiral Grierson is here with me as well." They were seated in a small breakout room off the main Cheyenne Mountain Operations Center. The major closed the door behind him.

"You've seen the reports?" Andrew asked.

"Yes, sir. It's not looking good."

"I've ordered evacuations of the major cities in the spread's projected paths. We may be able to save some, but I'm afraid we're going to lose a lot of people before this is over."

Allison knew he was right. They were facing a crisis unlike any the world had ever experienced. It wasn't spinning out of control yet, but she knew unless they could stop the spread, it soon would.

Admiral Grierson spoke up. "Mr. President, the evacuation orders are on the street and being executed as we speak." Keaton Grierson was one of six geographic combatant commanders, each a four-star admiral or general tasked with operational responsibility over a specific portion of the globe. The crisis was unfolding on the North American continent, so NORTHCOM—Grierson—was leading the fight. "We'll get as many people out as we can."

"Keep pressing, Keats. We need to stop these things."

"Stopping them may become problematic, sir," Allison said. So many had died in such a short span of time, it was simply sickening.

Worse, nothing they were doing seemed to make a difference. "Their numbers seem to be growing at an exponential rate."

A pause at the other end of the line. "Theories?"

"Nothing yet, sir," Grierson said. "We believe they're leaving the Kansas City area behind. As soon as we can, we'll drop teams back into the city to try to ascertain a point of origin, or find evidence of a cause. Hopefully they'll discover something actionable."

"I've ordered the CDC and Vanguard to examine the bodies, Mr. President," Allison added, "as soon as we're able to get our hands on some. CDC will do an initial analysis, and we'll fly them to Dugway and let General Rammes's team take a closer look." Allison noticed the questioning look from Admiral Grierson and realized—a little too late—he wasn't read-in to the Vanguard program. *Well, he is now*, she figured.

"Perfect. Thank you, Allison."

The relationship between president and vice president changed from administration to administration, the nature of it depending heavily on the personalities involved, as well as on the political promises made on the campaign trail to appease all those who would hopefully cast their vote for the winning team. Some VPs served their tenures as nothing but figureheads, and others wielded their own power outside of the Oval Office, but in this administration, the relationship was much like a commanding officer and his or her second in command. Allison Perez was second in command of the good ship United States of America and would take the helm if and when required. Allison would be no political figurehead—that much Andrew had made perfectly clear when he'd offered her the job. Professionally, they saw eye to eye, as a good commander and his second should. Their personal relationship was close. Not romantic in any sense, but both knew they would stand back-to-back and fight off the hordes together, if it came to that.

After Kate died, Allison filled a role as a sounding board and a shoulder to cry on when the press corps was nowhere near. There were times, in the months following Kate's death, when Allison knew that if she so wished, she could take their relationship to another level, but she chose not to.

Allison had married young and thought she'd found the man who'd stand next to her forever. The demands of being married to a Coast Guard pilot, however, turned out to be more than he'd signed on for, and in time, the marriage simply faded away.

She wasn't lonely by any means—she didn't have time to dwell on such things—but there were times she wished she could've done things differently.

But to Allison, wishing was nothing more than an excuse for poor planning. The past is the past, and nothing can change it. The future is what one makes it. And the present—today—is the most important of all. Right now, he was the president, and she his vice. As long as they were both in office, she knew that's how their relationship would stay. To allow it to progress to something more—even though she'd considered it—would be unprofessional, and she doubted Andrew would allow it, either.

She knew him, though, probably better than any other member of his staff. She could tell his mood by the tone of his voice, by the look in his eyes. She could read him.

And right now, she needed to speak to him in private. Something in his voice . . .

"Admiral, I need the room, please."

"Yes, ma'am," Grierson said. He stood and exited the room without question.

CHAPTER 17

Ever since the hideous radiological attack unleashed in Cleveland had murdered thousands of innocents, the American public had practiced citywide evacuations. What was once considered an obsolete, feel-good civil defense program—good for nothing more than making the public feel like there actually was an orderly way to get out of the way of hundreds of Soviet nuclear weapons that would soon be dropping on their heads—had been transformed by the urgent necessity of national survival into an actual, functioning program. The Department of Homeland Security had provided every major city with an evacuation plan designed to cover a number of possibilities, portions of which were practiced once a month.

Cleveland had been an example of mass public panic. People tried to run, to get as far away from the spreading cloud of invisible death as they could, and hundreds had died in the process. The entire nation had watched as it happened. Watched as the highways clogged and ground to a standstill. Watched as people had dropped dead, choking and spitting blood, clawing their eyes from their sockets. Watched mothers and children die leaning against their cars, hopelessly stranded in the sea of automobiles lining the highways for as far as the eye could see, while the dirty cloud spread. The sobering fact that more people had died trying to get away from the area than had died the instant the devices had exploded around the city had been a wake-up call. People had watched. And knew that next time, it could very well be them.

Six months ago, the entire city of Chicago had been evacuated. There were problems, but not on the scale some had expected. The exercise had gone surprisingly well.

But it had taken three days.

It was just an exercise. People knew it wasn't real.

Hugo knew there were going to be problems. The major cities—New York, Chicago, Los Angeles, Denver, San Francisco, most of the larger metro areas—were much more prepared than the smaller cities, as they were more lucrative targets. At least they were before this night. Right now, there were six other cities he wished had had more time to prepare. The entire country knew about Kansas City—and when the sirens sounded, people wouldn't react like it was an exercise. They would panic.

He prayed most could be saved.

Minutes after Hugo had stepped from the situation room, the sirens began wailing in Topeka. Five minutes later, in Des Moines. Then, in Omaha. St. Louis. Wichita. Springfield was last.

A mass exodus began.

The things entered Topeka forty-five minutes later. There were no soldiers there to delay their approach. There hadn't been enough time.

The hideous sound of demons feeding filled the Kansas night.

CHAPTER 18

Carolyn pressed herself against the interior wall of the Chinook's cargo area, hugging her knees tightly against her chest with two trembling arms. The rear hatch of the big chopper was still open, and the cold night air swirled around her, making every inch of exposed skin feel like ice. She was shivering uncontrollably, not only from the cold, but also from the absolute terror of what she'd just witnessed.

She could tell they weren't flying very high, as the lights from what little population there was in this part of Kansas farm country slid below them, the rapid *thwap thwap thwap* of the dual rotor blades propelling them forward. Toward where, she didn't know. And didn't much care.

The three remaining members of her team—also cold and frightened—were huddled together on the other side of the chopper's large interior. As far as she could tell in the dark, there were also about ten soldiers in the cargo area, the ones lucky enough to get away. They sat quietly, rifles between their knees, eyes looking straight ahead at nothing in particular. Carolyn knew their thoughts must be with their fellow soldiers—their brothers and sisters in arms—those who'd been left behind.

To fight.

To die.

The thought of all those people being killed by those *things* made her stomach turn. The yellow eyes—hundreds, thousands of pairs of pinpoint evil, bounding across the tarmac in the darkness. What she'd seen couldn't be real. It couldn't have happened! But she knew it had happened. And more than that, she knew she was one of the lucky ones. If she'd fallen instead of Matt . . . She shivered as she remembered his head ripped from his body as easily as a grape plucked from a stem. She remembered the crew chief . . . His eyes, as he was pulled from the open ramp. Whatever those things were, they were very, very real.

Noticing she was shaking, one of the soldiers handed Carolyn a heavy wool blanket. "This should help, ma'am," he said. She thanked him, and he walked back to his seat.

She covered herself, leaving only a small opening around her face to breathe.

The big Chinook slowly turned to the right, banking ever so slightly. Carolyn instinctively looked out the rear hatch to give her inner ears the assurance that, yes, they were actually turning, and she saw it. A single clawed hand grasping the edge of the chopper's back ramp.

She blinked her eyes, praying she was just seeing things.

She wasn't.

Two yellow orbs burned back at her from the blackness.

It had somehow managed to gain a handhold on the underside of the chopper after throwing the crew chief out the back.

And now, it was climbing inside.

Carolyn screamed as the beast passed her, scrambling forward into the hold. It hadn't seen her. Covering herself with the blanket had saved her life.

Startled by her scream, the soldiers turned, oblivious to the beast moving toward them. The first two were thrown out the open rear of the chopper—spinning through the blackness to their deaths below—before they had time to react.

The creature was moving fast, clawing and tearing as it went.

The next soldier brought his weapon to bear, but he too was flung toward the rear, and he skidded across the metal floor until his body disappeared into the darkness. His rifle slid across the floor, thudding to a stop against Carolyn's feet. She looked at it, for an instant wishing she'd learned how to handle a gun. She grabbed the rifle, which to her surprise was much heavier than she thought it would be.

The cargo hold of the chopper was filled with shrill, terrified screams as the members of her team scooted toward the front, toward the cockpit. The soldier farthest away from the beast opened up with his M16, spraying a volley of three-round bursts into the creature, which reeled back and let loose a horrible, thunderous roar, waving its long arms as if to knock the bullets away. Small, chunky clouds of gore blossomed behind it as the supersonic shells exited its back. But it didn't go down.

Carolyn, holding the rifle in her left hand, crawled on all fours toward the very rear of the chopper and huddled against a heavy bag of equipment strapped down to the floor near the ramp. She crouched low to stay out of the beast's field of view, trying desperately not to scream. The cold wind from the rotor wash pummeled her face.

The other soldiers started firing. The muzzle flashes from their M16s lit the interior of the cargo hold like strobe lights, capturing each movement as a still picture, a single moment of terror. The creature dropped to its knees as the shells slammed into its body. Sparks flew from the metal beside Carolyn's head, and she realized she was in their line of fire. She crawled around the heavy equipment bag, trying to shield herself. The metallic *ting* of spent rounds bouncing around her was almost as loud as the bursts from the soldiers' M16s. The sturdy bag thudded against her as some of the rounds hit it. She was only feet from the edge of the chopper's rear ramp, and the empty blackness outside. She held tightly to the bag as the chopper began to jink wildly to the left and to the right, its rotors' noise changing pitch—growling—with each abrupt movement.

She peeked over the bag and saw the creature crawling into the cockpit. The soldiers were desperately trying to fire at the thing as they skidded across the floor, working to maintain their balance.

She watched in horror as one long, clawed arm sliced through the air and crunched into the pilot's helmet. The big chopper dropped sickeningly, Carolyn's stomach rising into her throat as she floated above the metal floor for an instant.

She looked out the rear ramp and saw the treetops whipping by, small bits of leaves and branches snapping off as the bottom of the Chinook slid across the upper branches. She could smell the trees. The scent of broken wood, green with sap.

They were going to crash.

Carolyn always heard that people who knew they were about to die would see their entire lives flash before their eyes.

As the chopper started to spin out of control, all she saw was the horrid face of a beast standing in the cockpit of the doomed Chinook, one clawed hand grasping part of what used to be the pilot, two bright yellow eyes fixed directly on her.

She heard thick branches snap. The screech of twisting metal.

And then everything went black.

CHAPTER 19

The OH-58 Kiowa Warrior scout helicopter was the last aircraft to escape the carnage at KCI. Its occupants were also the last two survivors.

Colonel Garrett Hoffman sat silently in the right seat, trying to comprehend what had just happened; his entire base of operations, hundreds of troops and civilians, had just been massacred by a wave of . . .

Things.

He'd heard the president's speech, heard that some kind of mutated rats had killed thousands of people in Kansas City. Incomprehensible, it seemed, until he saw them with his own eyes. By the thousands.

So many, thousands, hundreds of thousands . . .

Moving faster than he thought possible.

The eyes, the goddamned glowing eyes . . .

His troops had stood their ground and pumped all the firepower they could throw at the beasts—and still they came. Climbing over their dead. In waves. Small yellow eyes glowing brightly in the night. Tearing into his troops. Killing them.

He'd watched as the Air Force peppered the tarmac with cluster bombs, tearing hundreds of the things to shreds with each pass. But still, they came.

He'd watched as the last choppers wallowed into the sky, carrying the lucky few who had managed to escape at the last instant. And then, as his own chopper had lifted off, he'd watched them completely cover the tarmac, their bizarre chattering and clicking filling the Missouri night, as they moved toward the terminal building. To kill whoever remained.

His entire base camp—the whole goddamned airport—had been overrun in a matter of minutes. It had been so fast, too fast to make any decisions. Too fast to move. Too fast to save anyone.

I left you all behind.

He was stunned, in a state of shock, and swept by a sickening wave of guilt. The airport had been his, and he'd lost it. Worst of all, he was alive, and his troopers weren't.

Part of him felt he should've died with his soldiers, but another part knew he was getting a chance to avenge their deaths. To kill as many of those fucking things as he could. Especially the *humanoid* ones.

He'd emptied his sidearm into the head of one of the two-legged devils, which had jumped at least twenty feet into the air to grab the right landing skid of the Kiowa, and watched as it fell dead to the cement below, rapidly torn apart and devoured by the rat-things swarming where his chopper had been just a few seconds before. They hadn't been briefed to expect anything with two legs, but whatever it'd been, Garrett knew he'd seen intelligence in its eyes. Behind the fury of its fiery gaze, it was thinking. He almost hadn't been able to pull his trigger fast enough to make the goddamned thing die.

Garrett couldn't wait to kill more of them, with his bare hands if he had to. The thought made him warm inside. Hate was an effective field dressing.

"Sir!"

The pilot was leaning toward him, yelling to be heard over the interior noise of the Kiowa's cockpit.

"We've got a Chinook down, Colonel, about three miles from here! We're closest to the crash site!"

Garrett didn't have a helmet, so he wasn't able to hear the pilot's radio traffic. "Okay, Captain!" he yelled back. "What are you waiting for! Let's move!"

The pilot banked the chopper hard, lining up their course with the last known position of the CH-47. The Kiowa Warrior's mastmounted sight—looking like a large basketball with glass eyes suspended above the main rotor—could see through the darkness with a low-light television and thermal imaging system. This chopper was designed to scout and search for the enemy, using the mounted sight to peek over hills and trees without exposing the entire aircraft to enemy fire. It would find the enemy, and the Apaches—the gunship choppers—would attack and kill.

The pilot skimmed the trees, using his night vision equipment to navigate obstacles and his global positioning system (GPS) readout to find the exact coordinates. The mounted sight swiveled left and right, searching for a heat signature—a fire—from the downed Chinook. To the south, the thermal imaging system picked up thousands of small heat signatures, moving fast to the north. The things, on the move. They were only a few miles from their position.

"Sir! If we're going to find them, we have to do it fast! The things are moving this way, about three miles from our position to the south!" The pilot pointed toward where the wave of things was approaching.

Garrett squinted through the darkness, trying to pick out their glowing eyes in the blackness below. At the speed they'd moved from the city to the airport, he knew they could cover three miles in just a few minutes.

"Got it, sir!" the pilot yelled as the thermal imaging site picked up the crash site. "About five degrees left, two hundred yards!" There was no fire, but the heat from the Chinook's two engines still glowed bright green on the screen. If there was no fire, the possibility of survivors was much higher, Garrett knew. *If* there were any survivors. He couldn't discern any movement on the screen.

"Take us in closer!" Garrett yelled. "Try to find a place to put us down!"

"Yes, sir! Looks like they went down in the middle of some trees! We may have to put down right here!"

"Do it!"

The Kiowa settled to the ground, its rotor wash kicking up grass and dust from the plowed field at the edge of the tree line. "Sir, you're going to have to hurry—"

"I know! If I'm not back by the time the things get here, you get your ass out of here! That's an order!"

"Yes, sir!"

Garrett jumped from the Kiowa and sprinted toward the tree line. As he ran, he looked to his left, trying to spot yellow eyes in the darkness. He couldn't see them.

Yet.

CHAPTER 20

The president wearily looked up from a blurry sheet of paper as the secretary of Homeland Security entered the situation room.

"Mr. President, it's happening in Topeka."

Andrew could hear the utter helplessness in Hugo's voice and see the matching desperation in the man's eyes. *Topeka. It's happening again, and there's not a goddamned thing we can do about it. Go ahead and say it, Hugo.*

"We started the evacuations about forty-five minutes before the things entered the city," Hugo said and then paused, the weight of the world brutally pressing down on his shoulders. "It wasn't enough time, Mr. President. We're going to lose Topeka."

The president glanced down to the statistics in front of him, squinting to read the numbers through tired eyes.

Kansas City, a city of over four hundred thousand people. Dead.

Lawrence. Nearly eighty thousand people. Dead.

Topeka. Over one hundred twenty thousand. Getting torn apart at that very moment. Dying.

Andrew knew there were five other major cities in the process of being evacuated: Omaha, Nebraska, 390,000 people; Des Moines, Iowa, nearly 200,000; St. Louis, Missouri, 350,000; Springfield, Missouri, over 150,000; Wichita, Kansas, 344,000. Combined with the surrounding towns and small communities dotting the map in the path of the things, the numbers were staggering. Well over a million of his fellow citizens, people he was sworn to protect, were in harm's way. Over half a million might've died already, in the short span of less than twenty-four hours.

Andrew looked past Hugo at the SECDEF and read the same desperation in his eyes. "Tank, what's the situation on the ground?"

"We're placing as many troops as we can around the five major cities under threat, Mr. President, regular army and National Guard. Right now, we're relying almost entirely on the local units for the deployments. They're not all combat units, but they all know how to fire a rifle." A fleeting old soldier's smile. "We'll be airlifting other units into the region by morning. Until then, sir, we'll have to stop their advance by air. Air Combat Command is moving as many strike aircraft into the region as possible." He stole a quick glance at his watch. "The first B-52 strike out of Barksdale should occur in about thirty minutes, directed against the wave heading toward Omaha. Similar strikes are planned against the five additional waves. Tactical aircraft are hitting them as we speak."

"Impact?" *Tell me something good, Tank.*

"Negligible, Mr. President. Hardly any impact at all." The SECDEF lowered his eyes, too full of the bitterness of failure to hold the gaze of his commander in chief.

"How can that be?"

Tank looked up again. "Sir, you saw our reports from Kansas City International. They blew right through the troops we had on the ground, and the air attacks had almost no effect. Until we bring more firepower to bear . . ."

"Okay, Tank. You're doing all you can. I understand that." The president looked up at the digital clock on the wall of the situation room. It was half past two in the morning. "I want details after the BUFF strikes." The B-52 was officially named the Stratofortress, but was more commonly known as the BUFF, which stood for *Big Ugly Fat Fellow*. Or *Fucker*, depending on who was asking. "I need to know if we're going to be able to stop them with conventionals."

"Understood, sir." Tank knew what the next step could be if conventional weapons failed, a scenario he wouldn't allow himself to ponder. Not yet.

"How long until they enter Omaha?"

"We estimate less than three hours, sir," Tank said. "Unless we can stop them, that is."

Less than three hours, the president thought. *Right before sunrise.* "Hugo, keep me updated on the evacuations. Keep pressing."

"Will do, sir."

Andrew leaned back in his chair, looking at the myriad of charts and displays arrayed in front of him. No president before him had ever watched the nation dying right before his eyes.

For the first time, Andrew began to wonder if this nightmare might require a nightmare solution.

CHAPTER 21

The heavy, choking stench of aviation fuel was nearly overpowering.

Garrett knew the fact that the chopper hadn't exploded on impact was a miracle. The *tink tink* of hot metal, though, meant there could still be an explosion at any moment. He'd have to move fast.

The wrecked Chinook was resting on its side, the rotor blades completely shredded and lying in pieces around the crash site. As Garrett moved toward the rear of the chopper, stepping over shards of carbon fiber rotor sticking out of the ground like husks from a blackened crop, he heard no moaning, no cries for help. Just the tinking sound of hot metal cooling in the evening air.

He shined his flashlight into the open rear of the chopper and was horrified at the scene the light revealed. The walls of the cargo compartment were covered in blood. Motionless bodies littered the interior. He could smell the blood, thick and coppery, mixed with the sickening stench of bile, the same haunting scent of a smoldering battlefield, an odor not easily forgotten by those who'd experienced the full brutality and violent aftermath of close combat. It was a smell he knew all too well, one he hoped he'd someday forget. "Is anyone alive?" he shouted, not expecting an answer.

He got none.

Garrett hurriedly checked each body for signs of life, knowing he was only going through the motions, but also knowing he couldn't leave without making sure. He owed them at least that much.

All dead.

From the look of the injuries, he figured the Chinook had hit the ground extremely hard. He'd seen the aftermath of aircraft crashes before, but none had been quite this bad; a couple of the bodies were twisted and mangled, missing arms and legs. The human body was incredibly resilient, but typically didn't fare too well when slammed into an immoveable object—like the ground. Inertia could be a real bitch when it came to flesh and bone.

Among the bloodied camouflage uniforms of the dead soldiers, he noticed civilian clothes. Kneeling to look closely at one of the civilian bodies, Garrett's eyes clouded with recognition as he shone his light into a dead face. He knew this man, but would sadly never know his name. One of the team members from the C-130. He quickly accounted for three civilians, but there'd been five, hadn't there? Yes, definitely five, including the brunette Marilyn Monroe. *Carolyn, that was her name. Legs. Carolyn Ridenour.* None of the bodies here were female, though. *Another chopper*, he hoped silently, *she must've made it out on another chopper.* The woman and her team didn't need to be at the airport in the first place, as it turned out, and now three of them lay dead in a wrecked chopper. Crappy luck, that was.

He felt a pang of guilt for treating her so gruffly on the tarmac, but he let it go. He had to. She was probably dead, like the rest. Just like his soldiers. And there'd been *hundreds* of them, many of whom he knew. He didn't know her from Eve. Never would.

Let it go.

Garrett stood and swung his light toward the cockpit. The entrance was too mangled to pass through, so he ran out the back of the Chinook and around to the front to check the flight crew. He discovered smashed cockpit windows and both pilots—obviously dead—hanging partway out of the twisted, crushed cockpit, along with, his light revealed, something else.

In an instant, he understood.

The horrific injuries he'd seen weren't all caused by the crash.

They'd been killed by the hideous thing that now lay broken and twisted beside the dead flight crew. When he shined his flashlight across the creature's mangled body, dead eyes glowed back at him as the beam entered through dilated pupils. Its mouth was wide, revealing rows of black, knife-edged teeth. A long, thin arm dangled at an odd angle in front of it, long claws spread wide, covered in bloody, dripping gore.

It was the same kind of beast he'd seen at the airport. The same kind he'd blasted from the Kiowa's skid as they lifted off. A monster. Something that couldn't possibly exist, yet it was there in front of him, as real as the ground beneath his boots, muted yellow discs staring at him. Mocking him.

Garrett shifted his light away from the thing's body. He'd seen enough. There were no survivors here. Most of the passengers—and most likely the crew, he knew—had died before the crash, killed by the thing hanging out of the cockpit. He turned to run back to the Kiowa—and saw the mass of glowing eyes in the distance. Racing across the darkened fields. Thousands of them. Small, yellow lights, bouncing and weaving, heading his way. And fast.

He heard the Kiowa's engine spooling up—the pilot had seen them, too. As Garrett watched the eyes bouncing in the darkness, he noticed something different. No chattering, no clicking sounds like he'd heard at the airport. The little bastards were moving quietly.

As he ran, Garrett judged the distance to the chopper. He knew he'd make it in time, but not by much. He fell to the ground, cursing himself for tripping over something in the dark. As he scrambled to his knees and spat dirt from his mouth, he knew now was definitely not the time to pull a goddamned Jamie Lee Curtis.

The eyes were close. So unbearably *close*.

He quickly got back to his feet and realized what he'd tripped over had felt soft. Like a body. He aimed his flashlight toward where he'd stumbled and saw the motionless body of Carolyn Ridenour, lying on her side. He knelt by her. "Ms. Ridenour? Carolyn!" He felt for her pulse . . . and found one. *At least she's still alive*, he thought, and flung her over his shoulder.

As he ran toward the Kiowa, he heard a moaning, an eerie, low sound, barely audible over the sound of the Kiowa's rotor noise. At first he thought it was Carolyn, but then he realized the sound was coming from a distance. From where he'd seen the things approaching.

The chattering and clicking suddenly erupted like thunder, and he knew he'd been spotted. He glanced over his shoulder, trying hard not to lose his balance as he ran with the added weight, and confirmed what he thought. They were coming right for him.

Garrett saw the Kiowa's pilot reach over and open the right-hand cockpit door as they approached, frantically waving at him to hurry.

The noise behind him was getting louder. With each step, he could feel the ground vibrating beneath his feet.

He knew the things were right behind him.

He threw Carolyn's body into his seat and climbed on top of her, cramming himself into the small cockpit just as the landing skids lifted off the ground. The chopper tilted forward as the rotor blades grabbed at the air, like spinning hands desperately grasping for purchase, and lifted off and away from the mass of creatures streaming toward them.

A set of long, sharp claws scraped the bottom of the Kiowa as it rose into the night sky, a thing barely missing a handhold as it leapt at the chopper.

Garrett held tightly to the unconscious woman huddled beneath his body.

He knew it had been close.

Too close.

•   •   •

As the *thwap thwap thwap* of the Kiowa receded into the distance, the chattering and clicking ceased. All that could be heard was the muffled thunder of thousands of ravenous beasts heading north across the farm fields of eastern Kansas.

The same sound could be heard from five other masses, as they raced across the trembling American heartland.

CHAPTER 22

The full evacuation of the Omaha area was under way, but it wasn't going well. Traffic to the north on I-29 and west on I-80 was at a complete standstill—both highways were filled with bumper-to-bumper traffic as the city's residents desperately attempted to flee what was approaching from the southeast. The situation only worsened as more and more people tried to take alternate routes out of the city, clogging the narrow roads and state highways with hundreds of vehicles.

People were panicky—they all knew what had happened in Kansas City. Cars full of families and whatever belongings they could grab lined the roads, each driver terrified they wouldn't make it out in time. Some were still in their pajamas. Accidents were inevitable. From the air, an unbroken string of taillights stretched to the horizon.

The same scene was unfolding in St. Louis. In Des Moines. Wichita. Springfield.

To the south of Omaha, a line of defense was quickly forming, composed of USAF security forces from Offutt Air Force Base and Army National Guard units from the surrounding area. They were lightly armed.

The Offutt AFB flight line was filling with strike aircraft, stopping to refuel and rearm. A-10s and F-16s thundered into the sky, heading south.

As they approached the base, Garrett watched the long blue tail of an F-16's afterburner rocket by him as the Viper screamed south, a pair of cluster bombs slung beneath its wings.

As the Kiowa settled on the ramp at Offutt AFB, the first bright flashes from a B-52 strike lit the southern horizon. A line of six of the mighty BUFFs from Barksdale AFB, Louisiana, were puking their heavy loads of high-explosive iron bombs from their fat bellies and wing pylons, shaking the ground with a thunderous roar that rolled across the cornfields like a massive earthquake.

As the first B-52 turned back toward Barksdale, the second bomber in line dropped its load of forty 500-pound general-purpose bombs. The remaining four BUFFs lumbered through the air, awaiting their turn on the bombing run, their turn to add to the fiery maelstrom erupting below. The press liked to call it "carpet bombing." To those who flew the old warhorses, it was called the "elephant walk"—one bomber after another, flying single-file in the sky, dropping their war loads.

For the first time in history, the oldest and mightiest symbol of American airpower was tearing into an enemy on American soil. It was a sobering sight.

As Garrett carried Carolyn across the ramp toward a waiting Humvee, all he could hear was the rumble from the B-52 strikes, the bomb blasts lighting the sky with an eerie orange glow.

He couldn't hear the sound of thousands of claws tearing into the soil, digging, digging. As the high explosives from the BUFFs blew hundreds of them to shreds with each detonation, the wave stopped in place.

A low moaning sound escaped from the open maws of the upright things, barely audible over the bombing's lionlike roar. Giving orders.

Soil flew through the air as each of the things tore into the ground with such ferocity, such urgency, that in a matter of minutes most had disappeared from view. They continued to dig, even as the 500-pound bombs continued dropping among them and unearthing hundreds with each earth-trembling blast, throwing their torn bodies high into the air and scattering pieces all over the once-peaceful farmland. Those that avoided the bombs continued to dig until they were far belowground, safe from the aerial onslaught being unleashed against them.

But they weren't trying to escape the bombardment. It was time.

To burrow.

To rest.

And more importantly, it was time to multiply.

At that same instant, the five other waves of creatures stopped in place and started to dig as well. A biological clock in the restructured brains of each of the things had hit an internal stop—the urgency to feed was replaced by an urgency to get underground, to hide. To prepare for the changes to come.

The high-altitude grumble from the B-52s' engines receded into the distance as they left their target area to recover at Barksdale.

When the sun broke the horizon announcing a new day, the American heartland was quiet once again.

Quiet as a tomb.

DAY TWO

CHAPTER 23

"Mr. President?"

Andrew lifted his head, surprised he'd actually dozed off for a few minutes. He quickly glanced at his watch, and found his few minutes had in fact lasted more than an hour. Jessie Hruska was standing by his desk, her hand resting on his shoulder.

"Sir, General Smythe is on the line from the NMCC. He has some new information."

Andrew reached for his secure phone, which had a direct connection to the National Military Command Center in the Pentagon. "Yes, General?"

"Mr. President, we've had a new development."

"Go on."

"Sir, the things have disappeared."

"Disappeared?"

"They're gone, sir. None of our monitoring equipment is picking them up. No infrared signatures, no ground radar contacts, no visual sightings. We think they may have gone underground."

"When did this happen?"

"About forty-five minutes ago, sir. The first B-52 strike was hitting them outside of Omaha and—"

"Forty-five minutes ago? Why wasn't I notified immediately?" He flashed an angry glance at his national security advisor, which he instantly regretted. He'd been awake for over twenty hours straight. Allison had noticed the fatigue in his voice, and called him on it. Now was not the time for the president of the United States to be asleep on his feet, she'd said, and as usual, she was right. Fifteen-minute catnaps could do wonders.

Jessie must've made sure he wasn't disturbed once he dozed off. She'd only woken him when it was absolutely necessary to do so.

The general was fumbling for words on the other end of the line. "Uh, sir, we weren't exactly sure what we were seeing. I wanted solid info before—"

"Okay, General. I understand." He looked apologetically at Jessie, and she smiled back. For just an instant, as he looked into her eyes, he allowed himself to feel a moment of affection for her. It was something he'd tried to avoid, tried to ignore, but it was getting more and more difficult.

Ever since the death of his wife over two years ago, he'd completely buried his whole being in the demands of the job—in part to deal with his loss, and in part to shield himself from those around him. A president, no matter what happened in his personal life, had to remain strong, especially in a time of war. Showing weakness, even when faced with the loss of someone so dear to him, was simply not an option. He had mourned, and the nation had mourned with him. But it had only been for a short time. No matter how much it hurt, he felt he had to put it behind him and move forward as quickly as possible, for the sake of his country.

As the months dragged on and he continued to bury his pain underneath the events of the day, it became less and less prevalent, even in the few quiet moments he was able to grab over the course of his grueling daily schedule. He thought of his wife less and less, which at times caused an incredible guilt to sweep over him.

After a year had passed, however, he began to feel a connection with his national security advisor. It was a connection that had grown stronger with each passing day. They'd worked side by side continuously during his administration, and there was rarely a day that went by when they weren't together in some capacity. Andrew knew, deep down, that Jessie Hruska cared for him. She was an incredible woman—strong, capable, and unafraid. She'd been a superb source of guidance and counsel to him and had helped direct the course of the nation in this time of war. More importantly, she'd been a source of comfort for him, especially after his wife had died. There had been many little moments like this, when she'd openly shown her compassion for him. He was finding it extremely difficult to keep his relationship with her on a strictly professional level.

She was striking—no man could help but notice her. But he was starting to look beyond the physical, to see inside. With subtle glances across a conference table or seemingly unintentional touches when they were standing close, he could tell she was feeling the same thing. The professional part of him told him it couldn't happen—shouldn't happen—but the man inside of him was telling him something entirely different.

And it was getting harder to ignore.

Andrew returned his thoughts to his chairman of the Joint Chiefs on the other end of the line as Jessie sat down across from his desk. "Go ahead, Ray. Continue," he said.

"Sir, when the B-52s hit the Omaha wave, we initially thought the strike had wiped them out. They were just . . . *gone*. But the other five waves we were monitoring disappeared at the same time. Their advances suddenly stopped, and all the infrared signatures disappeared in the span of a few minutes."

"You said you think they went underground?"

"Yes, sir. We've got people on the ground in the area of the Omaha strike. They're reporting the bombing killed hundreds of the things. They've recovered a number of the bodies for analysis as well, sir."

"Good. Maybe we can figure out what the hell caused this."

"Yes, sir. Some of the things were in the process of going to ground when they were killed by the strike. From the looks of it, the ones that survived the bombing escaped by quickly tunneling underground. We assume they're still there, Mr. President."

"How deep did they go?"

"We're trying to ascertain that right now, sir. We've got ground imaging radar being flown into the area. If they're not too deep, we can bomb the bastards out."

"And if they're too deep?"

"We're working on that, sir."

"The same thing happened with the other five waves? At the same time?"

"Yes, sir."

"Were they under attack as well?"

"The B-52s weren't hitting them yet—tactical aircraft, cluster bombs, no heavy bombardment. It wasn't making much of a dent in their numbers."

"So what you're telling me is they went to ground for some reason other than being under attack?"

"Yes, sir, it would appear so."

"How long until we have the ground radar in position?"

"It should be outside Omaha within the hour, Mr. President."

"If we *can* kill them, General, I want air strikes lined up and ready to go as soon as we know. If they're too deep, I want options."

"Understand, sir."

"Thank you, General." The president disconnected the line and pushed another button connecting him to his secretary of Homeland Security. Hugo McIntyre's voice came on a few seconds later.

"Yes, Mr. President."

"Hugo, what's the status of the evacuations?"

"Sir, it's not going as well as we'd hoped."

The president listened as Hugo McIntyre told him the bad news. Even though the exercises had gone relatively well, and the American people were much more prepared for a citywide evacuation now than they'd ever been in the past, he'd known it wouldn't go smoothly. The people knew what was coming, and some had panicked. The highways were jammed with traffic, hopelessly stalled by wrecks that were taking much too long to clear. Many had died in the rush to evacuate, and it was possible many more would die as the process continued. It was inevitable.

The president knew it would be a game of numbers. A cold calculus. The number to die in the evacuations would be much less than those who would die if the things made it into the cities. They'd already lost over half a million people in a little more than twenty-four hours. That number by itself was hard to stomach, but Andrew Smith knew it could be much, much worse. If the things hadn't stopped when they did . . .

"Hugo, I want those cities cleared. I don't care what kind of resources you need to do it. We have a pause right now, and I don't know how long it will last. So far, the things have only been active at night. If this remains so, we have about ten hours before they start moving again."

"We're doing all we can, sir."

"I know. Keep pressing, Hugo."

"Yes, sir."

The president ended the call. "Jessie, I want the bodies of those things completely analyzed. I want to know what made them, I want to know what makes them tick, and I want to know how to kill them."

"Yes, Mr. President." She turned to leave.

"And Jessie?"

"Yes, sir?"

"Thanks for letting me get some sleep. I needed it."

"You're welcome, sir." She smiled. For an instant, it seemed like she was going to say something else, but the moment slipped away as she turned to leave.

Andrew watched her leave, wishing he'd met her in another time and another place, where he could tell her how he felt. As the door swung shut behind her, he felt incredibly alone. He needed a partner now more than ever, someone he could talk to without a professional barrier, someone who could listen to his doubts, listen to his fears, and help him shoulder all the burdens resting solidly, and completely, on his shoulders. Since Kate's death, he hadn't had that kind of closeness with anyone. She'd guided him through his military career and through the first tough year of his administration. Always there, always listening, always understanding. Oh, how he needed her now.

But Kate was dead and gone. And she would never come back.

Alone in the situation room, the president covered his face with his hands as the tears slowly streamed down his face.

CHAPTER 24

Carolyn screamed.

In front of her was a beast standing on two crooked legs, its long, clawed arms reaching for her, glowing eyes burning right into her own eyes like two fiery shafts of pain. She tried to run, but couldn't. She felt its cold, leathery hands grasp her head, felt the pain as its claws dug into her cheeks and scalp, and sickeningly realized she was about to die as the thing began to twist. She heard the bones in her neck snap as her head was wrenched from her shoulders—

"Ms. Ridenour? Carolyn, wake up, it's okay. You're safe now! Carolyn?"

She opened her eyes—*a hospital*? A man was leaning over her. He was wearing a white coat, and a stethoscope hung from his neck. She could smell the distinctive medical stink that she hated so much: heavy disinfectant, sterile, suffocating. "Where am I?" she asked.

"You're in a hospital in Omaha, Ms. Ridenour. My name is Doctor Tanner."

"What happened? Why am I—"

"There was a crash, Carolyn. You were brought here after your helicopter went down. Do you remember?"

She did.

The snapping tree branches. The smell of sap.

The yellow eyes.

Her memories came flooding back. "There was a thing in the chopper! It killed the pilot—oh God, it killed the soldiers! They were shooting it, but it wouldn't die! It got into the cockpit and grabbed the pilot and—"

Doctor Tanner held her steady. "It's all right now. It's dead."

She didn't want to ask the next question. "Is anyone . . . My team was on that chopper—"

The doctor stood. His face said it all.

Carolyn's heart sank. All of them, dead? "Did anyone survive?"

"No, ma'am. I'm very sorry."

Carolyn closed her eyes tightly as the faces of her team flashed through her mind. Her memories of them were all smiles, laughter, and camaraderie. They'd been her coworkers. They'd been her friends.

She tried to suppress the sobs rising in her throat, tried hard to stay strong. A tear ran down her cheek as she felt someone sit down on the side of her bed.

"Ms. Ridenour?"

She opened her eyes and saw a soldier sitting by her side. She immediately recognized him as the Army officer she'd met at Kansas City International—Colonel Hoffman. "You were at—"

"Kansas City. The airport. I met you when your team arrived."

Carolyn remembered seeing the things sweep over the tarmac, killing everyone in their path, jumping on the helicopters trying to take off. She didn't think anyone could've survived. "You made it out?"

"Yes." He looked down at the floor. "I was on the last chopper to get out."

She knew the operations at the airport had been his responsibility—he'd been in command. She felt incredible pain from the loss of her team, but she could only imagine the torment he felt from losing his soldiers. There'd been so many of them.

And he'd been the last one out.

The doctor spoke. "Ms. Ridenour, you're a very lucky lady. Colonel Hoffman here found your crash site and got you out of there just in time."

"Just in time?" She didn't like the sound of that.

"We found your chopper right before it was overrun." Garrett was looking up again. "I tripped over you trying to get out of there, as a matter of fact."

"You were thrown from the crash site, Ms. Ridenour," Doctor Tanner said. "Luckily, you've only suffered some minor cuts and bruises. It could've been much worse."

Carolyn looked Garrett in the eyes. "You saved me?"

"I tripped over you."

Now I remember, she thought. *You're an asshole.* "Well, I guess I owe you a debt of gratitude for not being too swift on your feet then."

"Yes, I guess you do." He was frowning.

Carolyn immediately felt guilty for poking at him. He had, after all, risked his life to save her and had apparently barely made it out alive.

"Look, I'm sorry for that. I really do owe you a debt of gratitude. I owe you my life, Colonel. Thank you for saving me."

"You're welcome, Ms. Ridenour." At the airport, he'd seen her as a nuisance, an officious civilian getting in his way. But after he'd pulled her from the field and held her in his arms in the chopper, he'd felt an attachment to her. He hadn't been able to save many of his soldiers, but he *had* been able to save this one woman. That, to him, was a small victory. A single victory in the face of what had been a black night of unimaginable horror.

He turned to the doctor. "Doc, is she good to travel?"

"Travel? To where?"

"I have orders to accompany Ms. Ridenour to Utah. Today."

"Ms. Ridenour is in no condition to travel, Colonel. She's survived a traumatic helicopter crash. She needs to rest. I need to keep her under observation for—"

"Doc, I don't think you understand," Hoffman said. "If the trip won't kill her, she's going to travel. Right now."

"By whose orders?"

"Somebody who has enough stars on his shoulders to make both of our lives a living hell if we don't move quickly enough."

Carolyn sat up in bed. Her temples throbbed in protest. "They want me back at Van—to go to Utah?"

"Yes, Ms. Ridenour," Garrett said.

"Carolyn. Call me Carolyn." She found herself looking past the Army colonel and seeing Garrett for the first time. He was tall with angular features. Quite handsome. His eyes were slate-gray, communicating purpose, determination, and warmth.

"Okay, Carolyn it is, then. Yes, they want you back at Dugway as soon as you can move. If the doc says the trip won't kill you, we'll head for the flight line as soon as we can get out of here. Now, I need my answer, Doc. Is she good to go?"

"She needs to stay here for observation. Her injuries from the crash weren't serious, but sometimes things can come up unexpectedly that we didn't catch in our initial—"

"If you haven't noticed, *Doctor*, thousands of people were slaughtered last night. There's a very good chance that thousands more will be slaughtered before we can figure out how to stop these things. Ms. Ridenour may be able to help us do just that. If she can move, she'll move! Now give me a fucking yes or no, or I'll find another doc who can give me an answer!"

The doctor was obviously not accustomed to having a good portion of his ass bitten off, and his face showed it. He stammered as he said, "I don't believe the trip will kill her. But if it does, it's your responsibility, Colonel, not mine." He turned on his heel and left.

Carolyn had already swung her legs over the side of the bed. "I feel fine, for Christ's sake. Where the heck are my clothes?"

"Now that's more like it!" Garrett grabbed Carolyn's folded clothes from a chair in the corner of the room and tossed them to her. "Get dressed. I'll inform Dugway that we're on our way."

Much to his surprise, Carolyn stood, dropped her hospital gown to the floor, and started to get dressed. He couldn't help but stare, for a second. A long second. He turned away when Carolyn paused and looked at him.

"What's the matter? Never seen a naked woman before?"

Catching himself before he said, "Well, yes," Hoffman felt his face flush and quickly said, "I'll go call Dugway."

"Good. I'll be ready in a min—" She fell to the floor in a half-dressed heap.

Garrett knelt beside her and helped her sit up. "Are you okay?"

Her temples were throbbing terribly. "I'm a little light-headed. And I've got one hell of a headache. You must've stepped on my head when you tripped over me."

"Yeah, I'm a hopeless klutz. You're really okay to travel, right? If you croak, it'll be my ass."

"Thanks for the genuine concern for my well-being, Colonel Hoffman."

"It's Garrett." He helped her sit on the side of the bed.

"Okay, Garrett, then. Yeah, I'm okay to travel." She pulled her skirt up to her waist and buttoned her blouse. "Did they happen to tell you why they needed me back so fast?"

"They have some of the things. Dead ones. The bodies are on the way there right now, and they want you to take a look at them." He paused. "And since I have nothing else holding me here, I'm escorting you."

Carolyn looked into his eyes and saw the pain. She reached out and took his hand. "Are you okay?"

He pulled his hand away and stood. "I'm as good as I can be. Hurry up. I'll be waiting outside the door." He pulled a cell phone from the leg pocket of his ACUs as he stepped into the hall.

Carolyn knew that talking to someone about what he was feeling was not on the top of his priority list at the moment. He was, after all, a soldier with a mission to accomplish.

As Carolyn hurriedly finished putting her clothes on, she couldn't help but wonder what they'd discovered that so desperately required her analysis. *Why Dugway? Why are they taking the bodies there?*

She remembered what the sergeant major had told her about the creatures staying out of the light and the hunch she'd had, right before the things had attacked the airport.

If her hunch was correct . . .

She ran into the hall and grabbed Hoffman by the arm. "Garrett! What are you waiting for? Let's go!"

Thirty minutes later, they were screaming westward in a C-21—a USAF Learjet—toward the Dugway Proving Ground in Utah.

CHAPTER 25

The sleek B-1B Lancer—called the Bone by those in the close-knit B-1 community—started its target run, rising slowly above the horizon from the north, wings swept back for high-speed efficiency. The bomber's long, graceful lines made it look like an angry gray goose in one hell of a hurry, its cockpit glass glinting in the sun like two infuriated eyes probing the terrain below. The on-board targeting avionics were controlling every aspect of this run, ensuring perfect speed and altitude, calculating exact drop points, constantly analyzing wind speed and direction, air density, and other environmental factors that could affect the flight paths of the forty ground imaging radar sensors it was about to pound into the silent, infested ground outside of Omaha, now some ten miles distant from its current location.

The technology developed to "see" deep into the ground had advanced rapidly over the past few years, driven by the necessity to find—and kill—those who made it their habit to cower in well-developed, well-hidden underground shelters.

Radio-frequency energy—radar—had been used to penetrate the ground for various civilian purposes before the war started, such as measuring the amount of water present in the soil or finding metallic ore deposits.

As was the case with most civilian scientific advancements, the technology lent itself perfectly to military use. Ground imaging radar technology, coupled with remarkable advances in computer processing and imaging capabilities, had rapidly progressed to the point of being able to take a detailed snapshot of what lay beneath the surface of the earth. Three-dimensional images of underground complexes could be produced with exacting, almost pinpoint detail. The underground targets could be seen, studied for vulnerabilities, and then destroyed.

The afterburners from the Bone's four powerful engines spouted long tongues of blue flame as the huge bomber nosed upward, condensation clouds enveloping the aircraft as it muscled and ripped its way through air, the rapid onset of g's slamming the flight crew into their seats. With the computers controlling the flight, they were just along for the ride.

The center bomb bay doors swung open and the rotary launcher immediately started pumping out long, finned cylindrical objects, which for a moment seemed to fly in formation with the rapidly ascending bomber before slowly pulling away in their own preprogrammed flight paths.

When the last of the eight objects was dropped, the bomb bay doors slammed shut and the Bone continued its looping flight path until it was flying inverted, its curved gray back facing the ground. The pilot returned the engines to military power, and the big bird of prey rolled back to level flight, heading away from the target area.

Inside each of the eight objects, a GPS receiver passed tiny course corrections to the fins, keeping the objects on course toward the release point.

Side panels were blown from the eight objects as they began their descents, each releasing five smaller projectiles that immediately maneuvered toward their own GPS targeting coordinates on the surface. Radar altimeters in the nose of each of the objects constantly pinged the ground, measuring their exact altitude. At a preset height just moments before impact, tiny rocket motors fired, adding the right amount of momentum to slam the hardened projectiles into the plowed farm fields, each sliding to a stop at a predetermined depth in the exact point on the ground they'd been programmed to hit.

In a matter of minutes, a geometric grid of ground imaging radar sensors had been precisely planted throughout the area where the things had gone to ground. Singly, each object could map one small part of the picture; employed en masse, they could analyze a large area of underground terrain.

Fifteen minutes later, the first high-fidelity underground images popped up on screens in the NMCC.

The things were there.

And they were deep.

CHAPTER 26

"Mr. President, they're located roughly two hundred feet below the surface."

"Can we reach them?"

"Not with conventional weapons, sir."

General Smythe's statement hung in the air like a stale fart. It wasn't what the president wanted to hear. Not yet.

Every president since Harry Truman had lived with the possibility of having to order the use of nuclear weapons. Most had taken it very seriously. Others—some who couldn't even remember where they'd left their launch codes, according to the press—had treated it as a nonpossibility or a necessary nuisance. Regardless of who the president was, however, that single, ultimate decision floated over each of their heads like a big, black radioactive cloud. It was always there. Always. Dripping little acid raindrops on their sanity in the middle of the night when there was nothing else but silence.

President Andrew Smith didn't have to face the mind-numbing threat from a hostile communist giant like many of his predecessors had, where the decision to unleash America's nuclear arsenal would be a final, ultimate act of mutual destruction. He did, however, have to face the possibility of unleashing nuclear weapons in response to a massive terrorist attack on the United States. It was the scenario of the times.

The attack against Cleveland was the closest he'd come to authorizing their use. The terrorist group that perpetrated the attack was known. Their base of operations was known as well. For a time, they presented a clearly defined target.

He'd listened to his advisors. Some were against using nuclear weapons, others were for it—the most vocal being his national security advisor. She'd nearly swayed him—her arguments made an awful lot of sense at the moment. *Strike with an iron fist . . . No one would dare attack us again like this . . . We have to make an example of these bastards!*

She'd said what he felt.

Watching the footage of American citizens—his citizens—dying before his eyes in such a disgusting, horrible manner made his blood boil like never before.

Mr. President, you have to strike!

He was the president.

Strike!

The decision was his, and his alone.

Sir, you must act now!

He'd learned that a decision made in anger was almost always unwarranted, and sometimes just flat wrong. As a young naval ensign, when one of his sailors would make a stupid mistake, he would step back from the situation and get control of his emotions before acting. He was tough, but fair. It was a character trait he'd developed early and employed often. He would, and sometimes did, drop the hammer when he knew it was required. But this particular hammer was more massive and destructive than any other hammer he'd ever used. With it, he could crack the earth itself. It could not be wielded by emotions. It had to be wielded by reason.

In the end, the strike he ordered had employed conventional weapons. And it had been effective.

This, however, was a totally different situation. Hundreds of thousands of American citizens had been brutally slaughtered by an enemy that so far seemed unstoppable. Killing them on the move had been a failure. Now, they were fixed in place. Their locations were known.

With every tick of the clock, the president knew time was running out. Every second that passed could be bringing them closer to the moment when the things would emerge from their underground hiding places to ravage his nation again.

He knew he couldn't let that happen.

"Are they moving at all?" Andrew asked.

"No, sir. The underground images we've received show they're staying put. For now," Ray Smythe added.

Andrew stared at the plasma screen in his situation room, showing a multicolored image of thousands of oval objects highlighted against a dark background. "What am I looking at here? Are those objects the—"

"Yes, sir. As far as we can tell, the things are encased in some sort of . . . cocoons."

"Cocoons?"

"Yes, sir. We're analyzing the data right now, but the initial reports seem to suggest the things have enclosed themselves in some sort of thick casings. We don't know yet if it's a protective measure they've taken because of the bombing or if it's something else."

"What are these casings made of?"

"The report says it's biologic calcification."

"In English, General."

"It's bone, sir."

"Bone?"

A pause. "Yes, sir."

Andrew Smith knew that bone could be broken. He had the steel screws in his leg to prove it. "Are any of the objects close enough to the surface to dig out?"

"Sir, most of the objects are stratified roughly one hundred ninety to two hundred thirty feet underground. There are a few less than one hundred fifty feet beneath the surface, but digging them out would be a time-consuming endeavor. With all due respect, sir, I'm not very comfortable with the thought that time is on our side. If they should emerge at nightfall—"

"I hear you, General."

Jessie, seated to the president's left, spoke. "Mr. President, I think General Smythe makes a good point. If they emerge before we have a chance to complete the evacuations, we could be facing another night like last night."

"We don't know if they're going to emerge. We don't know if they're going to stay there for an hour, a week, or a goddamned month, for that matter." The president paused. "But I do agree if they were to emerge right now, we'd be hard-pressed to keep them from doing what they did last night. What's the status on the evacuations?"

"It's not going smoothly, Mr. President," Hugo McIntyre said. "The highways out of each of the threatened cities are hopelessly snarled. We're losing a lot of people just trying to get them away from the immediate area." He looked down at the surface of the table in front of him, as if looking for a better answer hidden in the highly polished mahogany. Only his reflection stared back. "If they were to emerge tonight, we're in a better situation than we were just twelve hours ago, but it's not good, Mr. President." He didn't know what else to say.

"Hugo, you've got to get those people out of there. Period. Is that clear?"

"Yes, sir."

The president turned his attention back to General Smythe. "Ray, is there any motion whatsoever? Inside the casings?"

"No motion, sir, but we've detected sounds. Faint, but audible. We don't know what to make of it yet."

"Okay, so we can assume since they're making noises, they're alive and well inside these casings. We don't know if they've encased themselves in these things as a protective measure or if it could be something else." The word the general had used initially to describe the casings—*cocoons*—made the president's blood run cold. "You said *cocoons*, General. Is that what you're supposing these things are?"

"Uh, no, sir. It was just what came to mind when I first saw the images, and—"

"If they are cocoons—which is a possibility that's just as reasonable as anything else right now—then we must assume they'll emerge again. Our task, ladies and gentlemen, is to kill them right now, before they have the chance to come back to the surface. I need to know how. Have we analyzed any of the bodies yet?"

"Sir, we've flown the first bodies we recovered to the Dugway Proving Ground in Utah, some of the rats, and one of the peop— humanoid things. Initial field tests by the CDC on the bodies revealed traces of a level 5 contamination—a biological warfare agent present in the tissue. The Vanguard team will be doing the full analysis."

Andrew had learned of Vanguard shortly after assuming office. They'd played a major role in the ongoing war on terror, pinpointing sources of chemical and biological weapons, helping trace possible locations of production, and developing countermeasures designed to keep the armed forces, and the American public, safe.

"You're telling me that this whole event was the result of a biological warfare agent? Why didn't the sniffer teams detect it? And why the hell am I only hearing about this now?"

"Sir, the traces were minuscule enough to prevent detection by the sniffer teams. There were also other substances present in the tissues that the CDC couldn't identify. I'm being told the level 5 traces are just one piece of a puzzle that still needs to be put together—the CDC can't put the puzzle together by themselves. Dugway can perform a more thorough analysis." Ray Smythe paused, his face showing an uncharacteristic degree of frustration. "I believed you'd been made aware of these findings, Mr. President."

"No, General, I was not." Andrew took a deep breath and calmed himself. He knew information flow didn't always work as advertised in rapidly evolving situations such as this. Most of the time, the information he needed would make it to his level, but sometimes, someone dropped the ball. He knew ripping into the general would serve no purpose—Ray Smythe was a fine officer who knew what his president needed to know. He'd obviously sent the information up the chain, and that particular ball had simply been dropped. Now was not the time for a tirade. "I want to hear the results as soon as they come in."

"Yes, sir."

"One more thing, Ray. I want one of those casings. I don't care how you get it, but I want it dug up, cracked open, and taken apart molecule by molecule until we can determine exactly what we're up against. And I want it fast."

"Yes, sir." Smythe paused for a moment, formulating a course of action. "Sir, we could use penetrating munitions—bunker busters—to get close to the most shallow of the objects, but we'll still have to do some digging to get to it."

"Your call, Ray. Just get me one of those casings." The president knew he was taking a risk. It was going to take time to analyze the bodies, and it was going to take even more time to get to one of the casings. In his gut, he knew it might be time wasted if the things emerged before they'd figured out a way to kill them while they lay deep in the ground.

Jessie spoke up again. "Mr. President, we can kill them now. We have the weapons that will do the job." She sounded oddly impatient.

The voice of Vice President Allison Perez filled the situation room, transmitted from NORTHCOM. "You're suggesting the use of nuclear weapons, Ms. Hruska, on American soil?"

Jessie turned toward the image of Allison Perez staring at her from another plasma screen. The national security advisor's eyes flashed bright green, full of fiery determination. "Yes, Madame Vice President. That's exactly what I'm suggesting."

CHAPTER 27

It was three o'clock in the afternoon when the C-21's wheels barked on the runway at the Dugway Proving Ground.

Carolyn slept for most of the flight from Offutt and felt remarkably better than just a few hours before, which, considering she'd barely escaped being eaten alive by a rampaging horde of monsters—not once, but twice—and survived a horrible helicopter crash, was a darn good way to feel. *All in a day's work*, she thought. *Yeah, right.*

She peered out of the small cabin window and saw General Derek Rammes standing next to a Humvee parked at the edge of the ramp. She could tell by the look on his face that she was going to have a lot of work to do. And fast.

"That must be General Rammes?" Garrett asked.

"Yes, that's him. He's the director of—" She caught herself before saying it. Even the term *Vanguard* was classified, and she didn't know if Garrett was cleared to hear it, much less know what the team actually did hundreds of feet under the Utah scrub brush.

He completed the statement for her. "General Rammes is the director of BSL-4 Vanguard. It's okay—I was in-briefed when I was ordered to bring you here. I'm cleared."

"Sorry. Security, don't you know."

"Yeah. Loose lips sink ships."

"Something like that. You'd be hard-pressed to find a ship out here."

"Gotcha. Not a very attractive place," Garrett said, taking in everything the surroundings had to offer, which didn't look like a whole hell of a lot.

"It grows on you," Carolyn said.

"Yeah, well, so does moss if you sit still long enough. Looks like he's waiting for us. We don't want to keep a flag officer waiting any longer than we have to. Let's go."

The pilot lowered the jet's small stairway, which doubled as the cabin door, and Garrett snapped a sharp salute as he approached General Rammes, Carolyn just a step behind. Rammes was short, stout, and built like a bulldog. "Sir, Colonel Garrett Hoffman, reporting as ordered."

Derek Rammes returned the salute. The two men shook hands. "Colonel, it's good to see you. I know what happened at Kansas City. Your boys put up a good fight."

"Yes, sir." Garrett looked at the ground, the feelings of guilt he'd been trying to ignore sweeping over him again.

Rammes knew how the younger officer felt. "I've lost troops before, too, Colonel. It's never easy. Soldiers die in wars. Innocent people under your protection die, too. Sometimes there's nothing you can do to prevent that. But now that you're here, and now that Carolyn is here, you'll have a chance to help us figure out how to kill those goddamned creatures. You can get your vengeance, son."

"Hooah, sir."

"Hooah is right, trooper."

Carolyn had heard soldiers say *hooah* before, but never really understood what it meant. To her, it sounded like getting sucker-punched in the stomach.

Rammes turned to Carolyn. "Thank God you're alive. I'm sorry to hear about the other members of your team. They were all fine individuals."

"Yes, General. They were." The vision of Matt's head being torn from his shoulders flashed through her mind once again, as it probably always would. It had been so utterly horrible.

They all climbed into the Humvee and sped away from the ramp toward the entrance to the Vanguard complex.

Speaking loudly to be heard over the noise from the speeding Humvee, General Rammes said, "We've got two of the ratlike creatures and one of the humanoids. The CDC discovered a level 5 in the blood and immediately sent the bodies here."

"A level 5?" Carolyn asked. Her hunch suddenly became less of a hunch and more of an actual theory.

"Level 5. Small traces, but it's there. We're trying to identify it right now. There's a lot of other crap in the blood that we're trying to nail down as well, but none of it's identifiable."

Carolyn knew *level 5* was the code word assigned to only the worst of the known biological warfare agents currently catalogued. Ebola, Marburg, smallpox . . . all level 4, and quite deadly, but science had devised even more horrid things. Level 5 meant the agent had been weaponized, changed at the genetic level to increase its effectiveness. The Vanguard complex was the only BSL-4 facility in the country cleared to handle level 5 material. The thought of that type of agent loose in the environment—regardless of which specific agent it turned out to be—chilled her to the bone. It was all nasty stuff. And that was a severe understatement.

As the Humvee screeched to a stop in front of the entrance to the Vanguard complex, Carolyn said, "General, I think I know what it is."

"You know what *what* is?"

"The level 5. I know what it is."

CHAPTER 28

Small wisps of smoke rose from the charred earth of the blast crater formed by the massive explosions from a series of high-explosive bunker-buster munitions dropped from a trio of F-15E Strike Eagles (affectionately called Mudhens) from Seymour Johnson AFB in North Carolina. It had been a very spectacular way to dig a hole. A big one, at that.

The Mudhens had been able to blast away roughly one hundred feet of prime Nebraska farmland, leaving the mining crews with a much easier task: to burrow the fifty-or-so feet that remained to the shallowest casing. If the explosions had reached any deeper, the ground shock might have shattered the casing, or worse, blown it into a thousand bits.

A young Army major stumbled over to the drilling supervisor, nearly losing his footing on the jumble of rocks and loose soil lining the surface of the crater. "How long do you think it'll take?"

"Probably three hours," he replied, wiping the sweat from his brow with a rag. "Another hour to set up the equipment and two hours to dig the thing out."

The major looked at his watch. Three hours would put them close to sundown. He didn't particularly want to be here when it got dark. "You've got to do it in two."

"We can only do this so fast, Major."

"In three hours, when the sun goes down, we could all be running for our lives." He looked down at the supervisor's heavy work boots. "Hope you can run in those things."

The mining supervisor thought for a second, shot a glance at the sun hanging over the western horizon, and then turned to his team. "Let's get on this thing, people! Let's move!"

CHAPTER 29

The elevator hummed as it slid down the long shaft to the Vanguard underground complex.

"It's Russian?"

"I think so, General," Carolyn said. "Soviet, to be exact. If it's what I think it is, we can trace it back to the Nazis, early 1945. The Soviets discovered a rudimentary sample of the stuff when they took Berlin."

"I knew the Nazis were developing some horrible things, but in 1945? Did they have the technology to make something that could cause all this?" Garrett asked. The mention of Nazis had a close personal meaning for him—he could still remember brushing his finger across the faded blue numbers tattooed on his grandmother's forearm. It was one of his earliest memories. She, and others like her, had been branded. Like cattle.

"No, nothing the Nazis had could cause this by itself. Our Russian friends were able to refine the agent over the years, though. They were very, very good at making some truly horrifying agents."

The elevator stopped at the bottom of the shaft, the Utah desert sitting a couple hundred feet above them. As the doors slid open, they were met with the stern gazes of two sentries, M16s at the ready.

"Identification, please, General."

General Rammes handed a coded card to the sentry, who slipped it into a small slot in a reader next to his undersized desk. Satisfied by the green light on the reader's panel, the sentry directed the general to a small eyepiece protruding from an oddly shaped piece of equipment on the wall next to the elevator. The retinal scan confirmed the general's identity.

"Identity confirmed, sir. Welcome to Vanguard, General Rammes." The sentry saluted smartly, and the general returned the courtesy.

"Thank you, Sergeant. I will personally vouch for Colonel Hoffman."

"Copy that, sir." Both sentries lowered their weapons, satisfied that all was in order. "And welcome back, ma'am. Glad to see you're okay."

"Thank you, Sergeant." Carolyn handed the sentry her own coded card, and peered into the retinal scanner. The readout confirmed that she was, in fact, Ms. Carolyn Ridenour.

"You're cleared to proceed, ma'am."

As the trio passed through the first set of heavy doors, which immediately slid closed behind them, Garrett said, "I've been in secure facilities before, but nothing like this."

"Colonel," Rammes said, "when you see what we deal with down here, you'll know why. Let's suit up."

"Yes, sir." He wasn't entirely sure he wanted to see what kind of horrors were being studied here, kept hundreds of feet belowground in this desolate area of Utah. He was, however, strangely looking forward to seeing the bodies of the things up close. He wanted to take a good look at the enemy that had killed so many of his soldiers. Carolyn helped him don his protective ensemble, a positive-pressure suit that covered him head to toe. He felt like one of the scientists from *E.T.*

"Carolyn, what has you convinced the level 5 is Soviet?" Rammes asked.

"The creatures were active during darkness and hid in the shadows when the sun came up. They're sensitive to light. That fact, combined with the mutation of both animal and human species that we've seen, points to a Soviet agent. We were able to get a sample smuggled out of their biological research facility in Kiev back in the late '80s. One of their researchers decided he had to get a sample to us."

They passed through the second set of heavy doors and headed down a long, sloping ramp to the next set of doors, right outside the facility's initial decontamination chamber.

"Officially, they called it agent 1Z65. Unofficially, they called it *Bliznetsy*. Gemini."

"Gemini?" Garrett asked.

"Their work was based on Mengele's experiments with—"

"Wait. Mengele? *Josef* Mengele?" Garrett was very familiar with that name. Mengele, the meticulous Nazi bastard who'd stood on the unloading ramp in his highly polished boots, holding a riding crop, deciding with a flick of his wrist which people would be sent to the gas chambers and which would be sent to hard labor—or medical experimentation—as soon as they stepped off the train. Nazi soldiers would move through the crowds of people, looking for those who met Mengele's twisted physical criteria for experimentation, the most prized being twins, who would immediately be taken from their parents, most likely never to see them again. His grandmother had been subjected to Mengele's extensive twin studies when she'd been held at the Auschwitz concentration camp in Poland. The endless experimentation. The endless measurement, study, and taking of blood. The endless terror. His grandmother had survived. Her twin sister had not.

"Yes," Carolyn said. "Doctor Josef Mengele. The Nazi 'Angel of Death' from Auschwitz. Apparently he'd done a great deal of the initial development work on the original agent. Our Russian friends decided to continue where he left off." She turned to face the general as they reached the final set of heavy doors. "I could be completely wrong, General. I need to dig into the numbers and see if my theory is correct."

"If you *are* correct, Carolyn, what does it mean?" Rammes asked.

"It means we're in more trouble than we thought."

CHAPTER 30

The sun disappeared below the rim of the blast crater, throwing the interior of the hole into twilight shadow as daylight slowly drained away. It had taken a little more than two hours for the mining crew to dig down to the nearest casing, and they were now in the process of hoisting the object up through the shaft they'd constructed.

The mining supervisor looked at his watch and frowned. He'd hoped the digging would've gone quicker, but they'd come across a tough layer of large rocks that had severely hindered their ability to go any quicker. They'd ruined three drill heads breaking through.

"How much time until it reaches the surface?" the Army major asked.

"It's on its way up the shaft right now. Probably another fifteen minutes at the most."

"Okay. I want you to release as many of your people as you can. Only keep the people you need to bring the casing up. Everyone else needs to get the hell out of here. Now."

"And once we get it out of the ground?"

"My people will take over."

The mining supervisor saw a large group of soldiers ringing the circular rim of the blast crater, all heavily armed. There was an olive-green truck backed up to the edge, its back open, ready to receive its cargo. A tracked vehicle was slowly crawling down the slope of the crater toward the hole, black diesel smoke belching from its exhaust. He figured it was going to be used to get the casing out of the crater.

"And then you need to get out of here, too," the major continued. "We've got transportation arranged. You'll leave all your equipment in place."

Good, the supervisor thought. *The quicker we can get out of here, the better.* Tearing down all his equipment and packing it out would've taken much more time than he was comfortable with.

Within five minutes, all the people the mining supervisor didn't need were scrambling up the edge of the crater, heading for waiting Humvees, which would take them away from the large area of buried casings and, hopefully, to safety.

The sun was sinking fast. The supervisor had seen the news reports and had watched the president's address to the nation. He knew what might happen if they were still here when it got dark. It wasn't a pleasant prospect.

The sound of the chain breaking was the last thing he wanted to hear at that moment. It was immediately followed by a scream.

The supervisor ran over to the hoist. "What the hell happened?"

"We have a break. It looks like the casing is jammed in the hole, boss. We just lost the fucking chain!"

"Fix it, and fix it fast! We don't have a hell of a lot of time. You got me?"

"Got it! We're on it, we're on it!"

One of the workers had been unfortunate enough to be standing in the wrong place when the broken chain sliced through the air, and it tore into his right arm like a steel whip. The supervisor could tell the arm was broken, and the jagged wound was bleeding profusely.

"Get that man out of here! Take him—"

"We've got him!" the major said. "Just get the goddamned chain fixed and get the thing out of the ground!"

A group of soldiers quickly carried the wounded man away from the scene and up the side of the crater.

An Apache attack helicopter thudded through the air above the crater, adding another dimension of surrealism to the whole situation. He was just a miner, for Christ's sake! This was all a bad dream. The feeling of dread he felt when the sun had slipped below the crater rim was building in intensity as he watched his work crew, now one man short, frantically try to replace the hoist chain. The hair on the back of his neck bristled with an almost electric fear. He looked at the long, sloping side of the blast crater and wondered how fast he could make it to the top.

He felt like his time was running out.

CHAPTER 31

Garrett had worn full chemical gear before, but it didn't quite measure up to the protective suit he was wearing now. It was lightweight and permitted much more freedom of movement than his heavy charcoal-lined chem gear, and the slow, constant airflow from his small backpack—providing positive pressure in case of a puncture or tear—kept him surprisingly cool. He, Carolyn, and General Rammes stepped through the portal to one of the many clean rooms in the Vanguard complex, the heavy six-inch-thick door sliding closed behind them. A series of interconnected locks slid into place.

In front of them lay the three bodies that had been flown to the complex earlier in the day, each separately encased in a thick Plexiglas coffin-like structure. Heavy rubberized gloves were inserted into the sides so workers could handle the bodies without direct contact.

Garrett was comforted by the level of protection this place employed to avoid any sort of release. If there were any bugs in those things he could catch, he knew the chances were infinitesimally small that something could actually get to him.

He was also struck by the whiteness of the place—he felt like he was in a dream world, where every bit of color had been sucked away, leaving only white. The only colors he could see were on the readouts of the computer screens that lined one wall of the room, and the faces inside the protective helmets.

Carolyn stepped up to the nearest Plexiglas coffin. "What have you got so far, Josh?"

Lieutenant Josh Ewing turned around from his station. "Carolyn! I heard what happened. Thank God you're okay."

"A little worse for wear, but not too bad. Just some scrapes and bruises. It could've been a lot worse."

"I'm sorry about your team."

"I am, too." Beneath her protective mask, Carolyn fought back the tears. Now was not the time to get emotional. Now was the time to focus. "General Rammes informs me there are traces of a level 5 in the blood. How close are you to—" The words stuck in her throat as she looked down at the thing in the Plexiglas box. It was more horrible than she ever imagined, now that she could see it up close.

One of the mutated rat-things—the size of a small dog—lay on its back on the white surface of the examining table, its legs splayed out. The right side of the creature was blown apart, probably, Carolyn thought, by shrapnel from the B-52 strike. The internal organs she could see were charred black and ripped into a mass of unrecognizable tissues, fused together by the searing heat of the shrapnel. The sides of the wound were what horrified Carolyn the most: the thing was covered with an incredibly thick layer of muscle. Dense muscle tissue, bound by heavy, cord-like sinew and tendon, ran the entire length of both sides of the open wound. The thing was built like a main battle tank.

"Carolyn? Are you all right?"

Josh's voice snapped her back to reality. She'd only seen the things in the dark, and never clearly enough to make out any detail. The thought of thousands of these things killing everything in their path made Carolyn shiver. "Yes, I'm all right. Ugly little bastards, aren't they?"

"*Ugly* doesn't quite describe it." Josh pointed to where the broken and smashed body of one of the humanoid things lay. "Our freaky friend over there won't win any beauty contests, either."

She had to force herself to look at it. Even smashed and torn from the bombing, the thing still resembled what she'd seen crawling inside the Chinook. The terrible beast that had killed her entire team. And almost killed her as well.

Although the sight of it filled her with terror, it also sickened her to realize that it had once been a living, breathing human being, mutated into a terrible beast by something they didn't quite understand yet. She was surprised the thought didn't sadden her . . . She was *glad* it was dead. It had ceased being human, and it had to be killed. It was as simple as that. After what she'd seen happen at Kansas City—and to Matt—there was no other solution. The things may have been human just a day before, but now they were a threat. Everything that had made them people was dead and gone as soon as they were transformed. They were now a threat that required complete extermination. Along with the rest of the mutated creatures.

She had to force herself to look away from it, as well.

"Like I was saying," Carolyn continued, "General Rammes said CDC found traces of a level 5 in the blood. Have you been able to nail it down?"

"Not yet. There's so many other compounds in the blood we can't identify that it's difficult to define the specific level 5. We *do* know it's a DNA-based agent—the DNA of each of the creatures has undergone a complete transformation. It's like they were reborn as an entirely new species." He reached into the Plexiglas box and pried the rat-thing's mouth open with his heavy, rubberized glove, careful to avoid the rows of razor-sharp teeth lining the thing's mouth. "Just by looking at it, you can tell this was a rat. The bone structure of the skull, the musculature surrounding the jaw.

It's all pretty much like your common field rat, only larger, stronger, thicker." He gripped one of the thing's legs. "The legs have been restructured for running—slightly longer in proportion to the rest of the body, and more muscle than you can imagine. The claws have also lengthened and thickened."

To Carolyn, they looked like a set of claws that belonged on a grizzly bear, not an oversized rat.

"The same can be said for our humanoid friend over there. You can tell it was once human by looking at it, but that's about as far as it goes. Its DNA has been completely restructured, as well, every sequence right in line with our little furry friend here."

"Josh, I think the level 5 may be related to 1Z65."

"Gemini?"

"Yes, Gemini."

"What makes you—"

"They're sensitive to light, right? They stay in the shadows during the day and only move in the darkness. The Gemini agent was initially designed to create a genetically bred army of night fighters, remember?"

"Yes, I remember reading about it, but that agent by itself doesn't explain the mutations we've seen."

"I agree, it doesn't. But, if it's combined itself with other agents—maybe naturally occurring compounds—it could've mutated into what we're seeing." She strode over to one of the computer workstations and began tapping on the keyboard, digging into the rows of numbers that spelled out exactly what the creatures were made of, in a language only a few could understand. Carolyn knew that language like the back of her hand. "The Soviets abandoned it because of what happened at Kiev, remember? They couldn't control it. The basic agent was much too unstable and unpredictable to ensure a uniform effect from its use." She continued tapping on the keyboard. "Come on . . . You're there somewhere . . ."

"But for a while, they still tried to refine it," Josh said.

"That's right. And that's why the sample was smuggled out to us. It scared the living hell out of one of their researchers. At least one of them had the smarts to realize they were playing with fire. I wish we had, too."

"You mean the New Mexico incident?"

"Exactly."

Garrett had been quietly listening to the discussion in his headset. "The New Mexico incident?" he asked.

Lieutenant Ewing explained. "Once the Gemini agent was smuggled out of the Soviet Union, we started trying to figure out exactly what made it tick. We needed to know how to protect ourselves from it, just in case the Russkies decided to drop a vial of it somewhere in the United States."

"So there's another place like this in New Mexico?"

"New Mexico was where it ended, sir. It actually started in a biological warfare research facility located about fifty miles north of here." Josh glanced at General Rammes, suddenly uncomfortable about telling this officer he'd never met about a highly classified subject, known only by a select few. It was definitely not meant to be common knowledge.

General Rammes spoke into the tiny microphone in his sealed helmet. "It's okay, Lieutenant Ewing. Colonel Hoffman is cleared."

"Thank you, sir." He continued. "The Gemini agent escaped one of their clean rooms and infected one of their workers. Unfortunately, their protocols weren't as rigorous as they are now—as I'm sure you've witnessed since you've been here at Vanguard, Colonel—and he was allowed to leave the complex before they knew exactly what had happened."

"You mean it got out into the open?"

"Yes, sir, unfortunately, it did. The agent's initial effect was a form of temporary insanity—massive, rapid chemical changes in the brain tissues causing a paranoia-like state—and the infected worker made it out of state before they caught up with him. The FBI got to him first and eliminated him, but the agents who killed him were also infected. They left the body in the trunk of a car and left it out in the New Mexico desert. At that point, the agents probably weren't thinking too clearly."

Carolyn's voice could still be heard in both of their headsets as she whispered to herself, "Come on . . . Almost there . . ."

Josh continued. "The New Mexico Highway Patrol found the car—and the body—and it was taken care of by the facility's rapid response team. The two infected FBI agents died in a car crash not long after they'd left the body. They went straight into a bridge abutment at a hundred miles an hour. After the fire, there wasn't much left. They were running—like that worker—from whatever Gemini was making them think. We got lucky that time."

Garrett could now understand why the Vanguard facility was built as it was—to prevent that type of event from ever happening again. He was suddenly very glad to be wearing his extensive protective gear. Carolyn's voice startled him.

"Oh dear God," she said.

General Rammes walked over to Carolyn's side. "What is it?"

"It's Gemini, all right. Just like I thought. But there's more . . ."

Josh peered over her shoulder, looking at the set of blinking numbers on the screen. "That can't be."

"The numbers don't lie, Josh."

"Twins?"

"Twins."

General Rammes sounded confused. "Twins? What are you talking about?"

Carolyn turned to the general. "Sir, have the things stopped? Other than getting out of the light, have they stopped?"

"Yes, they stopped last night." He suddenly realized Carolyn wasn't aware of all that had happened. "All five waves of the things stopped at the same time—"

"Five waves?"

"Five separate groups, headed straight for the five nearest cities. They all stopped at the same time and burrowed underground."

Carolyn sighed heavily, as if she knew the answer to her next question. "General, I need to know if they've . . . Are the things in any sort of chrysalis? Cocoons?"

Rammes's brow furrowed behind his protective mask. "The creatures are encased in some sort of thick, bone-like casings. They're trying to bring one up for analysis right now." He glanced at his watch. "If they're on schedule, they should have it on a plane to our location within the hour." Rammes wasn't sure he wanted to hear the answer to his next question. "How did you know about the casings, Carolyn?"

"Are the five cities evacuated?"

"It's ongoing, but—"

Carolyn's voice was calm, cool, but her eyes flashed bright with fear. "General, if I'm right, as soon as darkness falls, we could be facing a much larger threat."

CHAPTER 32

Floodlights illuminated the crater as the sunlight dimmed even further. The sun was sliding below the horizon. Just a sliver of its fiery brilliance remained. Like an eye slowly closing.

The mining supervisor wiped cold sweat from his brow—he was scared to death. The repairs to the chain had gone quickly enough, but the casing had jammed in the hole three more times, wasting valuable minutes as the crew worked to dislodge the object without breaking the chain again.

Time had officially run out.

"How far?" the major asked.

"Less than ten feet."

Both men watched as the hoist chain slowly spooled up, raising the casing at an almost mind-numbing pace.

"There it is!" they shouted in unison.

Suddenly, the top of a curved, grayish object revealed itself at the opening of the shaft. Within a few seconds, it was completely out of the hole, swinging in its harness a few feet off the ground.

"That's it," the major said. "Get your people out of here!"

"With pleasure. All right, people! Let's get the hell out of—"

"It's cracking!" One of the workers quickly backed away, staring at the object like it was an atomic bomb ticking away toward detonation. A long, jagged crack was visible on its smooth surface.

The major ran over to the hoist and grabbed the worker by the arm. "Was it cracked when you brought it out?"

"No! There were no cracks! I just saw it happening!"

The worker's statement was verified a second later as a loud cracking noise split the night, the fissure on the surface of the casing visibly widening. Both men took a step back, startled.

Suddenly, the workers who remained ran headlong up the side of the blast crater, clawing and kicking at the dirt.

The major regained his senses. "Everybody out! Out of the hole now!" As he ran toward the sloping edge of the crater, the mining supervisor just a step behind, he felt a strange vibration in the ground beneath his feet. His blood ran cold.

The climb to the top of the crater seemed like crawling out of the Grand Canyon—it suddenly seemed much steeper, much deeper than it really was. He barked orders as he climbed, his words coming in raspy breaths. "Evacuate! Evacuate the area!" Behind him, more loud cracking noises echoed in the pit as the casing began to open.

As he stumbled across the edge of the crater, he heard a loud chattering noise, a strange clicking. Joined a second later by another series of the same noises. Unnaturally loud. Chilling.

The major turned and saw pieces of the casing lying scattered at the edge of the hole.

He also saw four yellow eyes burning like flames in the shadows outside the floodlights' lamps, bouncing up the side of the crater. Incredibly fast. Toward him.

It was the last sight he saw.

THE THIRD NIGHT

CHAPTER 33

Andrew sat alone in his situation room. He'd just sat through one of the most difficult war cabinet meetings of his administration. Again, as he'd done after the brutal radiological attack on Cleveland, he'd listened to arguments for, and arguments against, the use of nuclear weapons.

But this time, the argument possessed an entirely different flavor.

This time, the target in question wasn't on the other side of the world. The target—*targets*, to be more accurate—were in the United States of America.

American targets.

On American soil.

Killing American citizens.

It was a course of action that had initially crossed his mind when the creatures made their first furious advances, seemingly unstoppable in the face of the conventional weaponry the military could bring to bear in such short order. He'd considered it for only a split second, knowing in his heart that it was the absolute last course of action he was willing to take.

He looked up at the plasma screen and spoke to his vice president. "Allison, has it really come down to this? Do nuclear weapons seem like a recourse we'll—*I'll* have to resort to if these things can't be stopped with conventional weapons?"

Allison was a valuable source of counsel for him. He could talk to her and bounce decisions off of her, like he could do with no other in his administration. He didn't have a warm relationship with her, like the personal relationship he'd developed with Jessie Hruska, but when it came to the most crucial policy decisions, there was no one else he felt comfortable talking with. As the old saying went, Allison Perez—the vice president of the United States—was only a heartbeat away from the presidency. She needed to be intimately involved in the major decisions of his administration because if the heart were to stop, she had to carry those decisions forward without skipping a beat.

"Mr. President, I don't believe we've reached that point yet. We've lost a large number of our people, and I know that alone is a compelling reason to try to wipe these things out as quickly as we can. But I think we need to take a step back from the situation and look at it objectively." He watched as she shifted in her chair and brushed away a strand of jet-black hair that had somehow escaped from the tight bun she wore at the back of her head. "We don't know this enemy yet. We haven't had time to study the findings from the analysis being carried out—at this very moment—on the dead bodies of the things. We haven't had a chance to analyze the casing that's being taken from the ground. All we know is we have large numbers of mutated animals and human beings on a killing spree in the middle of the country. What caused it? We don't know. How long will it last? We don't know. Are they going to start moving again, or will they be underground for an extended time? We don't know. What I urge you to avoid is making a decision based on incomplete information. If we were to use nuclear weapons—"

The president interrupted her. "*I*, Allison. *My* order, and no one else's."

"Yes, sir. If you were to use nuclear weapons now, and it later turned out from our analysis that the things only had a forty-eight-hour lifespan, well . . . You get my drift, sir."

"You're saying we need to know more before we take drastic actions. Permanent actions."

"Exactly. Sir."

"What do you suggest?"

"We allow the evacuations to continue and provide any and all support we can to make them as smooth as possible, with the understanding that more people are going to die. We have to accept that.

"Second, we wait for the analysis results to come in. Like you've said before, we need to know what makes these things tick. We need to know how to kill them. In the meantime, we pound the hell out of them with the conventional capabilities we have if they resume their movement."

The president thought for a moment, resting his chin on his palm. "And if we can't stop them?"

"Then, sir, we cross that bridge when we come to it. There's too much we don't know right now, which makes it impossible for me to provide you with any viable courses of action."

"I know you're right, Allison. But I viscerally dislike not having options."

"As do I, Mr. President. As do I."

The president leaned back in his chair, stretching his arms. It seemed like his whole body ached from lack of sleep. Getting older, he thought, was a definite pain in the ass. "You disagreed with Jessie Hruska pretty strongly."

"It's not that I simply disagreed with her, Mr. President. I'm concerned that Ms. Hruska isn't providing you with the correct option at the correct time. Her advocacy for the use of nuclear weapons—on American soil—was very premature in my view. Like I said, it's not—"

"—the correct course of action based on the information we have to date." The president finished her statement for her. "You don't have to sell me any further, Allison. I agree with you."

He could see Allison pause, considering what she was about to say next. It didn't take her long.

"There's something else, sir."

"What is it?"

"I spoke to General Smythe immediately following the meeting. He told me the information regarding the discovery of the level 5 contaminant was, in fact, up-channeled."

"The first time I heard about it was when Ray Smythe told me himself. Who did he—"

"Sir, Ms. Hruska has taken it upon herself to channel all communications—minus mine, obviously—through herself first. She's controlling access to you, sir."

The president was dumbfounded. That was definitely not how the communication flow was designed to work. "Are you sure of this?"

"Yes, sir. I'm sure."

"I'll take care of it," the president said. But he figured it was explainable. She'd let him sleep, waiting to wake him until it was absolutely necessary when there was new information streaming in. It was obvious she was trying to protect him, keep him from being overburdened. The president decided he'd speak to her about it when they were alone the next time. "Is there anything else, Allison?"

"No, sir."

"Thank you for your input. I value it more than you can imagine."

"Thank you, sir. Just doing my job."

"And I've got to get back to doing mine."

An instant before the president terminated his communication with the vice president, the secretary of defense—with Jessie Hruska—burst into the situation room.

Tank's eyes were wide with fear. "Mr. President, they're emerging. It's starting again."

CHAPTER 34

"Carolyn, you mentioned twins earlier. What did you mean?" Garrett asked.

She was standing over the charred and torn body of the humanoid thing sprawled on a stainless steel examining table in front of her. She could see Garrett's reflection beside hers as she stared through the thick Plexiglas. "It was what the Gemini agent was designed to do: genetically produce an army of superhuman night fighters. Two at a time."

"Two at a time?" He was listening, trying to concentrate on what she was saying, but Garrett couldn't help but stare at the thing on the table. In the artificial light of the lab, every single detail jumped out at him—every little crevice and fold in the fiendish face, every misshapen lump of restructured bone stretching against the skin, every single coarse hair covering its body—revealed in full Technicolor detail. He'd seen the things in the dark, in the shadows, lit only by frantic muzzle flashes. They'd been almost dreamlike in a way, blurred figures in the night moving so incredibly fast, with only pairs of intense yellow eyes slicing through the blackness to mark their passage. But in this brightly lit laboratory, the thing took on a new reality. It was no longer a nightmare creature from a bad dream. It was real.

He was repulsed by what he was seeing, but still, it fascinated him. He could see that it had been a person once; tattered clothes hung from its misshapen body, pieces of a leather belt clung to its waist, and what appeared to be a high school class ring was buried into the mutated flesh of the thing's right ring finger. For all he knew, he may have passed this person on the street or driven past him in his car just a few days ago, but now, the *it* that person had become was just a dead, rotting monster.

"Garrett? Are you listening?" Carolyn asked.

"Sorry. Seeing this thing up close is really—"

"Yeah, I know. He's quite a looker, huh?"

"Not your type, I hope."

"No, not quite. I prefer a man who won't eat me on the first date." Carolyn unlatched the outer covers from two of the gloves attached to the case. "Josef Mengele was fixated on twins. He'd run endless experiments on them."

"I know. My grandmother was at Auschwitz. When she arrived, she had a twin sister."

When she arrived. The meaning was obvious. "I'm sorry. I didn't know."

"It's okay. My grandmother survived the camp. She didn't talk about it much, but when I was older I started to research it on my own. I found a lot of material describing Mengele's experiments with twins. I could never find anything that explained what he was trying to prove, though. Lots of theories, but nothing concrete."

"The real reason died with him," Carolyn said. "The bastard suffered a stroke while swimming in 1979. Brazil. Nazi hunters didn't find the body until 1985. I personally think he was just a sick Nazi bastard who was trying to perfect Hitler's 'master race' by trying to understand and exploit the genetic triggers that produce twins. That's my theory." Carolyn reached inside the Plexiglas box and carefully pulled a strip of burned fabric away from the thing's charred flesh. "Josef Mengele sent most of his experimental data to Berlin for safekeeping when things started going badly for the Nazis. The Russians stumbled across it when they entered the city. It wasn't until the late 1950s that they started trying to expand on the good doctor's work." Carolyn tossed the piece of fabric aside. "Gemini was designed to transform a person into a completely different being, a different species. A species designed to see in the dark." Carolyn pulled more fabric from the thing's body. "Back then, fighting at night was much more difficult than it is today. No night vision systems. Having an army of killers that could own the night would've given the Soviets an incredible advantage." She tossed the fabric aside and started on another strip. "Part of the genetic code would trigger a reproduction sequence at a certain time. The things were supposed to double their numbers at timed intervals."

"A reproduction sequence?"

"Not what you're accustomed to when you think reproduction. There was no physical mating involved." Another strip of fabric pulled free, tearing off small bits of mutated flesh from the exposed ribs. "Have you ever seen pictures of a cell dividing? Maybe in junior high health class?"

"Yes. Freshman year of college, too."

"Sorry. I wasn't trying to be patronizing. Were you a—"

"Biology major."

"So you know what I'm talking about, then."

"Not really. I switched to political science the next semester. Feel free to patronize."

Carolyn smiled. "Now imagine that cellular division happening on a much larger scale. Millions upon millions of cells. All at once."

"You mean the things would divide?"

"Basically. One mutated human being would split into another mutated human being. An exact replica." Another patch of burned fabric ripped free. "The things would grow a twin. Pretty efficient way to make an army, don't you think?" Carolyn reached inside the exposed chest cavity with her heavy gloves, poking through a shattered portion of the formidable rib cage.

"How far did the Soviets get with it?" Garrett asked.

"Far enough that one of their researchers felt compelled to risk his life to warn us about it." She closed her eyes for a moment, concentrating on what she was feeling for in the thing's chest cavity. "They were able to reproduce a small number of human mutations—even got the reproduction sequence to work—but they couldn't control it. The things mutated far beyond what they were trying to produce. The process couldn't be controlled." She continued searching with her hands, digging through the torn flesh. "They discovered the things would mutate incredibly fast in response to any harmful agents they were exposed to. They were resilient, like bacteria adapting to an overused antibiotic." Her arms were into the thing almost up to her elbows. "They were afraid they wouldn't be able to kill the things if they allowed the mutations to continue. So they disposed of them." She opened her eyes. "There it is . . ." She started pulling.

"What in God's name are you digging for?"

"Damn! I can't get it out." She yanked hard, causing the thing's body to rock over on its side, a charred arm bouncing in the air as if it was still alive. "Put on the gloves."

"What?"

"You heard me. I need help."

"If you think I'm going to—"

"Oh, for Christ's sake. You're a soldier. Open the covers, put on the damn gloves, and help me pull this thing out." She grinned at him. "Don't worry, soldier. You won't break a nail."

Without another moment of hesitation, Garrett unlatched the covers, shoved his hands into the heavy gloves, and reached inside the thing's chest cavity. He was glad he couldn't actually feel anything through the heavy rubber.

Carolyn guided his hands with hers, folding his fingers around a large, soft object.

"There. Now get a grip on that thing and pull."

After three or four strong tugs, the object ripped free. The inside of the Plexiglas box was spattered with a thick, dark brown liquid that ran down the side of the smooth surface as the thing's heart tore free in a gush of foul, dead blood.

Garrett stared at the object in his hands. "What is *that*?"

"It's a heart."

"It's huge."

"Not huge. It's two hearts." Carolyn spread the mutated mass apart, revealing two separate heart-shaped lumps of muscle. Two sets of torn, hose-like arteries hung from the tops of the brown muscles.

"These things have two hearts?"

"No, this friendly fellow had already started to divide when it was killed. It starts with the internal organs."

"Jesus Christ."

"No, more like Josef Stalin. Or Nikita Khrushchev. Leonid Brezhnev, too. They were all involved in it. The program spanned a number of years." Carolyn pulled her hands from the gloves, leaving Garrett holding the mutated hearts by himself. "Spent a lot of Mother Russia's rubles, too."

"Can I put this down now?"

Carolyn couldn't help but giggle, amused by the look of disgust on Garrett's face. "Sorry. Yes, you can drop it. If we kept looking through its insides, we'd find more doubled organs."

"You also said something about cocoons?"

"The initial divisions are fast, hard to control. The Russians never figured out how to slow the initial divisions, and neither did we. As the generations build, the divisions take on a more predictable pattern, occurring at a set interval. In time, when the things started to divide, they'd encase themselves in a chrysalis. Like a caterpillar turning into a butterfly. It provides protection while they're vulnerable."

"The things underground, the casings—they're cocoons?"

"I'm almost certain. The things went to ground, spun themselves some cocoons, and began the rapid process of cellular division." She pointed toward the humanoid corpse. "Like our friend over there was doing."

"If you're right—and I hope you're not—we're going to be in a load of trouble when the things emerge."

"I'm right, Garrett. It all adds up." She glanced at the Plexiglas container holding one of the mutated rat bodies. "I can't explain everything about this, but the basic evidence is just too strong to ignore. It has to be a form of the Gemini agent. It *has* to be."

General Rammes cleared his throat. His face was ashen. When he spoke, his voice cracked. "Carolyn, you were right. They're emerging from the casings." He paused. "Hundreds of thousands of them. Maybe millions."

"Dear God." Garrett felt like all the air in the room had been suddenly sucked out, collapsing his lungs like a well-placed sucker punch.

"Carolyn, you need to look at this." Lieutenant Ewing handed her a sheet of paper. "It's blood-borne. The mutation is passed through the blood."

Garrett looked back at the brown-splattered Plexiglas container and was again very happy he was clad in a protective suit and had used heavy gloves.

The color in Carolyn's face quickly faded as she read the entire computer analysis. Her mouth hung open in disbelief.

"What is it, Carolyn?" Garrett was almost afraid to ask.

"It's Gemini, all right, but there's more to it. Highly aggressive . . . accelerated mutation . . ." She continued to read. "Twenty-four-hour replication timeline." She looked at Josh.

"I ran it three times, Carolyn. The results were the same each time."

"Does this mean these things are going to double in number every twenty-four hours?" Garrett asked.

"Yes." She paused. "By tomorrow night—"

General Rammes finished her statement. "By tomorrow night, there'll be twice as many."

"Yes, sir. Every twenty-four hours, if we can't stop them, we'll have to deal with twice as many as the night before."

"How do we stop them, Carolyn?" Rammes asked.

"I don't know yet. But now that we know what the basic cause is, we have an idea of where to start."

"How long?" Rammes knew how many cities were threatened. He also knew that conventional weapons more than likely wouldn't be able to stop them. The alternatives weren't something he wanted to consider.

"We're just starting, sir. It's going to take some time—"

"Time, Ms. Ridenour, is the one luxury we don't have. The lives of millions of people depend on us. On you. And—"

"Don't you think I know that?" Carolyn's face flushed with anger. "I've seen what these goddamned things can do, General. I watched them slaughter hundreds of people at the airport! I watched one of them, *one* of them, kill a whole helicopter full of soldiers—and my team—even though they were pumping it full of goddamned bullets!"

The general's eyes grew wide at first, then squinted as his own anger grew. It wasn't every day that he took this sort of verbal abuse. More like never. Especially from a civilian.

Garrett put his hand on her shoulder. "Carolyn . . ."

She shoved it away. "No! I'm not finished!"

"Ms. Ridenour, I strongly advise you to—"

"Advise me to do what, General? Wave a magic wand and instantly kill all these things? Well, that's not going to happen, *sir*. We've played God for too long, and now it's coming back to bite us in the ass. Hard." She pointed a trembling finger at the humanoid thing in the Plexiglas case. "That's what happens when people like you decide to act like the Creator and fuck with things that shouldn't be fucked with, General."

"We didn't make these things, Ms. Ridenour. The Soviets—"

"Of course! The Soviets! It's all their fault! The godless communists trying to destroy the free world for no other reason than they were fucking nuts! Maybe you don't remember, *General*, but there were two major players in the Cold War. We had a part in it as well. It was tit-for-tat, wasn't it, General? They make a new bomb, we make one that's better. We make a new poison gas, they make one that's better. They make a better fucking killer bug and we—"

"Stop it, Carolyn. Stop it now." Garrett gripped her shoulders and spun her around to face him. "The general needs to know how we can stop these things and how long it will take us to find out how. He needs to tell the president." He stared into her eyes. "More people are dying right now. Innocent people." He saw her eyes soften. "Get a hold of yourself and give him an answer."

Garrett loosened his grip as he felt her body relax.

Carolyn turned toward General Rammes. "I'm . . . I'm sorry, General."

"She's been through a lot, sir."

"Shut the fuck up, Lieutenant Ewing."

"Yes, sir. Shutting up."

The room was so quiet that Garrett could swear he could hear his Timex ticking away on his left wrist.

"That was a pretty thorough ass chewing, Carolyn. I haven't been braced like that since I was a cadet at West Point."

She stammered, "S-sir, I—"

"It's okay, Carolyn. You have been through a lot. We're all tired, and there's bound to be some short tempers around here."

Carolyn looked down at the floor, ashamed at her outburst. "There's no excuse for what I said. You had nothing to do with this, sir. I was out of line."

"Yes, you were out of line. And so was I." He smiled broadly at her, and she smiled back. Water under the bridge. "Now, I have to call General Smythe and let him know what you've found. The president needs to know how we can stop these things, Carolyn. He wants a viable option that doesn't include blowing our own country to smithereens."

"You said the Soviets had produced a number of these mutated human beings, Carolyn. How did they . . . dispose of them?" Garrett asked.

Carolyn looked back at the shattered body of the humanoid thing in the case. "Just like that," she said. "They blew the hell out of them."

CHAPTER 35

Lake Murray, just north of Little Rock, Arkansas, is the home of some remarkable channel cats, weighing in at thirty to forty pounds; they're an angler's dream if one is lucky enough to snag one.

Tonight, both men felt luck was on their side.

"Good night for it."

"You bet it is." He threaded a chunk of raw chicken liver on the thick steel hook, careful not to stick the barbed end through his finger. The heavy lead weight plunked into the water, and the bait started its slow journey toward the bottom and into the waiting mouth of one of the huge, whiskered bottom-feeders. That was the plan, anyway.

"Here, fishy, fishy, fishy . . ."

"Yeah, that'll work."

"Just watch. They love this stuff."

"They like leeches, not chicken liver."

"I don't see you reeling anything in."

"Neither are you, genius."

High above the men, a full moon slowly slid through the night-time sky. Neither man noticed the small black specks crossing in front of it. Just a few, at first.

"They don't like chicken liver."

"I caught a twenty-pounder on this same lake last year, with liver."

"You were lucky."

"Nope. They love it."

"Leeches taste better."

"And how do you know that?"

"I just do."

"You just do?"

"That's right."

"Been eating your bait again?"

"Would you please quit yapping? You're ruining the moment."

A pause, and then a muffled laugh.

"What's so funny?"

"Ruining the moment? I didn't know we were on a date!"

"Whatever. Be quiet."

More black specks crossed in front of the moon. Many more.

"You're not gonna make a move on me, are you?"

"If you don't shut the hell up, you're going over the side."

"A momma's boy like you? Push me over the side?"

"You keep my momma out of this, and I'll keep *this* out of your momma."

"Here we are, out in the middle of nowhere, and you're grabbing your crotch. Now I'm worried."

"Stop yapping."

"Okay. I will. I'll stop yapping."

"Stop."

"Okay, I'll stop. I really will."

"Damn it! Would you quit already?"

"Wait . . . Did you hear that?"

"I can't hear a thing with your lips flapping."

"I'm not kidding! Listen—do you hear it?"

The sound was distant, odd—like a flag whipping in the wind. Thousands of flags.

"Is it the wind?"

"What wind! There's not a breath of—"

"Well, what the heck is it?"

"I don't know! It almost sounds like—"

Neither man had time to scream as they were covered with a flurry of talons and serrated beaks ripping and tearing at eyes, throats, and flailing arms.

It was over almost as suddenly as it had started.

The small boat was covered in blood, its occupants gone.

The full moon no longer cast its soft light on the lake below. It had been blacked out by an immense flock of mutated birds heading southeast toward the center of Little Rock, Arkansas.

CHAPTER 36

General Ray Smythe sat in the bowels of the Pentagon in the NMCC, frowning at the stream of reports from the NORTHCOM command center flashing up on the screens in front of him.

The five waves of things from the night before—now doubled in size—were back on their original courses.

Omaha was in the process of being eaten alive. The long lines of cars still trying to escape the city were systematically being emptied by the thousands of mutated creatures tearing through eastern Nebraska. He knew Lincoln, roughly an hour's drive west from Omaha on I-80, would be hit later that night.

The University of Nebraska was there.

So was his daughter.

The cities of Wichita, Springfield, St. Louis, and Des Moines would also be hit that night. Thousands of people had tried to leave during the day, but it was fruitless. The interstates were hopelessly jammed with traffic, and the side roads and state highways just weren't able to handle the incredible rush of traffic. Most of the evacuees were stuck in place, unable to travel, except by foot. They didn't have a chance.

The general knew the ground forces arrayed around the threatened cities were going to be lost as well. The lesson from the previous night was all too clear: ground forces didn't have a chance. They could stand their ground and kill hundreds of the things, but they would only be delaying the inevitable. They would be overrun and slaughtered just like the long lines of fleeing civilians they were trying to protect.

"General, the video-teleconference with the president will start in five minutes." The aide stood by his general's side, watching him stare at the map of the advance. Stare at the city of Lincoln. He knew the general had a daughter there. "Sir, is Laura—?"

"Yes. She's still there."

"Maybe she left when the sirens sounded, sir. If she was one of the first ones to hit the road, she'll have a good chance of—"

"I just talked to her fifteen minutes ago. On her cell phone. She's stuck in traffic, Jerry."

"We'll stop them, sir. She'll be okay."

Ray Smythe looked up at his aide, a pained look of resignation crossing his face. He knew his daughter probably wouldn't be alive by the time the sun rose again. "Thanks, Jerry. That'll be all."

His direct line to the national security advisor rang, and he picked it up. There was a momentary delay as the line went secure. "This is General Smythe."

"General, this is Jessie Hruska."

Ray had grown to like the national security advisor over the last few years. He admired her direct approach to things, her low tolerance for bullshit, and the general manner in which she conducted herself. The last couple of days, however, he'd changed his opinion of her. She wasn't functioning as well as she should in a time of national crisis. She'd failed to pass important information to the president, and, as a result, made him look like an incompetent ass.

"Yes, ma'am?"

"I wanted to talk to you before the conference started. The president is desperate to find a way to stop these things without resorting to . . . other options. I think you know what I mean."

"Yes, ma'am, I know exactly what you mean."

"We're not going to be able to stop them using conventional weapons, General." It was a statement, not a question.

"That's correct, Ms. Hruska. We're hitting them from the air right now, but it's not having much of an effect on their advance. Just like last night." The Air Force was throwing all the heavy and tactical air power they could at the waves. It wasn't working.

"What do you suggest, General?"

"We don't have a lot of other options available right now, Ms. Hruska. Our ground forces will try to delay the advances to give the evacuations time to proceed, and we'll continue to hit them with everything we've got from the air."

"And we're dropping conventional munitions, correct?"

"Yes, ma'am."

"There are other weapons we should consider, General. Nonnuclear weapons."

The general paused. He knew what weapons the national security advisor was referring to. Old Russian weapons. Soviet, to be more accurate. Crated up and taken to the United States after the fall of the Soviet Union to keep them out of the hands of the terrorists.

Chemical weapons.

Tons upon tons of the stuff.

Over the last decade, they'd destroyed quite a bit of it, but had only made a dent in the overall inventory. It would take a couple of decades to dispose of it all properly.

"We're talking about using those 'other weapons' on American soil, Ms. Hruska. We don't even know if they'd work against these things."

"But they might."

"Yes, they might. But I'm not ready to make that recommendation to the president. Not yet."

"We're running out of time, General. We've lost Kansas City, we're losing Omaha, and we're going to lose four other major cities by sunrise—not to mention all the small towns and cities that have already been destroyed—and there's no stopping it!" She paused. "The things should be entering Lincoln within the hour, correct?"

"Yes."

"General, you have a daughter going to school there, don't you?"

For a moment, Ray Smythe couldn't believe his ears. "Excuse me?"

"Your daughter attends the University of Nebraska. Correct?"

"Yes, *ma'am*, I do have a daughter there." *You bitch! How dare you bring her—*

"We have to try to save her, General."

"Just what the fuck do you want me to do, Ms. Hruska? Poison the entire midsection of the country just to save my daughter?"

"No. I want you to take whatever actions necessary to save not just your daughter, but the sons and daughters of all the other people who will lose their children tonight if we're not able to stop these things."

Ray Smythe imagined his commander in chief being compared to Saddam Hussein gassing his own country. The situation was entirely different, but he couldn't get that vision out of his mind. He also couldn't get his daughter's face out of his mind, the face of a tiny baby he could hold in one arm. A little pig-tailed girl learning to ride a bike. Birthday parties. First date. Prom night. Heading off to college.

"General, I want you to offer that option to the president."

"Ma'am, even if I did, and even if the president approved it, it would take time to—"

"If you don't suggest it, then I will."

Their discussion was interrupted by the general's aide. "Sir, we've got reports of something happening in Minneapolis."

"Hold on, Ms. Hruska." The general turned toward his aide. "Minneapolis?"

"Yes, sir. It's happening there, too. Started about thirty minutes ago. The 911 calls are starting to pour in from all over the city."

"That can't be! None of the waves are anywhere near Minneapolis right now!"

A young Army sergeant ran up to the aide and handed him a sheet of paper.

"Oklahoma City. It's happening in Oklahoma City, too, sir."

"What? There's no way they could've gotten that far that fast without us knowing about it!"

The aide took another sheet of paper. His hands were trembling.

"Little Rock. They're in Little Rock."

"Sweet Jesus," the general mumbled to himself. "This can't be happening."

On the screens arrayed on the walls of the NMCC, the faces of the president, vice president, SECDEF, secretary of Homeland Security, and national security advisor suddenly appeared. The video-teleconference had started.

The president spoke. "General, what's our current status on the ground?"

General Smythe looked at the phone in his right hand—and then at the face of Jessie Hruska on the plasma screen on the wall—and placed the handset back in its cradle. He knew with a sudden clarity what he was going to recommend to his commander in chief. He cleared his throat.

"Mr. President, we have some new developments."

CHAPTER 37

The president couldn't believe what he'd just heard: there were now three additional major American cities under attack! Three cities that hadn't been evacuated at all—no preparation, no warning—because there hadn't been a *need* to! He wearily scanned the population demographics that had been hurriedly provided by Hugo McIntyre.

Minneapolis—nearly 340,000 people.

St. Paul—one half of the famed Twin Cities—had a population of over 270,000 people. There were no reports from there yet, but the president knew they would come.

Oklahoma City—well over 400,000 people.

Little Rock—almost 184,000 people.

Three cities—soon to be four when St. Paul was hit, which it almost certainly would be—with over one million American citizens under attack.

"These cities are nowhere near the five existing waves. How in the living hell did these things get that far, that fast? And how did we miss it?"

"Mr. President, we're trying to ascertain that right now. We don't know where they came from." Ray Smythe was reeling from the new information flowing into the NMCC. He was trying to keep his thoughts focused on what was happening, but in the back of his mind, he couldn't help but think about his daughter stranded in traffic outside of Lincoln, Nebraska. A doomed city.

The president's voice boomed. "Ladies and gentlemen, I want answers, and I want them yesterday! We've got three new waves attacking our citizens hundreds of miles away from the waves we've been tracking. 'We don't know where they came from' is *not* a good answer! It's absolutely unacceptable. Am I making myself perfectly clear?"

The *yessirs* came fast and furious.

"Mr. President, I think we need to reconsider the possibility that this may be some sort of coordinated attack," Hugo McIntyre said. "It doesn't make sense that these things could've moved so quickly—traveled hundreds of miles—without us seeing them. Whatever caused this travesty to erupt in Kansas City must have been released in these three new cities as well."

"Released? Are you saying this is all part of a coordinated biological attack?"

Ray Smythe spoke next. "Sir, the initial information we've received from the Vanguard team suggests the mutations were caused by a Soviet biological warfare agent called 1Z65. It doesn't explain everything that's happened, but they're almost certain this agent has something to do with it."

"Could this Soviet agent have made it into terrorist hands?"

"Doubtful, but it's a possibility, Mr. President." Tank took the next five minutes to explain the history of the 1Z65 agent. "The Soviets lost control of it when one of their scientists smuggled it out of the Soviet Union and brought it to us, and we had an accidental release as well. The Russians—and we—destroyed all remaining samples of the agent in the mid-1990s, sir."

"You mean all *known* samples."

The SECDEF sighed. "Yes, sir, all known samples."

Ray Smythe broke in from the NMCC. "Sir, we've got an update from Minneapolis. The animals are different from what we've seen so far. They're birds, sir."

"Birds?" The president's tone was incredulous. If the next thing he heard was that a truck full of teddy bears had come to life in San Francisco and had started eating people with a little sourdough bread on the side, he wouldn't be surprised one little bit.

"Yes, sir. Initial reports from Little Rock and Oklahoma City—and now St. Paul—are stating the same thing. Birds, Mr. President."

Visions of Alfred Hitchcock's thriller immediately filled the mind of every member of the president's cabinet. Except this wasn't a movie. No cheesy special effects. Real blood. Real death.

"We could've missed them." The vice president joined the discussion.

"What do you mean, Allison?"

"Mr. President, if the mutation has been passed to birds—which it's obvious it has been—it could've happened last night, or the night before, and we're only encountering them now. If it happened in the vicinity of Kansas City, they could've traveled that far. We have to assume they can travel at an increased rate of speed, just like the mutated creatures in the five existing waves. I don't think we can assume this is a coordinated attack with complete certainty. This could be related to the initial mutations."

"It doesn't matter if it's a coordinated attack or not," Jessie Hruska stated. "We can figure that out later. Right now, we have the five existing waves on the ground—and now three new waves in the air—that all need to be stopped. If they're not, we're going to lose millions of our people."

"The Vanguard team is trying to figure out exactly how to do that right now, Ms. Hruska."

"With all due respect, Madame Vice President, we don't have the time to wait. We need to act now. Tonight. We need to discuss the other options available to us." Jessie Hruska's eyes flashed bright green, full of determination. "I think we all realize by now that conventional options are not working. General Smythe, do you agree?"

"Yes, ma'am." He paused, finding it hard to believe he was about to suggest deploying chemical—and possibly nuclear—weapons on American soil. Weapons that would certainly kill thousands of innocent citizens . . . but, if successful, would save millions more. "Conventional weapons are not stopping them. We're throwing everything at them that we can, and they're still advancing. The ground forces, Mr. President, are being sacrificed; they don't have a chance against these things. Not with these kinds of numbers. They just can't stop them."

"What are you suggesting, General?" the president asked.

"I agree with Ms. Hruska that we need to consider other options available to us. One, of course, is nuclear weapons . . . which I feel is an option of last resort, Mr. President."

"As do I, General. Your other option?"

"Chemical weapons, Mr. President."

The president immediately turned to his SECDEF. "Tank, am I to understand we have chemical weapons in the inventory?" Once he'd assumed office, he'd been briefed on a number of things that only a president and a select few in government were allowed to know. Some of the things had made him wince. Others only became known after he had dug a little deeper and found the right career bureaucrat to pressure. It was an unfortunate—and natural—consequence of big government: some things passed from administration to administration, from president to president, without ever coming out in the open. He hoped chemical weapons weren't one of them. The tone of his question suggested that heads were going to roll if he didn't get the right answer.

"No, sir. Not . . . exactly. We have ex-Soviet weapons in storage awaiting destruction. They could be brought to bear in minimal time, if we decide to do that."

"What kind of agents?"

"Mostly nerve agents, Mr. President. There are some quantities of sarin, some VX, but the majority is soman."

Over the years the president had been briefed numerous times on enemy chemical capabilities—especially during his time in the Navy—and he knew soman well; it had made up the majority of the Soviet Union's chemical warfare arsenal. It was a nasty nerve agent made by combining sarin with another chemical weapon known as lewisite—a blister agent. Also known as GD, soman had been initially developed as an insecticide in Nazi Germany in 1944. They found it worked just as well on people as it did on bugs. "Tank, correct me if I'm wrong, but soman has a very short lingering effect, right?"

"Yes, sir. It doesn't hang around very long."

"Where are we storing it?"

"Sanbourne Army Depot in Utah, Mr. President."

"How quickly can we deploy it?"

"Almost immediately, sir. Your predecessor directed that some of it be kept in ready-use status. Just in case."

"Ray, I want you to make preparations to—" The president stopped when he saw that his chairman of the Joint Chiefs was no longer looking at him from the plasma screen. His face had been replaced by an Air Force colonel's.

"Sir, this is Colonel Jerry Taggart. I'm General Smythe's aide."

"Where the hell is General Smythe?"

"Mr. President, the general just received a phone call from his daughter. She's stuck in traffic outside of Lincoln." He paused. "Lincoln is being hit right now, sir."

For a moment, the president didn't know what to say. He'd watched the numbers build on the status boards—hundreds of thousands, if not millions, of his citizens had either died or were soon to die—but it hadn't been personal yet. *Her name was Laura.*

He'd met the general's daughter on a number of occasions. He remembered her as an attractive young lady, ready to take on the world as she prepared to leave Washington, DC, for the University of Nebraska. Andrew knew she probably wouldn't survive to see morning.

"Colonel Taggart, please tell the general . . ." For one of the few times in his life, Andrew couldn't find the words he so desperately wanted to say. They were stuck in his throat.

"I understand, Mr. President."

"Thank you, Colonel." The president cleared his throat. "Here are your orders. I want you to make immediate preparations to employ the soman nerve agent weapons against the ground waves. You will stand by for execution orders from me. Is that clear?"

"Clear, Mr. President."

The president turned his attentions to the rest of his cabinet. "If we use this agent, I need to know what the effects will be on the surrounding population. I want to know weather effects, I want to know duration, and I want to know expected casualties. Brief me in an hour."

Jessie smiled as she left the situation room—General Smythe had come through for her after all! Using his doomed daughter as a motivator had worked brilliantly, just as she'd hoped it would. She hurried to her office. She had work to do.

CHAPTER 38

General Rammes hung up the phone and hurried over to Carolyn and Colonel Hoffman, both huddled over one of the rat-thing's bodies in its thick Plexiglas container, slowly cutting into the body to discover its secrets. His voice startled them.

"We've got a live one."

"They captured one alive?" Carolyn said.

"It's fifteen minutes out right now. They'll bring it down as soon as they land."

"Humanoid or animal?"

"Animal." He looked at the creature in the container, now fully splayed open from the neck to the lower abdomen. "Like this one. One of the rats."

"That's awesome!"

Awesome? Garrett was a little surprised at the enthusiasm in Carolyn's voice. *Scientists can be so weird sometimes.*

"They captured it about ten miles north of Omaha," Rammes explained. "Still had a chunk of casing stuck to it, so it couldn't move as quickly as the others. It was a straggler."

"How'd they capture it?" Garrett asked, amazed that anyone would have the *cojones* to get anywhere near one of the things without blowing the living hell out of it. Or the luck to avoid getting eaten first.

"Special Forces."

Those two words were all the explanation Garrett needed. Those guys had balls big enough to handle anything, including a mutated rat with a taste for human flesh.

"They jumped on the thing with a steel ammo box." Rammes smiled, glad that guys like that were on our side. "They drove it to Offutt—before it was overrun—and put the box in the backseat of a Strike Eagle. It's been on its way here—at Mach 2—for the last thirty minutes. Barely got out in time."

"Omaha is being attacked?" Carolyn's heart sank. Although it had been hours, she felt as if she'd just left there.

"Yes. Looks like Lincoln is going to get hit any minute, as well. They're heading west awfully damned fast," Rammes said.

"My God." Carolyn was afraid to ask if any of the people still in the city had managed to escape. So she didn't.

"General Smythe informed me the president has ordered preparations to use chemical weapons against the creatures. Some of the old Soviet crap we're keeping over at Sanbourne Depot. Soman."

"Soman? We don't even know what kind of effect it will have on the creatures, General! These things are built to mutate rapidly against any kind of threat. The Russians discovered it when they were playing with Gemini. They might just adapt to it and—"

"The other option discussed was nuclear weapons, Carolyn."

The temperature in the room seemed to drop a few degrees.

"They're considering nukes? On our own soil?"

"Conventional weapons are having little effect, Colonel, like you saw for yourself. To make matters worse, we've now got three more major cities under attack, four if you count St. Paul. Minneapolis, Little Rock, and Oklahoma City."

"How can that be, sir? The waves are nowhere near any of those cities."

"Birds, Colonel. Giant flocks of the things."

Carolyn immediately understood the gravity of the situation they now faced. If the mutation had spread to birds, the expansion of the creatures might be impossible to control. The thought chilled her. The excitement she'd felt learning that they were going to be able to examine one of the things alive quickly vanished, replaced by an indescribable feeling of dread.

They could spread incredibly fast now—multiplying every twenty-four hours, doubling in number—attacking every population center in the United States. Next would come Canada. Mexico. Fly to Central and South America. Fly across the Bering Strait to Russia. Fly south to population-rich Southeast Asia—China, Japan, Korea. Fly west to India, through the Middle East. Fly south toward Africa. Fly north toward Europe.

Suddenly, she thought Australia would be a nice place to settle down.

The tinny, electronic voice of Lieutenant Ewing filled their protective helmets. "General, the Eagle just touched down. The thing should be on its way down in about ten minutes."

"Okay, Carolyn, what do we do with it?" Rammes asked.

"Soman. We expose it to soman."

"You don't want to do any other experiments on it first? What if the soman kills it? Then we've lost the chance to see if there's any other way to kill these things."

Carolyn sighed. "General, if I'm right, we'll still have that chance."

CHAPTER 39

The knock on her office door startled her.

She quickly hung up her secure phone, rattling the handset against the cradle in her haste to terminate the call. "I thought I told you I wasn't to be disturbed—"

The door opened, and President Andrew Smith poked his head in. "Jessie?"

"Mr. President!" She stood. She was flustered, not only because she'd just sniped at the president, but because she'd nearly been caught doing something that in the old days would've earned a quick trip to the gallows and a nice leisurely swing at the end of a rope. If, that is, they'd been able to decipher what she was saying to the person at the other end of the line. "I'm sorry, sir. I didn't know it was you."

"That's all right. May I come in?"

"Of course, Mr. President."

Andrew stepped through the door and closed it behind him.

Jessie could see he was tired—extremely so—and he obviously needed to talk. Inside, she smiled at the opportunity being presented to her. She could almost visualize the president standing on a silver platter as he took his first few steps toward her desk. "What can I do for you, sir?"

The president sat down on a leather couch placed to the right of her desk against the wall. The leather made a *whoosh* as his weight settled in among the comfortable cushions. "I wanted to get out of that situation room for a minute or two." He rubbed his eyes. "And ask you a few questions."

Jessie walked to the couch, and stood. She didn't want to appear too eager.

The president patted the cushion beside him. "Sit down, Jessie. Please."

She moved with feline smoothness, nearly slinking onto the couch, sitting to his right. She immediately crossed her legs, right over left, being sure to allow her skirt to rest atop the middle of her right thigh, her right calf flexing as she pointed her foot slightly toward the floor. She was presenting herself in full splendor, and it took so little effort to do it. She was pleased when she saw the president quickly look at her legs and then look away. Like a shy schoolboy sneaking a glance.

She tucked her red hair behind her left ear, making sure he could look unobstructed into her luminous green eyes. She didn't speak. She wanted him to speak first. To give her an opening to exploit. A crack to reach into.

"Jessie, I know this may seem a little out of the ordinary, but I trust your judgment. I wanted to talk to you alone, away from the situation room." He paused, obviously struggling with his words. "I need some feedback."

"Sir?"

"You and I—"

She smiled inside as she saw the crack start to form.

"—we've been through a lot together."

"Yes, we have." No *sir* this time. No *Mr. President.*

"You've been an incredible source of counsel for me, something I've appreciated more than you can know."

She knew he was thinking about his wife's death. She'd been there for him, trying to comfort him in little ways, as he dealt with her death. *Oh, if he only knew who was behind his wife's death.* "Thank you. I know it's been hard." Her voice was soft, smooth. As smooth as the skin of her delicate hand, which she placed over his. It was a bold move, but she knew it was time.

She tried hard not to smile openly when he took her hand in his.

"Jessie." He was looking into her eyes as he spoke. "I don't know how to say this."

Andrew was trying to fight back an urge he was almost certain he wouldn't be able to ignore any longer. The last few days, he'd needed the kind of emotional sounding board his wife had provided for him throughout their years of marriage. Every struggle, every crisis, she'd been there. Her soft words and soft touch had kept him steady.

Holding Jessie Hruska's hand in his, he felt the same kind of attachment he'd once felt with his wife. Not just physical—even though the touch of her hand was having an electric effect on him that he couldn't ignore—but emotional, as well. He'd come to realize that he wasn't the same person without his wife by his side, and he needed that touch, that connection, if he were to continue to function effectively through this crisis.

But it wasn't just the crisis. It was his heart and soul. When he'd buried Kate, he'd buried a part of himself with her. A part of him was now empty, a black void in his being that cried out to be filled. To be alive again. To *feel*.

As he stared at Jessie, sitting on the couch just inches from him, her warm, soft hand in his, he felt the void starting to fill once again.

Maybe she was the one.

Having a relationship with someone in his administration—someone in his direct chain of command, to use Navy terms—was not something he took lightly. *Admiral* Smith had kicked people out of the Navy for doing much the same thing.

But now, things were different. His wife was dead and gone, even though he didn't like to use those exact words. "Dead and gone" seemed much too harsh . . . but it was true.

Jessie squeezed his hand, ever so slightly. Her eyes were soft, alluring.

Kate was never coming back.

Jessie's perfume was pleasing, almost relaxing in a way.

It had been a long time now—

Her lips were full and red, slightly moistened.

—and Jessie Hruska was right here.

He wasn't at all surprised when he felt the warmth of her lips against his.

It was meant to be.

He wasn't surprised either to find himself leaning into the kiss, enjoying it, tasting it, feeling every single moment of it, and he wasn't surprised when she responded to him, her hands stroking his face, sliding down his chest, her touch soft and gentle. Timid, yet purposeful.

He felt an incredible sense of relief wash over him, as if a giant weight had been lifted from his shoulders.

A part of his past life had quietly slipped away with a simple kiss; a part of his life that he'd so dearly loved and cherished, a part of his life that had choked him with unimaginable, unbearable pain, slid away into the past by the simple human touch from the beautiful woman sitting on the couch with him.

He was no longer burdened.

He was a man again.

Their hands began to move within the restrictive folds of clothes, stroking, touching, exploring. Their mouths opened, tongues deeply darting and tasting, bodies pushing against each other with an urgency that was quickly rising in their breasts, hearts beating rapidly, lungs taking short raspy breaths quickly, when they could. Piece by piece, their clothes fell to the floor, to lie in a heap on the plush carpet in the office of the national security advisor to the president of the United States of America.

To Andrew, the lovemaking that followed was one of the most moving experiences of his life.

He felt free.

To Jessie, the necessary physical act—although pleasurable—was the silver platter.

He was not free. He was *hers*.

As the president of the United States lay on top of her, sighing with an orgasmic shudder, Jessie knew he was pounding nails into his own coffin.

She dug her fingernails into his back, like a lioness gripping its prey right before it sinks its fangs into the doomed animal's neck.

She climaxed quickly. More than once.

CHAPTER 40

The steel ammo box had served its purpose well but didn't look as if it could hold the demon inside very much longer. Its sides were dented in places, but not like your normal everyday ammo box. It was dented from the inside out.

The thing trapped inside had slammed its powerful body against the sides, trying desperately to escape, with enough force to bend steel. For the pilot of the Strike Eagle, who'd been forced to fly with the thing sitting in his backseat, just a few feet away from his own hind end, the flight had been just a little too long. Screaming along at over Mach 2 hadn't been fast enough for his liking.

Even through their protective environmental suits, they could hear it: talons scraping against steel, gnawing teeth clicking and clacking against the heavy lid, low grunts vibrating through the floor as it slammed its body against the side of the box.

The thing wasn't the least bit pleased to be stuck in the ammo box. As a matter of fact, it was downright pissed.

The ammo box lay on the floor next to an open Plexiglas container. A ring of armed soldiers surrounded it, their rifles aimed directly at the padlocked lid. Just in case.

Garrett asked the question that was surely in the minds of everyone in the clean room at that moment: "How the hell do we get it out of there?"

He didn't particularly want to be anywhere near the ammo box when the lid was removed, and he was pretty sure even the guys with the rifles felt exactly the same way.

"Sergeant, is that box airtight?" Carolyn asked.

Without taking his eyes off his sights, the soldier answered, "No, ma'am. Not completely."

"Then we'll gas the little bastard right in the box." She turned to Josh Ewing. "Josh, get the guest room ready for our little friend, will you?"

"Yes, ma'am. Will do." Josh stepped to a touch pad at the far end of the clean room, pressed some numbers, and stepped back as the wall slid up into the ceiling, revealing a hidden chamber.

It was a simple room: white walls, a stainless steel toilet in the corner right below a stainless steel sink. What looked like a hospital bed sat in the middle of the room, with enough space around it to handle all the medical equipment you would find in a normal hospital. The entire space was behind a thick wall of Plexiglas.

To Garrett, it looked like what you'd find in a prison infirmary. Or a psychiatric ward. "Guest room, Carolyn?" he asked.

"That's what we call it. It's a confinement chamber. Used for treating people who've been infected—or exposed—to something we don't understand yet."

"Doesn't look like you've 'treated' too many people in it."

"We've never used it. Never had to."

Garrett was surprised to see part of the inner wall slide away and see Josh Ewing step inside—he hadn't seen him open a second door right next to the sliding wall. The entrance, obviously.

"If that thing gets out, is the door strong enough to hold it?"

"I hope so," Carolyn said.

"You hope so?"

"Look, genius, we can either put the box in that room and gas it, or you can walk over there and open the ammo box yourself and try to put our little friend in an examination box, just like his dead buddies. Your choice."

"I think I like the room idea a little better."

"I thought you would." She turned toward the general. "Sir, how are they going to deploy the soman?"

"The Russians weren't very complex in their delivery methods. The stuff is in a bomb—small explosive charge splits the casing at a preset altitude. A rainmaker."

"Concentration?"

"Depends. Delivery radius—depending on the specific weapon—can extend from a few hundred yards to almost half a mile. The concentration will be heavier toward the center of the radius, diminishing as you move away. Most of what we've kept in ready-use status is the smaller-radius variety. There's still a few of the bigger weapons, but not many."

"They'll be air-dropping it?"

"Yes. We've got a couple hundred of the bombs ready to use."

She quickly changed her plan. "We'll have to get the thing out of the ammo box. If the creatures in the field are going to have this stuff rain down on them, then I want to expose this little bastard to it the same way."

"That's not going to be easy." After speaking those six words, Garrett knew he was now in the running for the Most Obvious Statement Ever Said award.

"I can do it." One of the soldiers with his weapon trained on the box spoke. "I can shoot the lock off. The thing will get out on its own."

General Rammes glanced at the lock on the ammo box—it was a typical US Army–issue combination lock. Nothing too substantial, and from the looks of it, about ready to fail. A well-placed round would probably do the trick. "Okay, trooper. You get the shot. If you miss, or if you hit the thing inside, I'll—"

"You won't have to, General. If I miss, I'll give you one of my stripes myself. I don't miss."

"Hooah."

"Hooah, sir."

"Carolyn, how long do you need to get the room ready?"

"Just a few minutes, General. They can take the box inside the room now."

"You heard the lady. Move!"

The armed men slung their rifles over their shoulders—as best as they could, considering they were wearing the same protective suits as everyone else—and reached for the box.

The sound was immediate.

Garrett and Carolyn froze in place. The sound was one they'd heard before. In Kansas City. The same chattering and clicking. It was an evil sound.

The soldiers hesitated for a moment, and then, as one, picked the box up and carried it toward the containment room entrance. They placed the ammo box on top of the hospital bed and left the room, making sure the lock was directly toward the small inner entrance door so their partner could have a clean shot.

Carolyn moved to a control panel on the other side of the containment room's transparent Plexiglas wall and started entering commands on a small drop-down keyboard. Garrett stood beside her. He could see the hospital bed bounce with every violent movement of the creature in the steel box, still desperate to get out and take a big, juicy bite out of whoever had put it in there.

Without having to be asked, Carolyn explained what she was doing. "We can control almost any variable in this room.

Temperature, humidity, light, airflow—any environmental variable we want to introduce can be entered here."

"Can you make it snow?"

"It's good, but not that good."

Two technicians carried a long, silver canister over to a receptacle in the wall just a few feet away. With a push of a button, the canister slid into the wall. Small locks snapped into place.

"Is that the soman?"

"That's the soman. Enough to kill every man, woman, and child in the city of Los Angeles. If it's delivered properly."

Garrett had been exposed to some pretty humbling weapons in his time, but nothing like this. He was amazed how a beautiful young woman like Carolyn could work in close proximity to such incredible evil and still be so alive inside. "Are you going to use that much?"

"No. It'll only take a small amount to duplicate what the creatures will actually be exposed to."

"Sorry. I'm new to all this."

"It's okay. I wish I didn't know so much about it myself."

But you have to, Garrett thought to himself. *We all have to know things we wish we didn't have to these days.*

It was a sad thought.

The America he'd grown up in had changed in so many ways. America was no longer a peaceful place, where people could chase after their dreams, raise a family without fear, and if they were lucky, enjoy the simpler things in life. Now, people had to think about survival. Twenty-four hours a day. They had to think about what they'd do if a terrorist attack occurred in their city—or small town—and how they would react. They had to wonder whether or not today would be the day that a mushroom cloud would rise into the sky. Maybe, they'd be lucky enough to have just time to squeeze their child's hand a little tighter. One last time.

It was a different world.

And it was why he had joined the United States Army.

Turning the other cheek had been tried for decades, and it had failed. The enemies lurking in the shadows had taken the time provided them by well-intentioned—yet incredibly naïve—politicians and used it to prepare. To plan. And finally, to act.

Thousands had died in the war on terrorism. America had grown different. Harder, not happier.

But still, even in the face of all the death and destruction that had been visited upon his country, America still remained the one place in the world where people believed in the meaning behind one single, simple word . . .

Hope.

Hope that things would get better. Hope that in the end, freedom would prevail and America—and the world—would be a safe place again.

Hope was holding his country together. It was a tenuous thing, but as long as people believed hope was still alive, it was as strong as the most hardened steel.

Hope was what Garrett saw when he watched Carolyn prepare the containment room for the soman gas. She still had hope. It was alive in her, in the way she spoke, in the way she moved. She was a beacon for others, a bright light that seemed to signal that all would be okay one day, as long as we didn't give up. *As long as we keep fighting until we can't fight any longer.*

As long as we keep fighting for the future.

Garrett knew every person on the Vanguard team was full of hope, in one way or another. Without it, they'd simply cower in a corner and wait for the end to come.

As he watched Carolyn punch in more commands, he had a sudden sinking feeling that the end, in fact, might be coming. All the hope in the world might not be enough to stop these things, unless people like Carolyn found a way.

He silently prayed that she would.

"General, it's ready. I'm going to release the soman as soon as our little friend pops his head out of the ammo box," Carolyn said.

"Soldier, you get your ass back behind that door as soon as you take your shot. They move incredibly fast."

"Yes, sir. No sweat."

"Lieutenant Ewing, get ready on that door. As soon as he's clear, you slam that thing shut."

"Yes, sir." Josh placed his finger over the button that would slide the inner entrance door shut. The outer door to the clean room was still open—he'd shut it, too, as soon as the soldier made his exit.

"Carolyn, are you ready?"

"Yes, sir. Ready."

Rammes turned to the other soldiers watching their comrade wrap his rifle sling around his left arm to provide added stability. "If that thing escapes, you kill it. Clear?"

As a single person, they answered, "Hooah, sir."

Carolyn was going to have to ask Garrett exactly what that word meant.

Rammes counted down. "On my mark. Three . . ."

The soldier centered his sights on the lock. It was moving slightly, as the creature in the box continued its frantic efforts to escape.

"Two . . ."

The soldier took a long breath, let it out only partway, and started a gentle pull on his trigger. His rifle was set for a single-shot burst. One bullet.

"One . . ."

The box jumped. The lock swung back and forth . . .

"Mark!"

189

"Stand by!"

The shot didn't come.

"Stand by . . . stand by . . ." The soldier waited for the lock to stop swinging.

The rifle's report was a dull thudding sound, masked behind the thick Plexiglas wall of the containment room. Sparks flew from the hardened lock as the bullet slammed into it, disintegrating it in a small shower of metal fragments.

The lid of the ammo box was flying open even as the largest piece of the shattered lock was falling to the floor.

The thing was out.

The mutated creature slammed into the ceiling of the containment room, about five feet above the hospital bed where the box had been lying.

Josh Ewing watched the rifle barrel retract from the entrance and mashed the button to close the inner door.

The creature spun in midair, looking straight at the entrance. Looking straight at the soldier with the rifle trying to get away.

It hit the floor and leapt at the sliding door. It moved as a blur, incredibly fast.

The inner door clicked shut just as the thing slammed into it. It cried out with a terrible wail, a scream of fury, as it hit the floor.

Out of the corner of his eye, Garrett saw the soldier dive out of the door to the clean room, tumbling across the white, polished floor. The second door slid shut behind him.

Josh Ewing stepped back from the control panel and shouted, "We're sealed!"

Carolyn hit a key on the keyboard, releasing the soman gas into the confined space of the containment room.

"All right, you little bastard. Take a deep breath."

In the instant before the soman rained down on it from the jets in the ceiling, the mutated creature looked through the thick

Plexiglas and saw the group of people standing just on the other side.

Yellow eyes, as bright as fire, burned with a hellish rage as it turned its head from person to person.

Its mouth opened, revealing long, black fangs glistening and dripping with saliva, a small string stretching to the floor in front of it, translucent and shiny. The noise erupted from its mouth, chattering, clicking, loud enough to be heard even through the four-inch-thick Plexiglas.

The soman fell from the ceiling like a gentle rain, a misting of small droplets, settling to the floor below.

The creature's eyes squinted as the powerful muscles in its legs tensed. Just as it was about to leap toward the Plexiglas viewing wall, the first mist of soman settled onto its back. Into its eyes.

The effect was immediate.

Silence. The chattering and clicking stopped.

At first, the creature seemed confused, not sure what to make of the wetness that was descending from above. It raised its ugly snout and sniffed the air—now filled with a strange camphor scent, the smell of rotting fruit—its restructured senses trying to categorize the new smell, the new feeling that was at that very moment racing through its nervous system, through its blood.

It blinked, as if someone had just kicked sand in its face. It scratched at its eyes with its long, black claws, rubbing and pawing at them with its front legs.

Its mouth was suddenly covered with a foamy mass of saliva, its long brown tongue slinging clumps of the foam from side to side. Its right front leg suddenly stiffened, stuck out to the side like it had been pulled by an invisible chain, and then it started to twitch, almost vibrate, as the first convulsions set in.

The creature's rib cage expanded and contracted grotesquely as the lungs started to fail, its mouth opened wide, trying to get a breath. Its tail stiffened behind it, and then began to vibrate along with the rest of the creature's appendages.

Death throes.

The creature rolled over onto its back, and a stream of pale brown urine shot into the air as the thing lost control of its bodily functions. A liquid mass of brownish-red feces literally erupted from its anus, spraying across the floor and splattering the side of the hospital bed.

Garrett watched in horror as the soman ravaged the mutated creature on the floor just fifteen feet away from him, watched as it quickly died from the gentle mist that had dropped from the ceiling. He knew agents like soman had been used against people before, and he was sickened to think that they'd died in much this same way.

Deep down, though, he was glad. Glad that the thing was dying. Glad that it was suffering. He knew he was watching the end to all the terrible events of the last few days, as the mutated thing sprayed its bodily fluids and bodily waste around the room in a maddening display of malfunctioning nerves. All the little controls that keep a body running like a top had been completely destroyed in this creature—in a matter of seconds—and the thing was entirely out of control, twitching and writhing on the floor like it had been stepped on by a giant's mighty foot. Squashed like a bug.

The convulsions were tremulous, and every single restructured muscle fiber in the thing's body vibrated with incredible intensity—

And then it stopped.

The fiery eyes dulled.

It was dead.

"Jesus Christ," Garrett muttered.

Carolyn turned toward him. "Are you praying, or just amazed?"

"I think a little of both."

"It's nasty stuff." She paused. "But, there's worse out there, believe it or not."

"Unfortunately, I believe you."

Lieutenant Ewing was watching a medical readout panel right next to the chamber's entrance. All the needles and dials had stopped moving. "All biometric functions have ceased."

"Is it dead?" Garrett asked.

"We'll have to wait and see," Carolyn answered.

• • •

The first B-52 lumbered off the runway at Hill AFB, Utah. Ex-Soviet chemical weapons filled its cavernous bomb bay and hung from its wing pylons. It was immediately followed by four other BUFFs heading toward their preplanned targets in the heartland of the United States of America.

The president had given the order.

CHAPTER 41

"How much longer are we going to wait?"

"I'm not too sure, Garrett," Carolyn answered. She glanced at Josh Ewing, and he shook his head. Still no readings from inside the chamber. "It looks like the soman did the job, but I want to wait a little longer before we call it a success."

"If it was going to come back to life, shouldn't we be seeing something on the monitors?" General Rammes was getting impatient.

"This is a new species, sir, one we know very little about. It's in this thing's genetic code—because of Gemini—to adapt to anything harmful. We don't know how long the process takes. If we had monitoring equipment connected to the creature's body, we could tell what was going on inside, but we're limited to the biometric sensors in the room. They can pick up a heart rate, breathing, some electrical activity, but not much else. We can't be entirely sure the thing is stone-cold dead by looking at the monitors."

"So when do we decide it *is* dead?" Rammes asked.

"The soman has been evacuated from the room. The environmental controls were set to purge it from the chamber at a rate comparable to how the agent would disperse in an open area. It's

been gone for about . . . fifteen minutes now. I want to wait a little
longer."

CHAPTER 42

"The president ordered the attack? I thought he wanted a briefing before he made any sort of decision!"

"I know, I know. He just ordered it about an hour ago." Tank knew what he was going to hear next.

"Doesn't he understand how many citizens we're going to lose if he drops that crap where the things are right now? We'll lose thousands of innocent people who're trying to escape from those things!"

"He knows, Hugo. He knows."

"We've got to convince him to let the conventional forces try to stop them, maybe until morning. It'll give us more time to get more people out of harm's way and—"

"The BUFFs have already launched, Hugo. They're in the air."

"Jesus. Is he hitting each of the ground waves?"

"Yes. Five B-52s, each heading toward a different wave."

"The things are in Lincoln right now. Everyone is going to die, Tank. People are still trying to get out."

"I know. The president's decision is final, Hugo. He made that quite clear."

"Does the vice president know?"

"I have to assume she does. He's kept her informed on every single decision he's made. I'm sure he consulted her."

"Why the quick decision?"

"You're asking the wrong person."

CHAPTER 43

"Mr. President, this is Jessie."

"Yes, Jessie." As he spoke to her on his secure phone in his situation room, Andrew could still smell her perfume on his skin.

"General Stone informs me the first B-52 will reach its target area in the next thirty minutes, sir."

The first target area was Lincoln. He knew there were still many of his fellow citizens on the ground. He also knew he'd signed their death warrants as soon as he'd ordered the strike, but it had to be done. She'd convinced him of that. No matter how horrible it was, it had to be done now, before events spiraled out of control. "Thank you, Jessie. Keep me informed."

"One more thing, sir. The vice president wishes to speak to you."

"Go ahead and put her through."

"Yes, sir." She paused. "Andrew?"

"Yes?"

"Are you okay?"

"I'm fine."

"I'll put her through now."

The president hung up his secure phone and waited for Allison Perez's face to appear on the plasma screen in front of him.

When her face did appear, she looked confused. And a little angry.

"Mr. President."

"Hello, Allison."

"You ordered the chemical strike?"

"Yes."

"I understood you wanted a briefing on casualties prior to ordering—"

"There's no more time for briefings, Allison. The things have to be stopped right now. It doesn't make any difference whether or not I saw the numbers. People are going to die. Innocent people. I fully understand that."

"We don't even know if the soman will kill these things yet. If it doesn't work, we will—"

"—suffer a nuclear holocaust on our own soil, Allison. That was my only other option, wasn't it? You heard exactly what I heard: conventional weapons will not be able to stop these things. And they're spreading, Allison, they're *spreading*."

"Mr. President, may I speak freely?"

"We're not in the military anymore, Allison. You don't have to ask my permission. I expect you to speak your mind. You know that."

"I also know, sir, that making a decision like this is your prerogative, and yours alone, as commander in chief. However, I do not appreciate being kept out of the loop."

Her statement surprised him. "How in the hell have I kept you out of the loop? You've been a part of every single briefing I've received on these things!"

"I'm your vice president. I should hear about important decisions from you, sir, not as secondhand information passed to me by the national security advisor. Especially when it's a decision like this, with thousands of lives at stake. I'm suddenly being held at arm's length, Mr. President, and that's not where I belong."

"I had a decision to make, Allison, and I made it. You're correct when you say it's my prerogative as commander in chief to make decisions like this. It's my call. If I feel a threat to the national security—no, the *survival* of the United States—warrants my immediate action, then I will take it, regardless of whether or not I've been properly briefed or whether or not I've called you personally."

"I understand that sir, but—"

"No, I don't think you do. We're facing a situation that no one has ever had to deal with before. No one! Our country is being eaten alive and we haven't been able to stop it. We have to take quick action—and if I deem necessary, drastic action—to stop it. If this chemical attack doesn't work, I've only got one option left. One option, Madame Vice President."

There was a moment of silence in the situation room as the two top leaders of the United States stared at each other through electronic eyes, seeing faces on the screen that neither had seen before.

"Then, Mr. President, let us both pray that this option works."

"It will, Allison, it has to."

"And if it doesn't, sir, I hope I don't find out about an order to use nuclear weapons by looking out my window and seeing a mushroom cloud on the horizon."

"I'll keep you informed, Allison."

The screen went blank.

• • •

Allison sat alone in the breakout room, struggling with her thoughts. She and Andrew had argued before—especially following the Cleveland attack—but never, never had he been so . . .

Different.

She'd seen him stressed. Seen him angry. After Kate's death, she'd watched him wrestle with his inner demons, struggling to find himself again after such an important part of his personal life had been so cruelly ripped away.

She'd seen the best of the man, and the worst. But through it all, he'd never kept her at arm's length. Especially not during a crisis.

Something was wrong. She wasn't sure what yet, but the gnawing ache in her gut was screaming a warning. She pressed a button connecting her to the NORTHCOM senior controller and asked to see Admiral Grierson. He entered the room a moment later.

"Keats, where's the nearest E-4?"

"Denver, ma'am. Sitting standby at DIA."

She'd flown to Colorado Springs on *Air Force Two*, a modified Boeing 757 the Air Force used for vice presidential—and at times, congressional—travel. It was a capable platform, but she needed something designed to perform a mission she hoped wouldn't be necessary.

Allison had learned over the years that hope, like wishing, was also a sign of poor planning. What she was about to do was highly irregular, but she'd answer for it later. She was the vice president, and if anyone didn't like it, they could kiss her Coastie ass.

"Bring it here."

"Ma'am?"

"Get me the fucking E-4, Keats. I'm going airborne."

• • •

High above the Nebraska farm fields, the first B-52 started its bombing run. The bomb bay doors slammed open, and the first of the old Soviet chemical weapons dropped from its belly. It was followed by many, many more.

CHAPTER 44

Ray Smythe was making the most difficult phone call of his life. On the other end of the line was his baby girl.

"Daddy?"

"It's me, honey."

"We're stuck, Daddy! There's wrecks all over the place and nobody's moving!"

For once, her cell phone reception was crystal clear. He was glad for that at least. "I know, honey. Try to stay calm. We've got soldiers west of you who are going to stop them. I promise." He'd never lied to his daughter before.

"I'm scared, Daddy, I'm so scared!"

"It's all right, honey. It's all right." He could hear the low rumble of the B-52's engines through her phone, as it thundered through the night sky above his daughter, dumping its load of death. He knew he only had minutes to say what he needed to say.

"Daddy, I—oh God, I can *see* them! I can see them, Daddy! They're coming! Ohmygod, ohmygod, I'm gonna die, Daddy! I can see their eyes!"

"Shhhh. Hush, little one." He'd called her that as a child. "I want you to listen to me, okay?"

"Okay . . ." Her voice was trembling.

"I want you to know that I love you, Laura. I love you more than anything in this entire world. Do you know that?"

"Yes, yes, I know that . . ."

"Your mother and I love you so much, and we're so very, very proud of you."

"Daddy, what's going to happen to me? What's going to—"

"I want you to close your eyes . . ."

" . . . Okay . . . ohmygod, ohmygod . . ."

" . . . And I want you to imagine something for me, real hard, okay?"

" . . . Okay . . ."

"I want you to imagine that I'm there with you right now, Laura. I want you to imagine that I'm right there. I'm right there, Laura, can you imagine that for me?"

" . . . Yes . . . Daddy, I'm so scared . . ."

"I know, I know . . . I want you to reach out your hand, Laura. Reach out your hand and imagine that I'm there and I'm holding your hand. I'm holding your hand right now, Laura . . . Can you imagine that?"

" . . . You're right here and you're holding my hand . . ."

"That's right . . . I'm right there and I'm holding your hand, Laura. I'm right there. Can you feel my hand? Just like when I walked you to school. Do you remember that? Do you remember when I held your hand when I walked you to school on your first day of second grade? Do you remember that, honey?"

"I remember . . . I was so scared . . ."

"You held my hand so tightly because you were scared, but it was all right, wasn't it? It was okay, wasn't it, Laura? You were safe with me, you were safe with me, Laura. Do you remember that?"

"Oh, Daddy, what's going to happen to me . . ."

She was crying. "Shhhh . . . Hold my hand, honey. I'm there holding your hand. I'm kissing your forehead, honey. I'm there and

I'm kissing your forehead and I'm telling you that I love you . . ." A single tear rolled down his cheek.

"I love you, Daddy, I love you . . ."

She screamed as the first bomb exploded overhead with a terrible loud crack.

"What's happening? What's happening, Daddy! What's happening!"

"It's all right, little one." He knew it would only be seconds now. "I love you, Laura. I'm there with you, baby. I love you. I love you so much . . ."

"Daddy . . . it's raining! I'm getting w— Ohmygod—I—"

Ray Smythe listened to his daughter die on the other end of the line. It was a sound no father should ever have to hear.

There were no more words.

There was a gurgling sound.

A sickening choking noise.

A loud crack as the cell phone hit the pavement.

Through the still-open connection, General Smythe listened to the rapid succession of *thump thump thump*s as the bomb casings split apart and spilled their deadly vapor through the air. He heard people screaming—loudly at first, and then more quietly, as if the screams were bubbling up through throats full of honey, thick and heavy.

In the background, the rumble from the B-52 slowly receded as it left the target area, banking to the south to recover at Barksdale. The rumble from its eight mighty engines was replaced with a strange clicking noise, a wicked chattering. Incredibly loud. Incredibly evil.

He held the receiver in his hand for what seemed like an eternity.

There was silence in the NMCC. Everyone in the command center knew what had just happened.

A father's heart had been ripped from his chest.

The sound of the general's phone being gently placed back in its cradle could be heard from every corner of the room. People stood in shocked and respectful silence for the man who'd led them through so many bad times.

The silence was broken when General Rayburn "Scythe" Smythe, chairman of the Joint Chiefs of Staff, decorated combat veteran and proud United States Marine, removed his sidearm, placed the barrel in his mouth, and gently squeezed the trigger.

CHAPTER 45

"Carolyn, I think it's dead." Rammes stood just outside the thick Plexiglas containment wall, staring at the crumpled body of the mutated rat. It hadn't moved for over forty-five minutes, and the biometric sensors were still blank.

"I think we can go ahead and get it out of there. I want to make a thorough examination." In the back of her mind, however, Carolyn didn't believe the thing could've died so easily. Since the Gemini agent was the foundation for this mutation, the creature should've mutated in response to the soman nerve gas. "Only one person goes in there, and they must be armed."

"What are you thinking, Carolyn?" Garrett asked.

"This doesn't make sense. I honestly didn't think the soman would kill it. All the data I've seen from the Soviet experience with Gemini led me to believe the creature would've mutated. It shouldn't be dead."

"You sound disappointed."

"No, not disappointed. Just a little confused." She looked at him through her plastic face mask and smiled. "I don't like to be wrong."

"I guessed that."

"Lieutenant Ewing, open the door," Rammes ordered. "Sergeant Wilson, get in there and get it to the examination container as quickly as you can. If that thing so much as twitches, I want your men to fill it full of lead."

"Hooah, sir."

Carolyn couldn't resist any longer. "General, just what the heck does *hooah* mean?"

"It can mean a lot of things, Carolyn. It can mean yes, it can mean great, it can mean shit hot, it can mean fuckin' A, it can mean—"

"Okay, sir. I get the idea."

"It's just a very strong affirmative."

"Got it, sir. Hooah."

"Very nice, Carolyn. I'll make a trooper out of you yet."

"That may be harder than you think, General. I don't like guns."

"That's okay. Neither do I."

Josh Ewing opened both sets of doors, and Sergeant Wilson, rifle at the ready, walked confidently into the room toward the dead beast. He inched up to the body, holding his rifle barrel right next to the thing's head. "Jesus! This thing made one hell of a mess. I'm glad I don't have to smell this shit."

"Pick it up and get the hell out of there, Wilson," Rammes said.

"Yes, sir."

Sergeant Wilson tried to pick the creature up with one gloved hand, but found it was stuck to the floor by the congealing mess of bodily fluids that surrounded it. He stood, slung his rifle over his shoulder, and stooped down to grab the body with both hands.

Carolyn saw the eyes first.

Two bright, fiery yellow orbs.

Before she could scream a warning, the thing was raising itself off the floor, clumps of its hair ripping away, stuck to the mess on the floor.

The biometric readings spiked.

It was alive.

"Get out of there! Get out!" Her warning was too late.

Sergeant Wilson was startled. He lost his balance and fell back on his butt, kicking with his boots to get some distance from the thing, trying desperately to untangle his rifle strap and bring his weapon to bear.

In a blur, the creature jumped at him and sank its fangs deep into his leg.

Sergeant Wilson let out a bloodcurdling scream. He raised his rifle above his head and brought down the butt of the weapon square on the thing's head.

It wouldn't let go.

"Jesus! Get this thing off of me! Get it off!" he screamed.

It was too late. The transfer had been made. The mutation of Sergeant Randy Wilson, United States Army, began almost immediately.

The other soldiers ran through the first entrance, rifles at the ready.

Sergeant Wilson fell back onto the floor, his head bouncing with the impact. His back arched, and he let out a tortured scream. Even now, just seconds after the infectious bite, the sound that escaped his trembling throat didn't sound entirely human.

The creature released its vise-like grip on its victim's leg, and crouched, preparing to jump.

Garrett pushed Josh Ewing out of the way, sending him sprawling through the air to land in a tangled heap against one of the examination tables, and mashed the button to close the inner door. It slammed shut just as the soldiers reached it, and just as the creature flew through the air, slamming onto the door with a sickening thud.

"Garrett! What are you doing! We've got to get him out of there!" Carolyn tried to reach the button herself, but Garrett held her back.

"He's already dead, Carolyn! He's already dead!"

Rammes ordered the remaining soldiers out of the entrance and closed the outer door. He walked to the Plexiglas and watched as the mutated rat jumped at him, slamming into the thick wall with a muted thud, snarling at him around oversized fangs, a foamy mass of blood—Sergeant Wilson's blood—ringing its mouth. A red smear ran down the inner surface of the Plexiglas to the floor, where the creature had landed.

A few feet away, Sergeant Wilson's body twitched and contorted in a macabre dance of death—but it wasn't really death, it was a transformation. Rammes watched in horror as what was once Sergeant Wilson tore at the environmental suit, ripping it into shreds with his new hands, now clawed and built for tearing.

Carolyn quickly walked to the soman control panel. She adjusted the dials and hit the release button. Within seconds the room was shrouded in a fog of deadly nerve gas.

Through the cloud, two sets of burning yellow eyes shone back at them, one set at floor level, the other at eye level. The transformed Sergeant Wilson was standing. He was now a *thinker*.

CHAPTER 46

The president called an emergency session of his war cabinet immediately after learning of Ray Smythe's suicide.

Assembled in the situation room were Hugo McIntyre, Tank Stone, Secretary of State Adam Williamson, and Jessie Hruska. The vice president and the directors of the CIA, the NSA, and the FBI were all video-teleconferenced in.

Jessie sat immediately to the president's right.

"We've suffered a terrible loss this evening. The chairman of the Joint Chiefs—and my good friend—Rayburn Smythe committed suicide in the NMCC upon learning of his daughter's death." He paused, unsure of what to say. He knew a good man had lost his daughter directly because of his decision.

"Mr. President, it had to be done," Jessie said. "The creatures were already on top of them—they'd almost reached the traffic jam where his daughter was stuck. She told her father she could see them coming closer." She gently placed her hand on the president's thigh, under the table. Out of sight. "She couldn't be saved, Mr. President. None of them could."

"How many did we lose?" the president asked, to no one in particular.

"Mr. President, there are no—" Hugo stopped midsentence.

"Go ahead, Hugo."

"All the evacuees from Omaha and Lincoln are dead, Mr. President. We don't have exact numbers yet, but the troops on the ground aren't reporting any survivors."

Andrew pushed that terrible news aside for the moment. He had to. "Did we kill the things?"

"Looks like it, sir. They dropped in place when the soman hit them. I think we've done it, sir. I think it's over."

"We've still got three more waves hitting us from the air, Hugo."

"Yes, sir, but now we know how to kill them."

"You want me to drop soman gas all over three—no, *four* more—cities that haven't had a chance to evacuate at all yet, and hope that we kill every single mutated bird in the air?"

"We can release the soman *in* the air, Mr. President. Defense is looking at modifying some of the old National Guard aerial spraying aircraft. Some are being used by the forestry service, a couple are in ready-use status at the boneyard, and—"

"How long before they can be used?"

Tank answered, "We can have a couple ready by tomorrow night, Mr. President."

"How much soman do we have left?"

"That's not a concern, Mr. President. The Soviets had enough of the stuff to blanket the entire globe a couple of times."

"Well, Tank, I guess I should thank the Russian president the next time I talk to him, then."

The secretary of state took this chance to interject. "Mr. President, the Russians are getting a little antsy. They're concerned that this situation may get out of control—and spread. And they're not the only ones."

"What have we told them?"

"They've been watching CNN just like everyone else on the planet, sir. They're not, however, aware of the Gemini connection.

They've inquired about helping us—humanitarian relief, border security, that sort of thing."

"I think those bastards have helped enough already."

Adam Williamson continued. "Like I said, sir, the Russians aren't the only ones showing concern over this. Our allies—especially Canada—are especially concerned about the spread of the mutations. Most countries have cancelled all international flights to and from the United States. Mexico and Canada have stated they're going to station troops along their borders, as well. They haven't closed them yet, but once Canada learns of the Minneapolis attacks, we can expect them to close their border."

"We have to stop this before the spread reaches outside CONUS." Andrew rubbed his face with his hands, the scruff of his day-old beard sounding like sandpaper against leather. He turned his attention to his CIA and NSA directors. "Jake, Steven, what are we showing on the threat boards?"

The director of the CIA, Jake Kesting, spoke first. "There's still no evidence, Mr. President, to assume a state-sponsored attack. We've been digging hard into the terrorist organizations; other than sending messages back and forth about how this is a message from Allah that the end is near for the Great Satan, there's been no chatter whatsoever claiming responsibility. Same for the domestic groups—they're silent."

"Sir, we *have* been intercepting some troubling communications from the Chinese," Steven Jacobsen said. "NSA has seen increased message traffic to their regional commanders over the past few hours. The units they're talking to are those units we assume would be used in an attack against Taiwan."

Andrew's gaze grew suddenly fierce. He focused it on his secretary of state. "State, you tell those bastards that if they even twitch toward Taiwan—if they even take a piss in the Taiwan Strait—I will not hesitate to blow their whole fucking country right off the face of the earth. You can use those exact words, Adam."

"Understand, sir."

"Tank, we need to get a new chairman up and running to take Smythe's place."

"Sir, right now the vice chairman is running the show—Admiral Burns. He's the logical choice to step up to the pla—"

Jessie cut him off. "General Metzger, sir. He's the right man for the job."

"Metzger?" the President asked. "Isn't he at STRAT?"

"Yes sir. General Thad Metzger is the commander, United States Strategic Command."

"Ms. Hruska," Tank said, his voice cool with contempt, "Admiral Burns, for the sake of continuity in this time of crisis, is the right—"

"Thad Metzger is a warrior, Mr. Secretary. Admiral Burns is a politician, a yes-man. He's not the kind of leader we need right now."

Andrew couldn't help but smile. He knew Burns personally from their days together on the Pacific Command staff, years ago. Jessie was right about him.

Tank didn't like being called on the carpet at all, especially by Jessie Hruska, and especially in the situation room in front of the president. His voice boomed low and loud. "Mr. President, with all due respect to Ms. Hruska, I strongly recommend Admiral Burns for this position."

"Tank, you know as well as I do that Don Burns is an administrative genius. I knew him when he was a captain on the PACOM staff. He's a hell of a staff officer, but he's one of the most uninspiring officers I've ever met. We need a leader, Tank. Get me General Metzger on the horn. Right now."

Allison spoke. "Mr. President, I agree with Mr. Stone that—"

"Not now, Allison. Tank, make the call."

"Yes, sir."

The president had made his decision. The time for arguments was over.

• • •

Allison watched, dumbfounded, as the president made another decision without even a whiff of consideration for what she thought. It was his prerogative as commander in chief, surely, but never had she seen him so blatantly disregard his own secretary of defense. Or her.

Allison didn't think Donald Burns was the right choice, either, but Metzger? Not her first choice. As well as she knew—or thought she knew—Andrew, Metzger shouldn't have been at the top of his list, either. Hruska made the suggestion, and Andrew had hopped right on board, almost like he was her friggin' lapdog.

Not the Andrew she knew. At all.

The Russians were getting concerned. The Chinese, getting frisky. Old allies beginning to turn their backs. The American Midwest had turned into a massive killing field. A crisis like no other, and the president no longer seemed like the man beside whom she'd agreed to serve.

Now high over eastern Wyoming and heading north onboard the E-4, Allison was glad she'd listened to her hunch. Something was definitely wrong.

She had a bad feeling it was going to get worse.

CHAPTER 47

General Rammes stood at the Plexiglas wall, watching as the thing that was once one of his soldiers walked right up to him, its face clouded by mists of the soman gas, staring right at him. Burning, yellow eyes. Full of hate, full of hunger. Full of intelligence.

The thing let out a low moaning sound, its lips parting to reveal row upon row of black, triangular teeth. Serrated at the edges. Like a shark's.

Without breaking his stare, Rammes said, "Carolyn, the soman isn't having any effect this time. Why isn't Sergeant Wil—" He paused, correcting himself. "Why isn't this *thing* going through the same death throes that the rat did the first time we used the gas?"

Carolyn was amazed at how quickly General Rammes had made the switch from "Sergeant Wilson" to "this thing." She realized, as Garrett had told her, that Sergeant Wilson was as good as dead as soon as the monster sank its fangs into his leg. The mutated creature standing just a couple feet away from the general was no longer human. It was no longer Sergeant Wilson. She regained her composure and answered. "Sir, what we've just seen is the Gemini agent mutating in response to the soman. The mutated rat is now immune to its effects. When it bit Sergeant Wilson, it passed this immunity on to him. Sergeant Wilson—it—is now impervious to the soman gas."

"Can we raise the exposure? Maybe overwhelm the thing's defenses and—?"

"General, I released the entire container of soman. There's enough gas in there right now to wipe out a good portion of the eastern seaboard."

General Rammes sighed. "I'll let General Smythe know. He'll have to tell the president to call off the attack."

• • •

At that very instant, General Smythe's body was being removed from the NMCC.

In the air above Des Moines, Springfield, Wichita, and St. Louis, B-52s were dropping their loads of ex-Soviet soman gas on the remaining ground waves of mutated creatures.

And on all the people who were still trying to escape.

CHAPTER 48

The commander, United States Strategic Command, was brought into the video-teleconference in a matter of seconds. Since Offutt AFB had been overrun, and USSTRATCOM headquarters had been abandoned, General Metzger was airborne. "Mr. President, this is General Metzger."

"Hello, Thad. I'm pulling you out of STRATCOM. You're taking over for Ray Smythe. You need to get your butt to Washington."

Surprisingly, he wasn't stunned by the announcement. Not even a little. "Understand, sir. We're airborne over Ohio right now. We'll divert to Andrews AFB immediately."

"See me when you get on the ground, General."

"Yes, Mr. President." He paused. "And sir, let me pass my condolences on to you regarding General Smythe. He was a fine man. I know he was a personal friend of yours."

"Thank you, General. I agree—he was a fine man."

"Yes, sir. STRATCOM out." The video link was broken.

The president turned to Tank Stone. "Tank, get him up to speed as quickly as you can."

"Yes, Mr. President."

"And get those aerial sprayers ready to go. Yesterday."

"Copy that, sir."

• • •

Inside, Jessie was beaming. Generations of effort, years of endless waiting and personal sacrifice to perform a mission once abandoned by those who'd originally launched it, had all come down to this moment . . . And in the end, it'd been surprisingly easy. First, she'd conquered the president of the United States—the most powerful man on the planet. And then she'd ensured one of her own—a person much like her—had been placed in a position of enormous power as chairman of the Joint Chiefs of Staff. The suicide of General Smythe had been a blessing in disguise—completely unexpected, but completely welcome. Her clandestine calls to her counterparts in foreign lands were also beginning to pay off. The Chinese. The Russians. Soon, she knew the intelligence agencies would be reporting on troublesome events in North Korea. Great Britain. France. Germany. A worldwide network of those who shared her vision was alive with advice whispered into the ears of other powerful men, just as she had done. No, *was doing*.

The events of the last two days had been completely unexpected—the whole situation had caught her off guard. She didn't know if the chaotic, fast-moving situation could be managed effectively yet, but chaos was never frowned upon by her and those like her. It opened doors to opportunity. Her time, *their* time, was now. As Vladimir Ilyich himself had once said, *It is impossible to predict the time and progress of revolution. It is governed by its own more or less mysterious laws*. Lenin was right. Mysteries were at work here, and the laws were in their favor.

She gently stroked the president's thigh, and was delighted to notice that he made no effort to remove her hand. She had him.

Even in the situation room, in front of his war cabinet, she *had* him.

It was a delightful thing.

The president was in a weakened state. His wife's death, which had been a beautiful example of planning on her part, had set the most powerful man on the planet on a course straight into her loving arms. Soon, he would be speaking *her* words, ordering *her* desires, and the world would be finally be prepared for the moment for which she'd lived her life.

She silently thanked the *Komitet Gosudarstvennoy Bezopasnosti* visionaries for designing such a useful tool as *Spetsial'naya Podgotovka 117*. If they'd known a derivative of their psychotropic SP-117 was to one day be given to the president of the United States himself . . . No one in the old KGB would've dreamt such a thing were possible. God knows they'd tried to do it before.

The KGB had passed into history.

But others, like her, had not.

For decades, her kind had sat dormant—sleeping, as it were— always scheming, awaiting the order to awake and strike.

The villages built in remote parts of the Soviet Union—crafted to resemble an American or British town, where agents would lose their Soviet identities and immerse themselves in the culture of their target country—now sat abandoned. Children, selected for their racial or physical characteristics, had been raised from birth in these villages, given their lives to the great cause, and when ready, traveled abroad with new foreign identities provided by the KGB. New York, London, Washington, even Beijing blindly welcomed the newcomers, the secret soldiers of the Soviet dream.

Her grandfather had been one such child. He lived his life waiting for an order. His son—her father—grew to accept the cause, as well, and he waited.

Jessie was American by birth, but a follower of the cause. Her father had taught her well . . . and she, too, waited.

The order never came from her true homeland, the land of her forefathers. The KGB's tentacles had once reached far and deep, much more than anyone ever imagined, into nearly every government across the globe. They were so close to realizing their dream . . .

But those tentacles withered and died along with the Union. Thousands of willing soldiers—the sleepers—were abandoned in place, left to fend for themselves, their mission no longer important. For some, though—for many—the cause was too great to abandon. All their sacrifices would not be in vain.

The fight would go on.

From father to son to grandson—and granddaughter—the cause was kept alive. In London, Tokyo, Paris, and Washington, the fight would go on. In Berlin, Beijing, and even Moscow itself, the fight would go on. The old ones in the Kremlin had passed on, and the new leaders—the bastards who'd allowed decades of glory to fade away and then greedily embraced the corruption and excesses of Western society—had abandoned them, and for that, they would suffer the same fate. The descendants of the coward Gorbachev and the drunkard Yeltsin, and the string of fools that followed them in the Kremlin, would feel the sting of their sins.

The entire world would tremble when they made their move, and the new world, the one envisioned by the Fathers of the Revolution, would rise from the ashes.

Her father, and his father before him, would be proud of what she'd accomplished . . . and of what she was prepared to do.

A tiny dose on the skin was all it took. For weeks, small amounts of the drug had drawn Andrew closer. A larger dose—a risk she was prepared to take—helped prod him to use the soman, something he never would've done on his own. With larger, more frequent doses, the president would be hers to use as she wished, clay to mold with her hands. In *his* hands lay the keys to America's nuclear arsenal.

For without fire, there can be no ashes.

CHAPTER 49

"When did *that* happen?"

"Just a little while ago, Derek. He was on the phone with his daughter. She was stuck in traffic just outside Lincoln when they released the gas." Admiral Don Burns didn't have to explain any further. The tone of his voice said it all.

General Rammes was shocked to hear of Ray Smythe's suicide, but he was even more shocked to hear the soman gas had already been used. "Don, are you telling me they used the soman?"

"Yes. Dropped it on the Lincoln wave, and the other waves as well. Looks like it's working. The things are dropping like flies."

"Those fucking idiots! Why didn't they wait for our analysis?"

Burns was confused. "What is it, Derek?"

"The soman doesn't work, Don. We exposed it to one of the live creatures, and it adapted to it. It dropped dead—at least we thought it was dead—and then it just came back to life. That's why I was calling Ray. So he could tell the president."

"Dear God."

"No shit. And there's more. The thing bit one of my troopers, and transformed him into a . . . into a *thing*. When it bit him, it passed its immunity to the soman on to him. We flooded the compartment with enough soman to kill a few cities, and it stood there and took it. No effect whatsoever. It doesn't work."

"We've killed thousands of our citizens. For nothing."

"Get on the horn to the president, Don. Tell him the creatures are going to be on the run again in about thirty minutes."

"I can't get to the president. Neither can SECDEF, for that matter, unless he demands to see him in person or the president contacts him directly. That bitch won't let anyone near him. I have to go through her."

Derek knew he was speaking about Jessie Hruska. "You're fucking kidding me."

"It gets better. They're replacing Ray with Thad Metzger."

"Metzger? He's a goddamned looney tune!"

"Apparently somebody at the top thinks differently."

"Metzger will go nuclear, Don."

"After what you've told me, we may not have any choice."

"We're trying to find another option. You've got to buy us some time here."

"I don't think there's a whole lot I can do. I don't have any access."

General Rammes thought long and hard before he spoke. He needed to choose his words carefully, for even secure lines were monitored at times. He knew one simple word should do it: "Coastie?"

There was a long silence on the other end of the secure line. General Rammes knew his old friend had immediately understood what he was getting at.

Insubordination was always a tricky subject. Especially when you were talking about directly circumventing the authority of the president of the United States.

CHAPTER 50

The president of the United States now had the blood of countless thousands of American citizens on his hands. He'd given the order to release the soman. An order at the time he'd felt was justified and completely necessary. No, essential.

Sacrifice some, in order to save many more.

But in the end, it had been a meaningless sacrifice. All the people had died for nothing.

"Mr. President, four of the waves are currently within the target cities. We're going to lose Springfield, Des Moines, St. Louis, and Wichita." The SECDEF rubbed his eyes, tired. "The wave outside Lincoln is continuing westward, roughly following I-80. We've started evacuation procedures in all the cities and towns along that path, from Grand Island to Denver."

"Evacuation procedures." The president spoke the words flatly, with no emotion. "It's not going to matter, Tank. It's not going to matter one bit."

"We've got to try, sir."

"And the birds?" the president asked.

"The birds are still fully engaged in Minneapolis-St. Paul, Little Rock, and Oklahoma City." He paused. "It seems to take them longer."

The president looked at his watch. Soon, the sun would rise over Washington, DC, signaling an end to the most horrific night in American history. A night when thousands of Americans had died. Some at the hands of the beasts. Many more at the hands of their own president.

"Tank, we've got a few more hours until they go to ground again. When they do, I want exact locations mapped out and targeted."

"Targeted, sir?" He didn't want to know what the president was thinking, although he was certain what he meant.

"Targeted. Fixed. Exact locations. We're going to have to move fast while we have daylight."

"Understand, sir."

"The birds, Tank. During the day, can we assume they will go to ground as well? Stay in the cities?"

"Possible, sir. Once we have daylight, we can find them. If they form some sort of cocoons—like the ground waves did—they'll be immobile long enough for us to locate most of them."

"Just as long as they're in the same general area, Tank."

This statement confirmed it. No pinpoint targeting. No conventional attacks. The president's meaning was crystal clear. "Sir, if we choose this course of action, I recommend we wait until the last possible moment. We need to allow as many people as possible to escape the immediate areas. Upwind. Away from the fallout."

"Start working on a plan, Tank. I want something ready by sunup."

"Yes, Mr. President."

As Tank Stone exited the Oval Office, he passed Jessie Hruska. She offered a greeting, but he didn't return it.

He closed the office door behind him.

"Mr. President?"

"Sit down, Jessie. Please."

She sat in one of the chairs placed in the center of the Oval Office, facing an identical set of chairs just a few feet away, the Great Seal of the President of the United States embroidered on the rug at her feet. "Tank looked like you'd just kicked him in the stomach. What happened?"

The president sat beside her. "I have to nuke them, Jessie."

She fought to conceal her excitement. "But, the soman—when I left, the reports said—"

"The reports were wrong. They're resistant to it. Vanguard released soman on one of the captured creatures, and it lived. If I'd have known, I wouldn't have ordered the attack."

"Andrew, you did what you had to do. You had to act."

"Too quickly. If I'd only waited an hour longer—"

"You'd only have delayed the inevitable. Those people were as good as dead, Andrew. We both know that."

"Have you ever seen what soman does to a person, Jessie?"

"Yes, I have. I know what it does. It's a horrible, painful death. But would it have been any less painful for them if they'd been attacked by the creatures? We've seen what they can do, too."

"I killed thousands of people who may have otherwise survived."

"You don't know that."

"Yes, I do."

"Bullshit. You made the right decision based on the information you had at the time. There's no other way to look at it, Andrew. Second-guessing yourself is not going to do you—or this country— any good. It's over. It's done. We know chemical weapons won't work now. We don't have to waste time considering that option any longer."

The president was tired. More tired than he'd felt his entire life. Her words were making sense. Yes, he'd made a decision when a decision had to be made. It had turned out to be wrong—terribly wrong—but at the time, it seemed like the most logical course of action.

They knew conventional forces wouldn't be able to stop the creatures.

They knew—now—that chemical weapons would be useless.

Not issuing the order *would* just have delayed the inevitable.

When the whole nightmare began, deep down in his gut he knew he would eventually be forced to resort to the release of the most powerful weapons ever devised by man, to stop the spread.

That time was now.

Jessie leaned closer, placing her hand on the back of his neck. She rubbed, gently, and his tension began to fade away.

As did Andrew Smith.

This was the strongest dose yet.

• • •

The first dim light from the rising sun shone through the thick bulletproof windows of the Oval Office. Her red hair reflected the morning light, thin strands of fire framing her perfect face. The president was transfixed by her beauty.

Even with all the death and destruction weighing so heavily on him, he found it impossible to concentrate on anything other than her at that moment.

Just her.

She took his hand. Her grip was soft, warm. Loving. Incredibly alive.

"Andrew?"

He looked into her eyes. The effect was hypnotic. He couldn't look away.

"You know what you have to do, Andrew."

"I know what I have to do." His voice was far away, detached.

"For your country."

"For my country."

She smiled. "For me."

"For you."

She leaned closer. Kissed him, long and hard.

He kissed her back.

This was the final test. She pushed him away. Slapped him. Hard.

The president of the United States looked up at her. His right cheek was reddened by the slap, but his face was blank. Like a child, waiting to be told what to do.

It was a success.

She had taken his wife from him, and for that she felt pity. He'd loved Kate so, and her loss caused him great pain. But it'd been necessary. The first lady of the United States had stood in her way and had to be removed. In war—even an ideological one—innocent people died.

She peeled a thin coating of spray-on latex from the palm of her hand, carefully avoiding contact with the outer layer. Another useful tool handed down from the KGB, and quite an ingenious manner to deliver the SP-117 derivative.

Before her sat the most powerful man on the planet. Utterly, completely alone.

And entirely open to suggestion.

Her feelings of pity were short-lived.

DAY THREE

CHAPTER 51

General Rammes stood no more than a few feet away from the most fantastic killing machine he'd ever seen. What had been Sergeant Wilson a few hours before now stood on the other side of the thick Plexiglas shield, yellow eyes burning furiously with a hatred and hunger that escaped description.

It just stood there. Staring back at him. Eye-to-eye. Unmoving, except for the slow rise and fall of its chest. The eyes didn't even blink.

Behind those eyes, Rammes could sense intelligence. It was a horrible creature, rebuilt for rapid killing, but there was something un-animallike about the eyes. There were thoughts running through its head. It was watching him. Examining him. Studying him. It was reasoning.

The interior of the room was now dark, as the creature had smashed the overhead lights about an hour ago. The things had an obvious aversion to light of any kind, but the fluorescent lights of the holding room didn't have the destructive effect that sunlight did. When the things entered sunlight, they died. They were true creatures of the night. Modern-day vampires mixed with the cunning of the wolf, the running ability of the gazelle, the strength of the grizzly bear, and the killing ability of a swarm of blood-frenzied great white sharks. Unstoppable, except when they were blown limb from limb. And there were so many.

Behind the creature, another set of bioluminescent eyes glowed from the darkness, the mutated rat slowly moving from one edge of the room to the next, its gaze fixed squarely on the general.

"It's waiting for orders."

"General?" Carolyn swiveled her chair away from the computer screen she had been studying for the last few hours.

"I said it's waiting for orders. The rat. It's waiting for orders from the bigger one."

"How can you tell?"

"I'm an old soldier. I can tell."

Garrett rose from his chair by Carolyn's workstation and stood by the general. "It makes sense, sir. I've seen it. The rats react to the bigger ones. They understand audible commands. When I grabbed Carolyn from the crash site, one of the big ones seemed to alert the others to my presence. It was a low, moaning sound. As soon as it let out that sound, the whole wave of the things turned in my direction." He shook his head. "It didn't dawn on me until what you just said."

As if on cue, the thinker let out a moan. Even through the thick Plexiglas, the members of the Vanguard team could hear it. They could feel it in their chests.

The rat began to scratch at the floor. Slowly at first, and then the motions grew more frantic. Its front paws, tipped by the long, black claws, tore at the steel floor, scratching away a layer of paint.

The thinker broke its gaze with the general and lowered itself to the floor. Its long arms began flailing at the floor, claws trying to dig through the steel.

"Carolyn? What do you make of this?" Rammes asked.

Carolyn glanced at the clock on the far wall. "It's time for them to go to ground. The sun will rise here in a few minutes."

"How the hell can they know that? They're hundreds of feet underground!"

"General, have you ever known what time it is, even though there's no clock in sight? Have you ever woken up just a few minutes before your alarm clock is set to go off?"

"Yes, I've done that before."

"Biological clock. In some creatures, it's as accurate as anything that comes out of the Naval Observatory. Quite amazing, actually." She stood next to the general, watching as the creatures scratched furiously at the steel floor. "Most of us only experience it in subtle ways, like waking right before the alarm clock goes off. Some people have more advanced awareness of it. They can tell the time of day even after being secluded from any normal source of time—the sun, a clock, anything. Some can even tell you what day of the month it is even after being secluded for extended periods of time. We've seen it in some POW cases."

"So you're telling me these things instinctively knew it was time to start digging?"

"That's right."

"Looks like the little bastards are going to be awful disappointed when they can't get through that floor."

CHAPTER 52

The city of Little Rock, Arkansas, was a bloody mess.

The Army Stryker vehicles entered Little Rock from the east and northwest on I-40, moving rapidly toward the portions of the city that had been under attack by the flocks of mutated birds.

There were cars leaving the city, but not many. Not many at all. Blackhawk helicopters circled overhead, their speaker systems thundering evacuation orders to the survivors below.

The scene was unlike anything any of the soldiers had ever seen. Bodies littered the streets by the hundreds, torn apart and shredded by the thousands of ravenous beaks that had eaten them alive during the night. Arms and legs were still recognizable, but the torsos were mangled. Eyes had been plucked from screaming heads, tongues torn out from shrieking mouths. Quick. Incredibly violent.

As the eight-wheeled Strykers entered the center of the city, the drivers were forced to slow to avoid driving over the dead. They slowly weaved through the city streets, trying as hard as they could to show some measure of dignity toward those who'd been their fellow citizens just a few hours before.

It was a horrid scene.

A scene that was being repeated in Oklahoma City and Minneapolis-St. Paul as the sun began its leisurely rise into the sky, marking the start of another day. A day of hiding for the mutated creatures. A day of planning for their human foes.

Soldiers spilled from the combat vehicles, rapidly spreading out to find any sign of the birds that had so ravaged the city. They ran to the shadowy places—the darkened buildings, the alleyways, the sewers. They searched the back rooms of buildings, the attics of houses.

It didn't take long to find them.

Where there wasn't direct sunlight, there were casings. Thousands of them. Small, oval-shaped cocoons, gray and hard as bone, completely harmless-looking, but inside—the soldiers knew—dwelt incredible evil. Changing. Growing. And if the last day was any lesson, multiplying. Doubling in number. Preparing themselves for another night of flying. Of feeding. And killing.

The ground waves, as they'd done twenty-four hours before, had stopped their advances and had encased themselves in the thick, bone-like cocoons. But this time, they hadn't gone deep. Most were just under the surface, no more than a few inches. Some were even visible, their curved surfaces breaking through the soil and dully reflecting the morning sunlight.

In very short order, their locations were mapped. Analyzed. Subjected to computer simulations of nuclear blast effects. To the new chairman of the Joint Chiefs of Staff, the data looked promising.

"This is Metzger."

"Hello, General. What do you have?" Jessie Hruska was comforted by the voice on the other end of the secure phone.

"The casings in the three bird cities are out in the open—in buildings, houses, the sewers—well within our reach. One weapon each should eradicate them."

"And the ground waves?"

"Different this time. They're not buried deep. They're almost entirely on the surface."

"On the surface?"

"Nothing deeper than a few inches. We don't know why, but they're there. We figure two to three weapons for each ground wave location should finish them off. If we hit them before sunset, this thing could be over."

The chance to destroy them before the sun set again was just the answer they'd been looking for. Ending it now, though, would ruin her plan.

The whole situation had been a blessing in disguise, the chance they'd all been waiting decades for. A worldwide crisis of unimaginable magnitude, developing rapidly, stressing every single means of control. Complete and utter chaos. The perfect playing field for all those placed in positions of power—or at least beside those positions of power— to shape the unfolding situation into the cataclysmic realization of destruction. On a global scale.

She knew she had to manage the situation. Controlling the president would be easy enough—he was now entirely subjugated to her every whim. It was those around him who worried her. The other members of his cabinet. And especially, the vice president. Allison Perez knew Andrew better than most and would surely be attuned to any personality changes. If Perez were close, Jessie could possibly arrange another "accident"—like the one that removed Andrew's dear Kate from the equation—but the bitch was nowhere near Washington, DC, completely out of reach. Jessie knew she had to act fast. Decisions had to be made.

"I'll brief the president, General."

"Copy. Metzger out."

Jessie quickly made her way to the Oval Office.

CHAPTER 53

"At sunrise yesterday, every single one of the things went to ground to avoid the sunlight. They dug deep and encased themselves in the cocoons. To multiply." Carolyn pressed her face mask against the Plexiglas wall, trying to see into the shadows.

"What are these things going to do, since they can't get underground?"

"I say we wait and see, General."

"Wait a minute. What's that on the big one's back?" Garrett asked.

A bubbling foam had appeared along the length of the creature's spine, slowly spreading across the thing's back.

Carolyn shined a penlight toward the back of the room where the mutated rat had been scratching. The same foamy substance was spreading out from its spine, as well.

She was shocked as the thinker suddenly stood, its eyes just inches from hers on the other side of the Plexiglas wall. Its mouth opened, revealing row upon row of glistening, obsidian shark's teeth. A low moan escaped its open maw.

She screamed and stumbled back, landing quite unladylike on her hindquarters. "Son of a *bitch*!"

"Are you all right?" Garrett asked as he helped her back to her feet. He was trying hard not to laugh.

"Yes, damn it, I'm fine." She pulled her arm away as he let out a genuine grade-A chuckle. "The thing just surprised me, that's all."

"More like scared the living shit out of you, I'd say."

She shot him a warning glance through her face mask.

"Oh, come on, now," Garrett said. "It was funny! We haven't had anything to laugh about in a while."

Her expression didn't change.

Oops, he thought, *not in a mood for humor. Better keep my trap shut.*

"They're making their cocoons," Rammes said. "Take a look at this—they've stopped trying to dig, too."

They watched as the rat crawled back into the security of the opened ammunition box, the foamy substance now covering most of its body.

The thinker turned and crawled under the examination bed, finding shelter. It too was rapidly being covered by the foamy mass.

Within minutes, revealed by Carolyn's penlight, both the mutated rat and the thinker had been completely covered by the thick foam, which was now starting to darken, from white to gray. It was solidifying. Hardening.

"When they're done, we need to take them out of there."

The statement made every single person in the clean room turn and look at her as if she'd just loosed one of the loudest lady-farts ever heard in human history.

Garrett spoke first. "You're kidding, right?"

"No. We need to see exactly what's going on inside those casings." She turned to Josh Ewing, who was, like everyone else, staring at her in disbelief. "Josh, I need a CAT scanner down here ASAP." She turned to the general next. "Sir, we should be safe until sunset—they won't start to emerge until then. If those casings start to crack even one millimeter, we'll blow them both to holy hell."

"Funny, that's what I was going to say. And Carolyn?"

"Yes, sir?"

"That was spoken like a true trooper. Hooah, Ms. Ridenour."

"There's that damn word again."

CHAPTER 54

His face.

As with every person she'd manipulated with the drug over the years, their faces were always the same: glassy, vacant eyes, mouths hanging open ever so slightly. They were puppets whose master had abandoned them. Left them motionless. Powerless.

As she walked into Andrew's field of view, she watched his expression immediately brighten and come to life. His puppet master had returned.

Now more than ever, she knew she had to keep him secluded, away from the others, lest they see him in his weakened state and decide to act. It wasn't going to be easy, but if she was successful, she wouldn't have to do it for long.

"Andrew?"

"Yes, Jessie?" Andrew fumbled with the papers on his desk, trying to appear occupied. After all, he was the president of the United States and being un-busy wasn't part of his job description. He knew he must've been doing something before she walked in. He just couldn't remember what it was.

"General Metzger reports they've mapped the locations of the casings."

The president's mind was foggy, as if he had woken from a long sleep. But if that were true, if he'd fallen asleep at his desk, why did he feel so exhausted? "Did they find the birds? Are they still in the cities?"

"Yes. Hidden in buildings, houses. Out of the light. They're concentrated, Andrew. General Metzger is confident they can all be wiped out with a single weapon each."

A single weapon each? he thought. *What kind of weapon? Is Metzger suggesting using nuclear weapons on American soil?* Gradually, the president's thoughts returned to their proper place. He'd considered—no, nearly decided—to use nuclear weapons himself. *It was the only way. Conventional weapons weren't working. They couldn't work. Didn't. Multiplying too fast. Too fast. Chemical weapons didn't work. Resistant to their effects now. Nukes are the only way. The only way to stop this. Stop it. Before it's too late.*

Jessie watched, fascinated, as Andrew struggled with his thoughts. She knew what he was thinking. Knew what he was remembering. She'd made sure he was convinced conventional weapons weren't the answer, which, in this case, was actually true. She'd also convinced him that chemical weapons were a possible answer—even though she knew using them before the Vanguard team had evaluated their effectiveness was taking a huge gamble. A gamble that had been paid with thousands of American lives. She'd hurried her president into making that decision, so in reality, the blood of the innocents was on her hands. So be it.

Her voice seemed unnaturally loud in the quiet of the Oval Office. "It's time, Mr. President. It's time to use all resources at your disposal to eliminate this threat."

"Get me General Metzger. Right now."

"Andrew, I just told you I talked to—"

"Jessie, I need to speak with him now, please." The voice was forceful, yet still clouded by the drug-induced connection he had with the woman standing before him.

He was a strong man, she knew. Probably the strongest man she'd ever tried to control. It wasn't surprising he would maintain some of the character traits that brought him to the presidency in the first place. They would be hard to undermine completely. But, they could still be controlled. Enough. "I'll connect him immediately." She reached for the secure phone on the president's desk and asked the person on the other end to immediately connect her to General Metzger in the NMCC. It was a good sign that the president had not simply picked up the phone and done it himself—he needed her to do it. For him.

"Metzger here."

"General, this is the national security advisor. The president wishes to speak to you. Stand by." She pushed a button on the phone and returned the handset to its cradle. "It's on speakerphone, sir."

He didn't object.

"Thad, this is the president. I understand you've located the bird casings."

"Yes, sir. Their locations have been mapped in all three cities."

"And the ground waves?"

"They repeated their digging from yesterday morning. However, they are barely under the surface this time. Some of the casings are even visible, poking out of the ground. These locations are also completely mapped. Unlike the birds, the ground waves are somewhat more spread out and harder to—"

"Destroy with a single weapon, General?"

General Metzger paused, suddenly uncomfortable with the president's tone of voice. "Yes, sir. It would take two, maybe three weapons to destroy each of the ground waves."

"And the birds, General? Can they be destroyed with a single weapon targeted against each of the cities?"

"Yes, sir. We've run their locations through numerous nuclear blast simulations. Completely eradicated them each and every time."

"And have you run the ground wave locations through the same simulations using multiple weapons?"

"Yes, sir. Similar results."

"What are the effects, General? What are the long-term consequences?"

"Well, sir, that depends on the timing of the attack."

"Explain."

"If we strike now, we'll lose significantly more people to the immediate blast effects. I've heard that the evacuations are ongoing, but moving slowly."

"So, you're suggesting we strike later, after letting the evacuations proceed for the rest of the day?"

"No, sir. That's your suggestion, not mine. I can't make that call."

"Then what is your suggestion, General?"

"Strike now."

"Now? When we'll lose so many more people?"

"Sir, we don't know when these things are going to emerge. They've done it at night, but what if they mutate into something that's not as sensitive to the light anymore? What if they can move freely during the daylight? We already know they've adapted to soman gas—something that initially looked as if it would kill them. What's to say with all certainty that they aren't adapting to sunlight right now while they're safely tucked away in their cocoons?"

A slight grin spread across Jessie's face. The general had made a convincing argument for the immediate use of nuclear weapons, and it had obviously had an impact on the president's foggy thought process.

"You have a point, General. I hadn't thought of that possibility."

"It's something we have to take into account, sir. We don't know what's going to happen next, but we know what we can do now to stop this thing once and for all."

"He's right, Andrew. If they adapt to sunlight and emerge in the next few hours, they'll spread incredibly fast—especially the birds. If they double in number—as they've done already—we won't be able to stop them."

The president didn't seem to mind that his chairman of the Joint Chiefs had just heard Jessie call him by his first name.

"General, I want the three cities infested by the bird casings hit before sundown. I'll authorize the use of nuclear weapons to do this. Single weapon, each city. The evacuations will continue throughout the day to allow as many people as possible to get out of the immediate area. You will use the smallest weapon possible to mitigate collateral effects."

"Yes, sir. And the ground waves?"

"You will use conventional weapons to strike them—use everything we've got. If they're just below the surface, we should be able to destroy them. Bomb the living hell out of them, Thad."

"Sir, I respectfully suggest you consider the use of nuc—"

"No! Not yet. If the birds survive, there's no way to stop them. I don't think there's any other option other than to use nuclear weapons against those cities. The ground waves are different. We may have to use nuclear weapons against them in the end, but not right now. And we won't need to as long as you throw everything we have against them." The president paused. "Do you understand my orders, General?"

"Yes, sir. I understand you want to use conventional weapons against the fixed locations of the ground waves. I also understand you are authorizing the use of nuclear weapons to destroy the fixed locations of the bird casings in Minneapolis-St. Paul, Oklahoma City, and Little Rock."

"That's correct, General."

"Sir, I need to confirm that you are authorizing the use of nuclear weapons. Please authenticate."

The old days of the "nuclear football" were long gone. A new system was now in place. Quicker. More reliable.

The president pushed a button on the side of his desk, revealing a sliding panel. It made a slight whirring noise as it slid out from under the thick, polished mahogany of his historic desk. The president placed his hand on a black panel. A small needle pierced the president's palm, drawing a tiny amount of blood for an almost instantaneous DNA analysis. "This is the president of the United States. I am authorizing the use of nuclear weapons." He pulled a small laminated card from his wallet. "Authenticate Romeo, Bravo, six, six, three, five, Delta, Sierra, two. Day code one, one, Kilo, Echo. Code word *eagle*. Final release is on my authority as president of the United States of America."

In the bowels of the NMCC, General Metzger had also placed his hand on a matching panel, which analyzed his DNA as he repeated the president's instructions. "This is the chairman of the Joint Chiefs of Staff. I have received orders from the president of the United States authorizing the use of nuclear weapons. Authenticate Romeo, Bravo, six, six, three, five, Delta, Sierra, two. Day code one, one, Kilo, Echo. Code word *eagle*. Final release is on his authority as president of the United States of America."

A few seconds passed as a supersecret computer located hundreds of miles away, deep underground, in a hardened complex below the shifting silt of the Mississippi River analyzed the data it had just received. A green light shone steady on each of the panels—one in the NMCC, the other in the Oval Office.

It was done.

The first step had been taken.

With the final release order, three American cities would soon be basking under the warm glow of nuclear annihilation.

The president removed his hand. "Thank you, General."

"Thank you, sir. I'll inform you when the assets are ready."

The call was terminated.

In a matter of a few short seconds, the world had crossed a threshold it had avoided crossing since the end of World War II.

"Andrew, you need to sleep now. You've done the right thing. You need some rest."

"I'm so tired."

"I know you are."

"So tired."

"Rest now, Andrew. Rest." She watched as the president's face returned to its former puppet visage.

It was time for the puppet master to leave.

She had calls to make.

· · ·

As Jessie left the Oval Office, Andrew sat alone at his desk, trying to comprehend what had just happened. He knew he'd done something he'd always dreaded, but it had come so simply to him . . . It had been so easy. He had used the panel numerous times during exercises and simulations, but it had never been for real.

But he'd done the right thing. She'd said so. She's right. It's the only course of action to take. Had to do it. Had to. It was so easy. So easy.

Down deep, a part of Andrew Smith was screaming a warning, but it was far too quiet for his heart to hear.

. . .

Her phone—*this* phone—was not monitored. It had taken a considerable amount of effort—and numerous personal connections—to ensure it was so. As she punched in the first set of numbers, she knew it had all been worth it.

"Yes?" An answer.

"This is One. The kindling is burning. In my house."

"When?"

"Today."

"I shall warm myself by the fire."

She hung up the phone. The memorized code words had been spoken in Russian, but their meaning was clear.

She repeated the calls to other numbers, speaking the same words in Chinese, Korean, German, French, Hebrew, and even English—with, of course, a British accent.

We shall warm ourselves by the fire.

There was no stopping it now.

CHAPTER 55

"Thad, this is Derek Rammes." It had been years since he'd talked to the man. He'd tried to avoid it as much as possible, but the current situation deemed any further avoidance on his part impossible. Using first names instead of rank or title made it easier to stomach—the fact that Thad Metzger was now chairman of the Joint Chiefs twisted his guts into a greasy knot. He'd disliked the man since their days together at the Point.

"Hello, General. How are things in Utah?"

"Beautiful. Just beautiful." *So much for using first names*, Rammes thought. "Listen, General, I've been having some difficulties getting information through to the president."

"Why?"

"I'm having to go through the damned national security advisor. She's got the president completely secluded from the normal communication channels and—"

"Things don't always work as advertised in a time of war, General Rammes."

No shit, Thad. He fumed. "I understand that, but this is highly irregular."

"Irregular in what way, General?"

"Access to the president of the United States is being controlled by a single person. The normal channels in place to get information to him are not being used. They were set up to function in a time of war, and like you said yourself, this *is* a time of war."

"But it's not a normal war, General Rammes. Not normal at all. We've never seen anything like this before, and the National Command Authority is functioning as it should in a fast-moving, fluctuating situation."

"That's a load of crap, Thad, and you know it."

"You need to remember who you're addressing, General Rammes."

"I know exactly who I'm addressing, Thad. I know you better than most, remember?"

"We're not cadets anymore. That was a long time ago, and we've moved on to other things, gone our separate ways. Some of us have progressed in our careers further than others and now find ourselves in positions of greater responsibility. You need to respect that."

"You're in that position because Ray Smythe blew his own head off, and furthermore, the only reason you got command of STRATCOM was—" *Careful, he is a senior officer.* Rammes knew he could be removed if he went too far, and now was not the time to get himself benched. "Look, General Metzger, all I'm saying is I'm uncomfortable with the way things are being run up there. I don't have a good feeling about the national security advisor and the way she's controlling access to *our* commander in chief."

Metzger sighed on the other end of the secure line, much like a parent who's tiring of explaining the same thing to an inquisitive child for the fifteenth time. "The president is being deluged by information. He's had to watch hundreds of thousands, if not millions of his citizens die at the hands of these monsters, and he's tired. He's exhausted. The information is getting to him, it's just being filtered appropriately."

"Filtered appropriately?" Rammes couldn't believe what he'd heard.

"Is that too tough a term for you to understand, General?"

"Oh no, *sir*, it's not too tough at all. I just want to know *what's* being filtered. If we come up with a solution to this whole mess, the president will need to know about it immediately. There's no time for it to go through some *filter*."

"You can rest assured that if you do find a solution, I will get your information to the president immediately. I also suggest you spend your time trying to find that solution rather than walking the thin line of insubordination with me. Do I make myself clear, General Rammes?"

You . . . are an asshole. "Clear. We're working on that solution now. Two of the casings are being analyzed as we speak. We're watching the catharsis process run its course, and hopefully we'll find a way to kill these things before we have to blow half the country to bits to stop them."

"Then, you'd better speed things up, General." The statement had an ominous tone to it.

"Why?" Rammes knew what the answer would be.

"We're launching today. This afternoon. Against the fixed locations of the bird casings."

"Thad, you need to give us a chance here. Don't let them do this. Not yet."

"It's already done. POTUS has given the order."

"Jesus Christ! Those cities are still evacuating!"

"We don't have a choice."

"Bullshit! We always have a choice! We're talking about nuking our own country, for Christ's sake!"

"This conversation is over, General Rammes."

The connection went dead.

Rammes pressed another button on his secure phone.

CHAPTER 56

"Madame Vice President, General Rammes is on the line for you. Button four."

"Thank you, Commander." High over the northwestern United States in her airborne command and control aircraft, the vice president swung her chair toward her secure phone. "Hello, General. Good news, I hope?"

"Ma'am, this is Lieutenant General Derek Rammes, commanding general of the Vanguard complex. I request level 10 communications protocol."

For a second, she was taken aback. But only for a second.

"Stand by." She removed a coded identification book from her briefcase and opened it to the appropriate page. "General Rammes, this is Ms. Allison Perez, vice president of the United States of America. Prepare to authenticate."

"This is General Rammes. I authenticate Maxwell, Donald, Lebanon, six, six, two, four. Day code is one, one, Kilo, Echo."

Good authentication. "Stand by." She muted the line. "Commander Williams!"

"Yes, ma'am?"

"Set me up for level 10, this line. Right now."

"Understand, ma'am. Level 10."

Allison held the receiver to her ear, listening to the soft clicking and bursts of muted static that signaled the recoding of the secure call. Level 10 was the highest level of encryption possible. It was used only in the direst of circumstances, where absolute confidentiality was required. Once the level 10 encryption code was used, it would have to be changed. Because of its secrecy, there were only three codes loaded and available for use at any one time. It would take the eggheads at the National Security Agency about six months to produce a new code to replace one of the three.

The Navy commander returned a few seconds later. "You're all set up, Madame Vice President."

"Thank you, Commander."

She heard the lock slide shut on the other side, and knew the commander was now guarding the door, armed with his sidearm. Use of deadly force was now authorized. No one would be allowed entry until she gave him permission.

"General, this is Perez."

There was a delay as the supersecret encryption equipment sent the four words she had spoken through a maze of highly sophisticated algorithms, scrambling sounds, scrambling the order, and then scrambling it again and again and again, until the only sounds transmitted to the Vanguard communications complex were a jumbled mess of static.

On the other end of the line, a set of identical encryption equipment rapidly put the electronic puzzle pieces back together. The vice president's voice came through the receiver with a tinny, metallic sound.

"Madame Vice President, I need to know if you're aware of the president's decision to release nuclear weapons against the cities infested with the bird casings." It was a tough call. If she knew, he would have compromised a highly secret code, and effectively ended his career. Worse than that, however, he would look like a bumbling idiot.

To put it in simpler terms, he'd just shot his wad.

When the general's words reached her ear, Allison couldn't believe what she was hearing. Her heart skipped a beat.

"General Rammes, I am not aware of any such order." If the order was valid, she'd been completely left out of the loop. Betrayed. By her own president. It wasn't supposed to happen this way. "Clarify."

A pause.

"General Metzger informed me of the order. It's going to happen this afternoon. I'm not aware of the exact time."

A pause.

"How certain are you of this, General?" She immediately regretted questioning him, because if he had even the slightest doubt, he wouldn't have used the level 10 communications protocol. Her words were already on their way, however.

A pause.

"As certain as I've ever been about anything, Madame Vice President."

A pause.

An electronic voice spoke from the receiver, announcing the call would only last another fifteen seconds, a safeguard to prevent a hostile listening station from intercepting a long enough stream of data to help break the code and decipher the message.

"I will contact the president immediately, General. Thank you."

A pause.

"You need to get us more time, ma'am."

A pause.

Ten seconds until termination, the voice announced.

"I'll do what I can, General."

Five seconds until termination.

250

A pause.

"Godspeed, Madame Vice President."

A pause.

The line went dead in her hand.

CHAPTER 57

The ramp at Barksdale AFB, Louisiana, was thrumming with activity. Trailer after trailer snaked its way to the waiting B-52s from the cavernous weapons storage bunkers, each trailer hauling tons of ordnance.

Munitions troops quickly filled the BUFFs' bomb bays and wing pylons with five-hundred-pound high-explosive bombs, soon to be dropped all over the American Midwest in a frantic attempt to kill the fixed ground waves, before they rose again with the coming of darkness.

On another part of the ramp, far away from the line of ancient, drooped-winged B-52s, sat three bat-winged B-2 Spirit stealth bombers.

Whiteman AFB, Missouri, was the normal home for these aircraft, but the fleet of B-2s had been dispersed due to the proximity of the creatures to their home base. They now sat at different bases around the United States. Some were being used for conventional strikes because of their massive conventional-weapons-carrying capabilities, but these three were being used for an entirely different purpose. A purpose they'd been specifically designed to accomplish during the latter years of the Cold War.

Small, cylindrical objects were being loaded into their bomb bays. Streamlined. Small fins at the rear. Glinting like fine sterling silver in the sun.

These objects had come from different munitions bunkers. Handled carefully. Cautiously.

One weapon was loaded into each aircraft.

Inside the supersecret bombers, flight crews went through their preflight checks, readying the billion-dollar war machines for flight.

The mission profiles were uploaded.

The targets were programmed into the targeting software.

The time to launch was set.

Only one more thing was needed for the aircraft to fly.

A final order from the president of the United States.

CHAPTER 58

The mutants were changing, but not as she'd predicted.

Carolyn stared at the screens in front of her as the medical scanning equipment slowly, painstakingly, swept over the casings, revealing what was inside on three-dimensional digital displays.

"Garrett, come take a look at this."

"Do I have to?"

"Come on. Take a look and quit being such a baby."

"I'm not a baby. Every time you tell me to look at something, you always have bad news."

"Look . . . here. The arm. Can you see it?"

Garrett stared intently at the screen. "Yep, looks like an arm, all right."

"No, look closely. Does it look like the arms we saw on it before?"

"Well, no, I guess it doesn't." It *did* look different, now that he looked more closely. "It doesn't seem to have the claws anymore."

"Right. And look at the bones. They're shorter. Not as thick. Look at the skull. It's thinning as well. Look at the teeth."

"So . . . you think the thing is shrinking?"

"It sure looks that way. It just doesn't look like it's . . . It doesn't seem to be splitting into two. Like they've done before. Like I expected."

"What about the rat?"

"Same thing. Look." She switched the display to show the scanning results for the mutated rat.

"It's much smaller. There's a lot of empty space in that casing now."

"Right. And here, Garrett, look at the bone structure."

"I'll be damned. Same thing, isn't it?"

"Sure looks that way. The bones are smaller, less dense than before." Carolyn paused. "You know, if I didn't know any better, I'd say the things were mutating back to their original state."

"What?"

"I'm saying, based on the readings we've seen for the last four hours, the mutated creatures are changing back into what they *were*."

"You mean to tell me those casings are going to crack open at sundown, and a normal rat is going to pop its head out?"

"I'm not too sure *normal* is the correct word, but anatomically speaking, it looks that way."

"Jesus. That means Sergeant Wilson—"

"That means Sergeant Wilson—or something that looks like Sergeant Wilson—will be in that casing when, and if, it cracks open."

"I don't understand this at all. Was there anything in the Soviet data that showed any sort of regression in their Gemini experiments?"

"Nothing. Not a thing."

"Well, it looks like you have another mystery to figure out, Carolyn."

She stared at the screen showing the casing containing what had been Sergeant Wilson. "Yeah, another mystery."

CHAPTER 59

The hidden keypad slowly slid from under the thick mahogany top of the president's desk. On it, he gently placed the palm of his hand. Around the underground situation room sat the secretary of defense, the secretary of Homeland Security, the national security advisor, and the newly frocked chairman of the Joint Chiefs of Staff, his four stars glinting from the bright overhead lights.

The president's voice was strained from lack of sleep—and from other reasons known by only one other person in the room—yet every word he spoke reverberated through the small buried command center as if he were speaking through a megaphone.

"Today, we have come to a turning point in this fight. We've found these creatures impervious to the effects of chemical weapons. We've found conventional strikes have been ineffective in slowing their advances. Right now, we have the opportunity to wipe them out where they lie. I have ordered a massive aerial bombardment of the ground waves. Their casings are barely belowground, and General Metzger has assured me we can blow them to pieces with high-explosive iron bombs. That order has already been given." Andrew paused, taking a moment to gather his thoughts before he spoke the words that no other president before him had ever been forced to speak. "I do, however, have one more order to give. In the cities of Little Rock, Minneapolis-St. Paul, and Oklahoma City, there is another threat we cannot destroy with conventional weapons. There are thousands of casings scattered in and around those cities. Casings of the mutated birds, aboveground, hidden in the buildings, and belowground in the sewers. If, as we have observed the previous two nights, these creatures emerge from their casings at sundown, in double the numbers we saw last night, we will have lost an opportunity to destroy them that we may never have again. I cannot let that happen. If we allow them to take wing again, we will not be able to stop them."

Hugo McIntyre spoke first. "Mr. President, if you order the destruction of those cities, you will essentially be signing the death warrants of thousands of American citizens. Maybe millions. Those cities are in the early stages of their evacuations and—"

"Hugo, I know. With God in heaven as my witness, I know."

"Mr. President, then let me suggest we wait until right before sunset, to allow the evacuations to progress as far as possible."

"The strikes will be timed to do just that, Hugo. We have three B-2 bombers waiting to launch at Barksdale. They will strike right before sunset at each of the three cities."

"Are the people going to know?" Tank's voice boomed, filled with emotion. "Are we at least going to let them know what we're going to do?"

Jessie Hruska responded immediately. "Would *you* like to be the one to let them know, Mr. Stone? Would *you* like to be the one who gets up in front of a camera and tells the American people that we're going to nuke three American cities?" Jessie's eyes burned bright as she stared at the SECDEF.

"Don't we owe them at least that much, Ms. Hruska? I mean, Jesus *Christ*, we're talking about blowing the living hell out of our own country, aren't we? Killing the same people we were put here to protect?"

Jessie fought to control her temper. She was so close, and no political appointees would stop her now. "Would it make it any better? Would telling the American people that we're very sorry we have to do this, but we're going to have to destroy three cities, and if you have any relatives there that are still trying to get out, you'd better get on your cell phones right now before it's too late? Would it make you sleep better at night? Would it?"

Tank took a second to compose himself before speaking. "Ms. Hruska. We represent the American people. We represent all their hopes, their desires, and most of all, their trust. They trust us to do the right thing, even when it's something like this, when we're faced with a problem that has no easy solution. If no one else in this room has the stomach to do it, bring me a camera crew and I'll tell them mysel—"

"That's enough!" The president slammed his fist on his desk. "That is *enough*. Tank, there's no time for speeches." He looked at his watch. "If I don't give this order in the next ten minutes, those bombers will arrive at their targets after sunset. After *sunset*, Tank. Am I clear?"

Tank stared at the president for what seemed an eternity. The man he'd grown to admire over the last few years no longer sat before him. The man he was looking at—with his finger on the nuclear button—was not that man. Not anymore. He'd changed. Transformed into something different. Cold. Almost unfeeling. The man he'd known would never have come to this decision so quickly. And more importantly, he would never have done it without the advice and counsel of his vice president.

Something was wrong.

"Yes, Mr. President. You are clear," he said. But he wasn't done yet. "Is the vice president aware of what we're doing, Mr. President?"

Andrew's gaze turned icy as he glared at his SECDEF. "No. She has not been briefed. Yet."

"May I ask why, sir?"

"There hasn't been any time, Tank."

"We've got time right now, sir." He glanced at the plasma screen on the wall. "It'll only take a second."

"Mr. President, you have to give the order now, sir. The bombers are waiting." General Metzger's voice sounded impatient.

"Sir?" Tank was not about to be ignored.

The president pressed a button on his secure communications panel, opening a line to the NMCC. A voice answered almost immediately.

"NMCC, General Blackburn speaking."

"General Blackburn, this is the president of the United States."

"Good afternoon, Mr. President."

"General, I am ordering the execution of operation Three Kings."

"Yes, sir. I understand you are ordering the execution of operation Three Kings."

"That is correct, General."

"Sir, I need to confirm that you are authorizing the release of nuclear weapons. Please authenticate."

A small needle pierced the president's palm once again, drawing a tiny amount of blood for instant DNA analysis. "This is the president of the United States. I am authorizing the release of nuclear weapons." He pulled a small laminated card from his wallet. "Authenticate Tango, Delta, seven, two, nine, six, Charlie, Bravo, one. Day code one, seven, Foxtrot, Xray. Code word, *falcon*. Release is on my authority as president of the United States of America."

Tank Stone took a step toward the president's desk. "Sir, why doesn't the vice president know?"

General Metzger stepped in front of Tank Stone and placed a hand on his shoulder. "Sit down, Mr. Secretary."

"Get out of my way, Thad."

"I can't do that, Mr. Secretary."

"Get out of my way, General Metzger, or I'll tear your fucking head off."

General Metzger pulled his sidearm and quickly affixed a silencer to the end of the barrel. "I think not, Mr. Secretary."

Tank paused, clenched his fists.

Metzger pointed his pistol squarely between the SECDEF's eyes. "You *will* sit down."

• • •

Unaware of what was happening in the situation room, General Blackburn placed his hand on his own panel, which immediately identified him through instant DNA analysis. "This is General Ryan D. Blackburn, senior controller on duty, National Military Command Center. I have received orders from the president of the United States authorizing the release of nuclear weapons. Authentication Tango, Delta, seven, two, nine, six, Charlie, Bravo, one. Day code one, seven, Foxtrot, Xray. Code word, *falcon*. Release is on his authority as president of the United States of America."

• • •

A steady green light appeared on the president's panel. The order had been received.

Tank tried to move past General Metzger, at the same instant shouting, "General Blackburn! Belay the—"

His statement was cut off by the puff of a silencer, and a bullet slamming into his forehead. Tank's body fell to the floor in a heap, a crimson pool spreading from the jagged exit wound in the back of his skull. His eyes remained open.

Hugo McIntyre sprang from his chair. "Jesus Christ! What the hell have you done!"

General Metzger nonchalantly swung the barrel of his pistol toward the secretary of Homeland Security. "Don't make a move, Mr. Secretary."

"Mr. President? What's going on there?" General Blackburn asked, hearing the commotion on the other end of the line.

The president stared at Jessie as he spoke. "Nothing, General. We're all secure." She smiled at him. "You have your orders."

"Yes, sir, I have my orders."

The president terminated the connection.

"Mr. President, I suggest a lockdown of all communications until this is over. We'd better get you airborne," General Metzger said.

"Yes. I'd better get airborne."

Hugo McIntyre couldn't believe what he was witnessing. "Mr. President! This son of a bitch just murdered the SECDEF, and you didn't even blink an eye!"

"He was trying to interfere with the president's legal orders to our nuclear forces, Mr. McIntyre," Metzger said. "I couldn't let that happen."

"Bullshit! He was trying to stop the madness, and you killed him! Why doesn't the vice president know about your order, Mr. President? Why was Tank trying to stop it? Why?"

Jessie Hruska calmly stepped over the lifeless body of the SECDEF and sat on the edge of the president's desk. "Andrew, you did the right thing." She pulled a surgical glove from her jacket pocket, along with a small vial. "You know that, don't you?" She uncapped the vial, placed a small amount of the drug on her finger.

"Yes. I did the right thing." His voice was flat, almost robotic.

"And I love you for it, Andrew." She slowly rubbed the drug into his skin, behind his ear.

"I love you too, Jessie."

"What in the name of God is going on here?" Hugo McIntyre asked, his mouth hanging open in disbelief.

"The cause lives on, Mr. Secretary." General Metzger moved closer to Hugo McIntyre. "Generations have patiently waited for this day, Mr. Secretary, right under your noses. The country we once served may have lost the Cold War, but the dream that gave it life still burns brightly."

Hugo McIntyre's voice was cracking. "My God, what are you talking about?"

"Andrew, Hugo may be a threat to you. To our national security." Jessie smiled and winked at Hugo McIntyre.

"Yes. A threat," the president repeated.

"You should order General Metzger to kill him."

"Yes," the president said flatly. "General Metzger should kill him."

Hugo McIntyre turned toward the door, but never took a step. The puff from a silencer was the last sound he'd ever hear.

General Metzger detached the silencer and holstered his weapon. He picked up the president's phone. "This is General Metzger. There's been an attempt on the president's life. We're going airborne immediately."

Jessie removed two pistols from the president's desk and placed one in a hand of each of the two dead bodies.

Metzger smiled at Jessie as he continued. "Mr. McIntyre and Mr. Stone attempted to assassinate the president. They're both dead. Get the Secret Service escort down here now, and inform the alert crew at Andrews we're on our way."

Jessie stroked the president's hair. "It's time to go now, Andrew."

"Yes," he said. "It's time to go."

CHAPTER 60

"Madame Vice President, there's been an attempt on the president's life."

"What did you say?"

The Navy commander handed her the message and gave her a quick synopsis. "It was in the situation room. The SECDEF and secretary of Homeland Security tried to kill the president. General Metzger shot and killed them both and then took the president to Andrews with Ms. Hruska. They're airborne right now."

This is wrong. Allison knew what she was reading couldn't be true. "Commander, tell the pilot to transition to orbit twenty-seven. Do not, I repeat, do not inform control that we're leaving this orbit."

"Ma'am?"

"You heard me, Commander. We're going to move, and we're going to do it quietly. No contact with control. Understood?"

"Yes, ma'am." He left the vice president's cabin and headed for the cockpit.

What she'd just ordered the pilot to do was completely out of the ordinary. He was never to leave a prescribed orbit without informing secret government air traffic controllers where he was headed. Although most aircraft transmitted their identification continuously via transponder, the vice president's aircraft—along with most high-level government aircraft—deactivated their transponders in a time of crisis. To use a term familiar to submariners, they were running silent and running deep. Orbit 27—where she'd directed the pilot to head—was a rare portion of the North American airspace that was not monitored by radar. It was a blind spot. A place to hide.

Allison Perez stared at the message in her hands.

If what she was thinking were true, she'd need to stay hidden. Maybe for a long time. She felt the plane begin to bank as it left its prescribed orbit and headed north toward Canada.

A knock on her cabin door startled her.

"Yes?"

The commander opened her door, with another message in his hands. His face was ashen. "Ma'am, the president has ordered execution of operation Three Kings."

"What is Three Kings, Commander?"

"You'd better read this one for yourself, ma'am." He handed her the message.

It was a nuclear strike.

The president of the United States had ordered a nuclear strike against three American cities—Minneapolis-St. Paul, Oklahoma City, and Little Rock.

She now knew beyond a doubt that something was terribly wrong. Not only had two highly trusted members of the cabinet been killed—supposedly after trying to kill the president—but Andrew had ordered the execution of a nuclear strike without even hinting to her that he was thinking about it.

"Thank you, Commander. That will be all."

The commander closed her cabin door on his way out.

Allison ran through the different possibilities. If there had been an assassination attempt against the president—by Hugo McIntyre and Tank Stone—there must've been a damned good reason for it. Chances were they were attempting to prevent the nuclear execution order she now held in her hands. *If* the story were true.

A second possibility was that Hugo McIntyre and Tank Stone had been framed. Someone had made it look as if they were killed during a botched assassination attempt. And those someones would be General Thad Metzger and Jessie Hruska, who were now with the president on *Air Force One*. And if *that* were true . . .

It didn't matter which scenario was true. They both came down to one thing—the president of the United States was under duress. He never would've given a nuclear execution order without consulting her first. His decision earlier to release chemical weapons without consulting her—although out of character—was still somewhat plausible. But nukes? No way. When he'd considered using nuclear weapons after the Cleveland attack, he'd bent her ear like it had never been bent before. This time, he'd kept her completely in the dark.

Hugo McIntyre and Tank Stone would never have tried to assassinate the president, under any circumstances. The more she thought about it, the more she knew it just wasn't possible. She'd known both men for years—worked with them during stressful situations. It just wasn't in their character to attempt something so *dastardly*. It would be like a nun robbing a convenience store. Just wouldn't happen.

That left her with her second possibility—that they'd been framed. Framed by Thad Metzger and Jessie Hruska.

Metzger was an unknown to her—she'd never worked directly with him. He did, however, have a reputation as a hard-as-nails street fighter who'd risen through the ranks by climbing over the bodies of his colleagues. She'd opposed his selection as CDRUSSTRATCOM specifically because of that, but the man had an incredible amount of support in Congress, and at the time, the president had been looking for any way to improve his standing with the legislative branch. Having never worked with Metzger left her with just his reputation. Reputations were word-of-mouth judgments—some accurate, some not. She'd never been able to evaluate him up close and personal. So, he remained an unknown.

Hruska, however, was another matter entirely. Allison had never liked the national security advisor. Why, she wasn't entirely sure . . . Just an odd feeling in her gut when she'd first met the woman years before. Hruska was capable, efficient, smart, and inquisitive, but there was something about her that simply didn't sit right with Allison Perez. Like drinking milk a couple of days after the expiration date—not yet sour, doesn't smell bad yet, but it still tastes a little off.

She remembered how vehemently Hruska had argued for General Metzger when the decision was being made for the next chairman of the Joint Chiefs. Hruska had been the first one to bring up his name, as a matter of fact. And the president had agreed much too quickly, in her opinion.

Hruska had been controlling the information flow to the president, as well, something he never would've allowed under normal circumstances.

It was all starting to become clear.

The president was being co-opted by the national security advisor. How wasn't entirely clear to her yet, but that wasn't important.

What was important was the president of the United States had just ordered a nuclear strike—on his own country—and was now airborne with one individual, or possibly two, somehow controlling his decision-making process.

Andrew Smith was quickly becoming less and less president of the United States and more and more a threat to its national security. No, a threat to its survival.

She had to make sure.

Allison pushed her comm button. "Commander, patch me in to *Air Force One*. I need an immediate videoconference with the president."

CHAPTER 61

The first bat-winged B-2 Spirit lifted off from the runway at Barksdale AFB in Shreveport, Louisiana, on its way to Minneapolis-St. Paul. In its belly hung a single silver object—remarkably small, considering the amount of destruction it was capable of producing—roughly thirteen feet long, a little more than a foot in diameter, with small fins at the rear.

The B61 nuclear bomb had been a mainstay of the United States' nuclear arsenal since the 1960s. Never before, however, had a load of B61s flown on an operational mission. Before the sun set below the horizon in the state of Minnesota, this weapon would detonate.

The B-2—a marvel of modern technology developed during the height of the Cold War—was designed to roam freely across the Soviet Union, undetected by radar, dropping its nuclear war load at will. Its basic structural design made detection by conventional radar almost impossible—supersecret radar-absorbent coatings made the bomber nearly invisible, but it could still be seen by the good old Mk1 eyeball. If an enemy could see it, he could kill it. For that reason, combat missions flown by the select crews of the 509th Bomb Wing—the unit to which the B-2s were assigned, the same unit that had dropped Little Boy and Fat Man on the Imperial Japanese during the waning days of World War II—were flown exclusively at night in the safety of darkness. The United States military still owned the night; no other country had been able to employ night-vision equipment with the precision and reliability to stop these invisible weapon systems, but they had—on occasion—been lucky. The Golden BB—a lucky shot—had taken down stealth systems in the past. But it had been just that: a lucky shot.

In the daylight, however, it was a different story.

The B-2s were big, black, lumbering targets. Vulnerable.

As the bomber turned north and began its slow climb toward its cruising altitude—its target roughly two hours away—the other two B-2s sitting in a secluded portion of Barksdale's ramp began their preflight checks.

The second bomber, once airborne, would reach Oklahoma City in about an hour.

The third bomber would hit Little Rock in forty minutes.

The clock was running.

CHAPTER 62

"Now that's odd."

"What's odd, Carolyn?" Garrett asked. It struck him funny that he would ask such a question, considering he was two hundred feet underground in a classified biowarfare research facility, dead tired from lack of sleep, studying the innards of two bone-like casings that held what were once a rat and a human being—both of which had mutated into some kind of terrible monsters and were now apparently reverting back to their original state. If that wasn't odd, nothing was.

"It's the brains. Look. They're different."

Garrett looked at the screen and didn't even try to pretend he knew what he was looking at. "You're going to have to explain this one to me. We never covered brain structure in infantry school."

Carolyn smiled. "Oh, really? That's a shock."

"Come on now, infantrymen have brains."

"Hooah?"

"Yes, *hooah*. Now show me what you're talking about."

She pointed at the screen. "Look, here. Near the center, inside the thalamus. That's not supposed to be there."

"What is it?"

"I have no idea. It's a mass of some kind, almost like a . . . Oh hell, I don't know." She rubbed her eyes. She too was suffering from lack of sleep.

"Why don't you go catch a few winks."

"I can't."

"You should. Even a few will do you some good."

"I'm not that tired."

"Yes, you are."

"There's too much to do and—"

"I know how you feel. You don't want to break away from what you're doing because if you do, you'll feel like you're shirking your responsibilities."

"It's not that, I—"

"Yes, it is."

"Garrett, there's going to be more trouble tonight if I don't keep working on this."

"There are other people here who can do what you're doing, Carolyn."

She glared at him.

He continued anyway. "You're exhausted. When you're tired, you can miss things. Important things."

"This is *my* baby, Garrett. I know exactly what I'm doing, and I'm not about to step away from it and let someone else do this. Am I tired? Yes! I'm damned tired, so are you, and so is everyone else down here. Countless people have died, and more will die unless we figure out how to stop this."

"Fifteen minutes of shut-eye. That's all I'm asking. Fifteen minutes, and you'll be amazed how you'll feel," he said.

Carolyn shook her head and turned back to her screen.

"Fifteen minutes, Carolyn."

She ignored him.

"Fifteen minutes."

Ignored again.

"All right, if you're going to be insolent about it, then I'll make you get some sleep."

Before she could say, *And just how are you going to do that?* Garrett barked orders to one of the guards.

"You! Over here!"

"What are you doing, Garrett?"

"I already told you," he said. The guard stood in front of him. "What's your name, soldier?"

"Specialist Blevins, sir."

"Blevins, you will escort Ms. Ridenour here to the back room. She's going to get some sleep." He glanced at Carolyn, and to both of them said, "That's an order."

"Yes, sir. Ms. Ridenour? Will you please come with me?"

"I will not leave my station."

The specialist looked at Colonel Hoffman, a questioning look in his eyes.

"Blevins, you have your orders," he said. "If you have to pick her up and carry her, you're authorized to do so."

"Ma'am?" Blevins said, hoping he wouldn't actually have to pick her up.

The look in Carolyn's eyes was beyond icy as her glance slowly bored twin holes through Garrett's skull.

But maybe he was right, Carolyn thought. She was tired. No, more than just tired. She was *spent.* She could be missing something important.

"All right, Specialist. I'll go. Lead the way."

Three minutes later, Carolyn was sound asleep.

Three minutes and thirty seconds later, in a chair in the corner of the clean room, Garrett was, too.

CHAPTER 63

Allison stared at the screen, waiting for Andrew to appear. A man whom she thought she knew so well had ordered a nuclear strike against three American cities without so much as a whisper to her.

A nuclear strike.

The very thought chilled her.

Although nuclear weapons had been a part of the American psyche since August of 1945—even if it seemed as if they'd been around forever—their actual *use* was something entirely different. She remembered the hokey Civil Defense films she'd seen on TV as a child, the "Duck and Cover" film clips that taught American children that the flesh-searing heat and unimaginable overpressure from a nuclear blast could be avoided simply by jumping under your desk at school. She remembered the pictures of the home fall-out shelters people had built during the 1950s, as if a robust version of a storm cellar would keep a family from being poisoned by radiation, or simply incinerated, for that matter.

She remembered the dreams she'd had as a kid: standing in her front yard looking up into the sky, watching the sun glint off the aluminum skin of what she knew was a Soviet bomber leaving stark, white contrails across the blue Colorado sky, and then seeing a small, black object falling from its bomb bay. She would stand and watch the thing fall, hoping she was far enough away, and then a fiery mushroom cloud would bloom in the distance. The beginning of the end.

She'd dream of a war that, thankfully, never happened.

It had been so surreal then. A fact of life parked in the back of everyone's minds, unavoidable, yet accepted. Dreamt about, but never experienced.

When she was growing up, there had been well over a thousand American missiles on strategic alert, ready to launch. Hundreds of American bombers sitting on alert ramps at Strategic Air Command bases around the country, their crews waiting for the Klaxon to sound, to call them to their aircraft so they could get the birds on their way to Mother Russia before they were obliterated on the ground. Command and control aircraft—the "Looking Glass"—flying twenty-four-hour airborne alert, ready to take the helm if Washington were suddenly destroyed by one of the many Soviet ballistic missile submarines lurking off the coasts of the United States.

It had been a scary time.

But the ever-present fear had been manageable.

Because nuclear war could never really happen.

Couldn't happen.

People weren't that crazy.

Or so she thought.

As she rose through the government after her time in the US Coast Guard—and her security clearance rose as well—she'd become aware of just how many close calls there'd been.

On both sides.

Too many times when a blip on a radar screen nearly started World War III. Too many times when a fail-safe system failed. Too many times when a collection of seemingly unimportant, unrelated events swirled together at just the right time to place fingers on buttons that would unleash Armageddon.

Somehow, those buttons had never been pressed.

Until now.

And it was the president of the United States pressing the button, against his own country.

The situation was grave. She realized that.

But not *that* grave.

Not yet.

She knew she had to act fast.

"Madame Vice President, the secure comm link is established. The conference will begin in ten seconds."

"Thank you, Commander."

Nine seconds later, the smiling face of Jessie Hruska filled her screen.

It didn't surprise Allison at all. In fact, she'd expected it.

"Madame Vice President, the preside—"

"Where in the hell is President Smith?"

Allison watched Hruska's smile quickly fade. "The president is in conference with the chairman of the Joint Chiefs, Madame Vice President, and he told me to—"

"Cut the crap, Jessie. I want to see the president immediately."

"The president is not available, Madame Vice Presi—"

"God *damn* you! Let me make this as clear as I possibly can. I am the vice president of the United States of America. I have requested to speak with the president—immediately—and I don't give a flying *fuck* who he happens to be in conference with at the moment!"

Hruska's smile reappeared. Reptilian. "Yes, ma'am. Please stand by."

The screen went blank.

"Commander?"

"Yes, ma'am?"

"I need the Eagle Seven Four comm codes. Now."

The naval officer quickly exited the vice president's cabin.

"Allison. Andrew Smith. What can I do for you?"

Allison was startled by the president's voice, as well as his odd, almost formal introduction. She turned to face the screen. "Mr. President, I need to speak to you about operation Three Kings." She noticed Hruska and Metzger standing at the rear of the president's cabin. "Alone," she added.

"There's nothing to discuss, Allison. I've ordered the strike to destroy the casings on the ground while we still can."

Allison noticed neither Hruska nor Metzger budged an inch. "You've ordered a nuclear strike against three American cities! Three *cities*! There are still innocent people on the ground who haven't been evacuated!"

"It had to be done, Allison. I had no other choice."

"Negative. There are always alternatives! You learned that after the Cleveland attack, didn't you? Nuking every Middle Eastern capital was the easy answer, but you *knew* there had to be another way."

"This is different. Our country is dying. We have to act now, before it's too late and—"

"I need to speak to you alone, Andrew." She'd never called the president by his first name unless they'd been alone. Never. But she had to get through to him.

For a moment, Andrew's face drew a blank. He was obviously confused. "I . . . I can't do that."

"Why, Andrew?"

"I can't."

Allison addressed the two people in the shadows. "Ms. Hruska, General Metzger, I need you to remove yourselves from the president's cabin. This is a private conversation, starting *now*."

"Allison . . ." the president said. "I . . . They have to stay."

That's it, she decided. It was time.

277

Allison stared intently into her screen, and into the eyes of someone she didn't entirely recognize anymore. She hoped at least a part of the man she'd known as President Andrew Smith still remained somewhere behind those blank, confused eyes. "Mr. President, Andrew, I need to ask you a question."

Allison watched Hruska emerge from the shadows. "The president is fatigued, Madame Vice President. This conversation has gone on long enou—"

"Who are you, his fucking nursemaid now? Andrew, are the Aussies on board with this?"

The president's face revealed a moment of clarity. "Are the Aussies on board with this? Of course they are. The Aussies are on board."

Allison immediately cut the secure comm channel.

She'd heard all she needed to hear.

• • •

The commander reentered the cabin, carrying a locked briefcase. "The Eagle Seven Four comm codes, ma'am."

"Thank you, Commander." Entering a combination known only by the vice president of the United States, Allison unlocked the case.

Inside was a plain manila folder holding a single sheet of paper signed by President Andrew Smith. "Commander, I need you to play back the final portion of my conversation with the president." She handed the single sheet to the naval officer.

With the push of a button, the commander listened to the president's words. He verified them against what was printed on the single sheet of paper and handed it back to the vice president.

"Verified, ma'am." He slipped a chain from under his uniform blouse. At the end of the chain hung a small metal key.

From her blouse, Allison removed a similar key hanging on a similar chain.

Using separate keys, they unlocked a small metal box inside the briefcase. Inside was a laminated card with a five-character code word imprinted on its face in bold, black letters.

"This needs to go worldwide. All comm systems, in the clear." Allison handed the card to the commander. "After transmission, I need a Flash Immediate Decision Conference with all ground and airborne command and control nodes. Got it?"

"Yes, ma'am."

"And find out where the hell *Air Force One* is." *Just in case*, she thought, hoping it wouldn't come to that.

She glanced at her watch.

One—possibly two—of the bombers would be in the air by now.

She hoped she wasn't too late.

CHAPTER 64

"Andrew?"

He didn't answer.

"Andrew! What did she mean?"

The president seemed confused, unable to focus. His body had gone slack in his chair after he'd spoken to Perez. "Jessie?" he said. "I . . . I don't understand . . ."

"Answer me!" She slapped him. Hard.

The president's head snapped back, a small string of saliva hanging from the corner of his mouth.

"She asked you if the Aussies were on board. What did she mean?"

The president stared at her like a dog that had just felt its master's boot in the ribs, not understanding what it had possibly done wrong.

General Metzger leaned against the wall of the cabin. He casually lit a cigarette. "You've used too much. He's too far gone." The first puff of smoke from his lungs obscured his face.

"Bullshit. He's still here." Jessie leaned closer. "Andrew, I need you to talk to me. I need you to talk to me now, okay?"

"Jessie? What did . . . I do . . . wrong?"

She cupped his face in her hands, holding his head steady so he had to look directly into her eyes. "You didn't do anything wrong, Andrew. But she said something to you, the vice president said something to you, and I need to know what it meant."

Andrew stared at her. One pupil slightly larger than the other. No response whatsoever.

Another puff of smoke. "It's not going to work. He's fried."

Jessie stood. The president's chin dropped to his chest. "He shouldn't be this way."

"He's weak. You overestimated him." Through the cloud of smoke, the ash tip burned bright for a second, and then disappeared.

"No! He's one of the strongest men I've ever met—I had to use more. But there's something wrong."

"Okay, so you say he's not weak, but here we are, flying on *Air Force One* with a head of lettuce sitting on the throne of the free world, drooling all over himself." Metzger dropped his cigarette into a water glass, the hot ash dying with a sharp hiss. "You're the goddamned national security advisor. What the hell did they mean? Are the *Aussies* on board? We don't consult with Australia when we order a nuclear strike!"

It didn't make any sense to her.

Are the Aussies on board with this?

Of course they are. The Aussies are on board.

Suddenly, she knew.

There was no other explanation.

"That *bitch*! It was a code phrase! It was a fucking *code*!" *He's still in there, all right*, she thought. Andrew—or at least a small part of the man he'd once been—was still in there, floating behind the curtain of obedience she'd wrapped around his mind. He'd reacted to the vice president's words, momentarily breaking through the curtain in response to the phrase Perez had spoken.

Are the Aussies on board with this?

Quite to Jessie's disbelief, Andrew still possessed the strength of mind to act on his own, to speak with his own voice. If only for a few seconds.

Of course they are. The Aussies are on board.

He'd communicated something to the vice president, using a simple phrase. Something preplanned. Understood by both, but by no others. A challenge. And a reply.

"A code? For what?"

"I'm not sure. A recall?" she asked.

"Impossible. The bombers have received their orders. There's no stopping them unless the president directs them to abort the mission using the same process he used to launch them. The order has to go through the proper channels. It has to come from him. I could get on the horn to the pilots right now and order them to return to base, and they would just give me the finger. As long as the commander in chief is alive, they won't take orders from anyone else. Not even the vice president."

"We have to be sure."

"I am sure."

"You're *under*estimating him." She mashed a button on the edge of the conference table, connecting her to *Air Force One*'s airborne communications center. "This is the national security advisor. The president wants current status on operation Three Kings."

The Marine colonel on the other end answered immediately. "Stand by one, ma'am."

Metzger checked his watch. "The first bomber should almost be to its target. The other two are airborne by now, as well." He lit another cigarette.

The colonel's voice sounded from an overhead speaker built into the ceiling of the president's cabin. "Ma'am, aircraft one is inbound to target, twenty-seven minutes from release. Aircraft two and three are en route to their release points . . . Aircraft two will reach its target in . . ." A pause. ". . . twenty minutes. Aircraft three will reach its target in seventeen minutes."

"Have there been any attempts to recall the aircraft?" Jessie asked.

"Ma'am?" the colonel answered, obviously confused. He knew only the president could order a recall. There had been no such order given.

"Has anyone tried to interfere with this strike!"

"The missions are progressing as planned, ma'am. No deviations."

"Thank you, Colonel. Keep us apprised." She closed the comm channel and turned to the general. "Okay, we know it wasn't a recall code. But what could it have been for?"

"It really doesn't matter," Metzger said, glancing at his watch again. "There's no stopping them now." He smiled, thin lips sliding back to reveal small, yellow-stained teeth.

If it was a code between the president and the vice president, Jessie thought, *there has to be something happening right now that we're not aware of.* She'd devoted her life to this very moment, the moment when the world would fall into an unrecoverable state of chaos, and she, and those like her, would enable the end of one chapter in history and the start of another.

So, so close.

But something was wrong.

She could feel it.

She couldn't let it fail now.

She turned to the president and pulled the vial from her blouse pocket, along with another surgical glove.

"How many of those things do you have?"

She ignored Metzger and placed an entire drop into her palm.

Andrew struggled to turn his head to face her, his eyes blank, expressionless. His mouth hung open in a drug-induced sigh.

She tilted his head back and with her thumb and index finger, spread his right eyelid wide open. The eye lolled lazily in the socket, unfocused.

"What are you doing? You're going to push him over the edge!"

"No. No, I'm not. He needs more . . . persuasion."

"We still need him," Metzger said. "He has to be able to function."

"He'll sleep after I get what I want. He'll be fine." Jessie held her hand over the president's open eye and tilted her palm. The drop trickled off the glove and into his eye. She closed the eyelid and held it closed.

She quickly repeated the procedure with his other eye.

The drug quickly entered Andrew's bloodstream. Jessie had never used this much of the substance before.

"It's time to talk to me, Andrew, time to tell me the truth." She kissed his slack, open mouth. "Tell me what you meant, Andrew . . . What did you tell her? She's a threat, Andrew. You need to stop her."

The president slowly raised his head and opened his eyes. The blankness was gone. They were clear and focused.

"Jessie?"

"That's it . . . Tell me, Andrew, tell me now . . ."

Metzger tossed his half-burned cigarette onto the floor and quickly lit another. He leaned back against the cabin and checked his watch for a third time.

Twenty minutes until their time would finally come. Three American cities would soon be incinerated by nuclear weapons.

He watched the second hand sweep across the face of his watch.

There really was no way to stop it now.

CHAPTER 65

"Excuse me, Admiral?"

"What is it, Colonel?"

"We just received an urgent message from Cutter." Cutter was the code name for the vice president.

"Cutter? Did you happen to ask her why the living hell she's taken her aircraft off of her prescribed orbit? I can't keep track of all the aircraft in my airspace with her roaming around on her own and disregar—"

"Sir, you need to see this."

Keaton Grierson took the message from the colonel's hand and quickly read it.

The simple, five-letter word immediately chilled him.

When he'd been stationed in Omaha, Nebraska, as part of USSTRATCOM a few years before, he'd run across the term *Aksarben* a few times. Apparently, it was the name of an old 1920s Omaha indoor horseracing track that had been used for different sporting events in the city over the years. *Aksarben*, it came to dawn on him, was *Nebraska* spelled backwards. He'd thought the trick was quite humorous.

This, however, was not.

The message spelled out S-U-T-O-P. POTUS—the acronym for *President of the United States*—spelled backwards.

Only one person could release this message.

And it had only one meaning.

"Is this verified, Colonel?"

"Yes, sir. Verified. The vice president is coming up on a Flash Immediate Decision Conference within the minute."

"Jesus Christ. Where are the B-2s right now?"

"Aircraft one is nineteen minutes from release over Minneapolis-St. Paul, aircraft two is twelve minutes from release over Oklahoma City, and aircraft three is nine minutes from release over Little Rock."

There's not enough time. "Colonel, I want every fighter in the air that's close enough to intercept vectored toward those three B-2s now!" He stood and headed toward the conference room two doors down from his office, the colonel a step behind. "Supersonic, weapons hot. Firing orders will come from me. Understood?"

"Most of them aren't armed for air-to-air, Admiral. They're striking the—"

"They can ram the friggin' B-2s if they need to!"

"Got it, skipper."

Grierson made it to his conference room just as the vice president flashed up on his screen.

"Gentlemen." Allison wasted no time. "The president is under duress. I have reason to believe that General Thad Metzger and Ms. Jessie Hruska have compromised the president. A short time ago, I challenged President Smith using the Eagle Seven Four codes, and he responded with the duress phrase. This has been verified by my onboard controllers. Because of this, I am exercising my authority under the 1974 Emergency Wartime Command and Control Act, effective immediately. Your orders are to take all necessary and prudent action to stop operation Three Kings."

The act was devised shortly after the resignation of President Richard Nixon in 1974. Its purpose was to provide a check and balance over the control—and more importantly, the use—of nuclear weapons. The theory was, a president whose mental faculties were less than reliable—as Nixon's reportedly were during the Watergate scandal and the days leading up to his resignation—had to be watched like a hawk when it came to using the "nuclear football." Under the original version of the act, the vice president could keep the president from executing the nation's nuclear forces if he or she thought the president was acting irrationally. Over the years, the act had been changed to prevent a president under duress from executing nuclear forces; the only way a president's order could be countermanded would be by a code phrase passed to the vice president from the president. The act was known only by the president, the vice president, and a few select military officers in key positions. The SUTOP message was the end result—a simple five-letter phrase that meant the president was under duress, and the orders he or she had issued were not to be followed. It was one of the most highly classified secrets the nation possessed.

"This is STRATCOM airborne. Ma'am, the aircraft won't respond to any direction other than from the president. The only way to stop them this close to their targets is to—"

Shoot them down. Keating Grierson broke in. "Ma'am, this is Admiral Grierson, NORTHCOM. I've ordered all fighters in the vicinity to proceed at max speed for the bombers. What are their rules of engagement?" *If they can make it in time*, he didn't add.

"Stop the B-2s. Any means necessary." Allison knew she'd just ordered Grierson to kill three aircrews, six highly trained airmen doing their duty. It wasn't a pleasant thought. But she knew if the death of those airmen meant saving countless innocent lives on the ground, then there was no other choice. "Am I clear?"

"Clear, ma'am."

"Admiral, I also need you to intercept *Air Force One*. Orders are to escort the aircraft back to Andrews AFB and keep it on the ground until the president can be taken to a secure area."

Grierson didn't want to ask the next question, but he had to. "If *Air Force One* doesn't respond?" He knew what the answer would be.

"You are authorized to shoot down *Air Force One*, Admiral."

CHAPTER 66

On board *Air Force One*, General Metzger received an urgent message from the cockpit crew.

"General, we're being instructed to return to Andrews."

"By whom?"

"The Northeast Air Defense Sector controller, sir."

All of a sudden, Metzger knew exactly what the code phrase meant. Somehow, the phrase the president had spoken to Allison Perez had allowed her—no, authorized her—to subvert the president's authority.

Are the Aussies on board with this?

—Are you under duress? 'Cause you're acting kinda weird there, mister, dropping nukes all over the place. This is our little secret word game, remember?

Of course they are. The Aussies are on board.

—I'm in a world of shit right now, and you'd better do something about it as quickly as you can, little missy. Now, I have to get back to drooling all over myself. Thanks for the momentary wake-up call!

Smart girl, he thought. A dangerous adversary as well, which was somewhat surprising, considering she was just a fucking Coastie. He'd like to kill her himself, if he got the chance. With his bare hands.

Metzger knew if they were being ordered back to Andrews, they'd eventually—if they refused—be forced to land, by whatever means necessary. The writing was on the wall, and he had to act fast.

"Colonel Jepperson, we have reason to believe the vice president has usurped her authority because she was in disagreement with the president's execution order for operation Three Kings. Disregard all further orders unless they come from the president, the national security advisor, or me. We may have a coup d'état on our hands, being led by the vice president."

"Sir?"

Glancing over at Jessie Hruska, he said to the pilot, "And I want you to listen very closely to what I'm about to say . . ."

• • •

"Ripper flight is supersonic. Time to intercept, uh . . . seventeen minutes."

Captain Brian Marshall, United States Air Force, had just pulled off a tanker, refilling his thirsty tanks after a strike against one of the areas of stationary ground wave casings, when he had received his orders, directly from Admiral Grierson himself.

He'd twice asked for confirmation before he realized the admiral was serious. Dead serious.

His flight—two F-35A Lightning II strike fighters—had immediately headed north toward Minneapolis-St. Paul to intercept the B-2 on its bombing run toward the city.

His two fighters were closest, and they'd drawn the short straw.

The bat-winged bomber was armed with a nuclear weapon.

His orders were to stop the B-2. To shoot it down before it dropped its bomb.

Kill two fellow airmen.

Maybe, two guys—or gals—he knew personally.

What a crappy day this was turning out to be.

An electronic voice sounded in his ears. "Ripper, this is Bandsaw. Target is at angels three-zero, heading zero-one-zero based on mission profile and last position report. I have no radar contact at this time. No response to mission abort order. Weapons free, I repeat, weapons free."

"Ripper lead copies," Captain Marshall said, answering the controller sitting in an orbiting E-3 Sentry roughly one hundred miles to the south.

If the E-3, with its gigantic rotating radar dome, couldn't pick up the B-2, his smaller radar wouldn't have a chance of finding it. The things were built to be invisible to radar in the first place. And they were.

He knew he'd have to spot it visually if he had any chance of killing it before it reached its drop point.

To keep the bomb from falling.

To keep Minneapolis-St. Paul from being obliterated.

He pushed his throttle to the max setting—it was already there, but he couldn't help but push it. His fighter was slicing through the air at one and a half times the speed of sound, his wingman half a mile off to his right, slightly behind and above his position.

"Ripper Two, lead."

"Two."

"Keep your eyes peeled, Harv."

"I'm lookin', Brian, I'm lookin'." A pause. "What the hell do you think is going on?"

"After what's happened the last few days, this shit doesn't surprise me one little bit."

Far below the streaking F-35s, their sonic booms rolled across the landscape, their supersonic shock waves slapping against the ground like an unseen, gargantuan beast galloping wildly across the plains.

"I don't like this, Brian."

"Me neither, Harv. Me neither. Sixteen minutes to intercept . . ."

CHAPTER 67

"General, *Air Force One* is changing course."

"What?"

"They're heading one-seven-zero, descending through thirty thousand feet."

"Damn. Any air assets in the vicinity?"

"Nothing in the air, sir."

"Send a scramble order to the nearest air defense unit. Their orders are to escort *Air Force One* back to Andrews AFB. If *Air Force One* doesn't comply, they're to contact me personally for guidance. Got it?"

"Yes, sir!"

In less than a minute, the Northeast Air Defense Sector command director's order was transmitted from the center. Ten minutes later, two Air National Guard F-15 Eagles leapt into the air armed for air-to-air combat, with orders to escort—or if it didn't respond, to force down—the aircraft carrying the president of the United States.

CHAPTER 68

"You got him, Harv?"

"Negative, lead. I can't see him . . . Nothing on radar, either. Not a goddamned thing."

"He should be at our twelve o'clock, straight ahead, two hundred feet below."

Captain Marshall knew they should be almost on top of the B-2 any second now, *if* the bomber crew had stayed on course, and *if* they'd maintained speed. If not, Ripper flight might blow right by.

The B-2 was a large airplane, and that was in their favor. It was the kind of shape that could be picked out of the sky at a distance, unless you happened to be at the same altitude. The flat shape of the bomber presented a very small profile when viewed edge-on. From their position two hundred feet above, they should be able to spot it against the top of the low cloud deck below.

For a split second, Captain Marshall saw something on his radar. "Harv, I just got a—"

"*Tally ho!* Got him!"

"Where?"

"At our twelve, right below the horizon!"

"I see him! Bandsaw, this is Ripper. Target in sight, Ripper is attacking!"

Inside the bomber were two fellow airmen, Air Force pilots doing their best to follow the order they'd received from the president of the United States, sweating in their flight suits and wishing they were somewhere else, doing something—anything—other than what they were doing right now.

Just as he was.

Screw the orders . . . I can't just blow him out of the sky without giving him a chance to disengage! It'll only take a couple of seconds. "Two, burn across his nose, see if you can get him to abort. I'll stay at his six." *And then gun the living hell out of him if he doesn't.*

Ripper Two flashed ahead, a long tail of blue flame shooting from the F-35's afterburner.

Ripper lead took position at the B-2's six o'clock position—directly behind—and armed his 25mm Gatling gun. Capable of spitting out 3,600 rounds per minute—sixty rounds per second—the rotary cannon could chew through the bomber with just a short burst. Since they'd been on a ground attack mission, their aircraft weren't equipped with any air-to-air missiles. The gun was all he had: 180 rounds of cold steel.

Captain Marshall watched as his wingman rocketed toward the B-2, positioning himself for a pass across the bomber's nose and then frantically pulling into a high-g climb when the massive bomber banked hard right, into his path, the two aircraft missing each other by a matter of feet.

As Ripper lead kicked right rudder and slewed his F-35's nose to follow the B-2, placing the bat-winged bomber in his gunsight, he noticed a glint of sunlight off to his left.

Below, and to the left.

No . . .

He reversed his turn, rolled inverted, and pulled back on his stick, dropping the nose of his aircraft.

And he saw it.

A small, cylindrical object, reflecting the sunlight and falling toward the cloud deck below.

The bomb.

The B-2 had released its weapon before they had a chance to stop it and then pulled away to escape the blast.

"Bandsaw! Weapon released! Weapon released! Ripper Two, get the hell out of here!" Captain Marshall shouted the words into his oxygen mask, grunting against crushing g-forces as he banked hard to turn away from the bomb, slamming his throttle to the stops and diving at a shallow angle toward the ground, keeping the tail of his aircraft toward the coming blast.

Through the cloud of vapor that enveloped his aircraft as he slammed through the sound barrier, he could see the B-2 diving away also, its two-person crew rapidly increasing the distance between them and the hell they'd released. Every second meant increased chances of survival.

As he screamed by the subsonic bomber, he knew the extra seconds he'd given them—to try to avert having to drill 25mm shells through a couple of pilots just doing their duty—had been a few seconds too many.

• • •

Twenty seconds later, the remaining residents of Minneapolis-St. Paul witnessed a man-made sun appear in the sky above their beloved Twin Cities, tearing a miles-wide hole in the cloud layer.

It had already happened over Oklahoma City.

And over Little Rock, as well.

For all the people left in those cities who'd turned their faces to the sky wondering if the jet engines' thunder was a sign of salvation from the horrors they'd seen, the last milliseconds of their lives became an insufferable eternity.

They felt the heat.

Thermal radiation, traveling outward from the fireball at over three hundred thousand kilometers per second, caressed them.

Searing. Blinding. Flesh-eating.

The fireball itself, tens of millions of degrees Fahrenheit, floated silently above them, expanding, reaching out with strange tentacles toward the earth, exploring its surroundings in its first wink of existence, gorging itself on the atmosphere around it.

Unimaginable, insatiable.

Milliseconds ticked slowly by.

Skeletons cleaned of flesh stood in place, some pointing, some staring eyeless at the ravenous brilliance, instantly vaporized as the detonation's roar embraced them. An ancient noise it was, cracking, rolling. The voice of Legion commanding.

I am become Death, the destroyer of worlds.

Silhouettes on pavement remained.

CHAPTER 69

Carolyn checked the time. Sundown would occur in thirty minutes.

Over the last few hours, she'd watched as the things inside the casings changed.

They hadn't doubled, as they'd done during the last three days.

There was a single creature in the humanoid casing, and a single creature in the rodent casing, but they were . . . almost normal. Both creatures now possessed a small, dense mass in the center of their brains, the purpose of which she couldn't ascertain. The rest of their bodies looked as though they'd returned to their premutated states.

The body of Sergeant Wilson—who she'd seen pacing back and forth in the containment chamber as some sort of hellish beast, who she'd seen soak up without any detrimental effects enough soman gas to kill a thousand people—looked human again.

Normal size.

Normal bone density.

Normal musculature.

And the rat, a run-of-the-mill sewer rat. Normal, except for the mass in the middle of its brain.

She'd watched her readouts record the gradual disintegration of the casings, a steady thinning of the thick, bone-like shells that, at their current rate of decomposition, would lose their integrity at roughly the same time the sun went down topside.

If the same thing was happening to the ground wave casings, and to the bird casings in Minneapolis, Little Rock, and Oklahoma City, they should've cracked open by now.

But they hadn't heard anything yet.

Nothing at all.

General Rammes had been topside for the last hour, apparently called away by something more pressing.

Carolyn couldn't think of anything more pressing than what they were doing right now, but he'd sure been in a hurry.

Garrett had gone with him, as well.

After Garrett's little scene with the security guard, forcing her to get some sleep, she'd gone out like a light. She'd been completely exhausted, and thirty minutes of sleep made a world of difference. She was energized, on top of her game, able to think clearly instead of trying to absorb all she was seeing and doing through a thick fog of total exhaustion.

Regardless, she couldn't explain what she was seeing.

There was nothing in any of the data they'd been able to glean from the creatures so far that would even remotely suggest the course of their current state of mutation. Or was it more correct to say, de-mutation?

It shouldn't be happening, but it was. Right in front of her eyes.

Both casings were locked in the containment chamber again, behind steel doors, and thick, impenetrable Plexiglas. Even though it appeared as if the two creatures were returning to normal—at least physically, apart from the unexplained brain masses—there were no guarantees of what would actually emerge when the casings cracked open.

Would it be just a normal field rat?

A normal Sergeant Wilson?

She didn't know what to expect, but she doubted it.

It was now just a simple waiting game.

Waiting to see what they'd become.

CHAPTER 70

Jessie gripped the edge of the small conference table in the president's airborne situation room as *Air Force One* dove from its cruising altitude, its four huge turbofan engines screaming like enraged beasts, yearning to tear free from their wing pylons and bolt ahead of the rest of the aircraft.

General Metzger sat in one of the cabin's large, padded chairs, staring at the president, who at that moment was slumped at the head of the conference table, eyes closed, mouth hanging open, oblivious to what was happening around him. Sleeping.

"How long until he's functional again?" he asked.

"An hour, maybe two. It's hard to tell." In reality, Jessie had absolutely no idea how long it would take. Andrew was proving to be stronger than any of the other men she'd conquered, and it had taken a much larger amount of the drug to force him to succumb to her will. As she looked at him, she was afraid he might never be fully functional again. She was definitely in unfamiliar territory with this man. The situation was unpredictable. For a few seconds, he'd thrown off the chains she'd wrapped around his mind and had been *the* Andrew Smith, aware of what was happening to him, and knowing he had to alert his vice president. Deep down, she admired his strength of will. But she also knew she couldn't afford to have the real Andrew Smith come to the surface again.

Not now.

Not when their moment was finally at hand.

If it happened again, she would kill him.

"We need him awake," Metzger said. "Without him, this is going to be difficult. When they start calling to speak to him—and *if* you've done your job, they should be calling soon—he's got to be ready. There can't be any mistakes."

Jessie's eyes blazed defiantly. "I *did* my job. The Russians, the Chinese, the British, even the peace-loving French are in the process of making moves right now that should inflame the entire situation." She smiled as she thought about how the process would eventually unfold, due in large part to her meticulous efforts laying the groundwork for the chaos that would surely ensue. "Their leaders will go ape once they learn we've nuked our own country to try to kill these things. From that point on, everything should start happening quite rapidly. Our people abroad have done their jobs, too. We've all waited for a moment like this to arise, and they were ready for it, just as you and I were."

Metzger lit another cigarette. "Let's hope you're right."

"Oh, I'm right, General. I'm right." Jessie shot a glance out a cabin window, gripping the table to keep her balance. She could see the horizon tilted at a crazy angle, the massive jet diving to a lower altitude to duck under the radar, and hopefully, to safety.

The pilot's voice came from the overhead speaker. "General, this is Colonel Jepperson. We've been in contact with Pasture. They're ready to receive."

"Very well. How long until we land?"

"Approximately thirty minutes, sir."

"Copy. Keep us informed."

When the president divulged the details of the duress phrase to Jessie—after she'd administered a dangerously large dose of the drug—Metzger immediately ordered *Air Force One* to head toward a supersecret government relocation facility located just outside of Louisville, Kentucky, code-named Pasture, an underground compound with all the command and control equipment needed to guide the nation during a time of crisis.

Metzger was old friends with the Kentucky adjutant general— the state's top National Guard officer—and had explained their need to land immediately at Louisville International Airport, home of the Kentucky Air National Guard.

He'd assumed—correctly—that the orders issued by the vice president hadn't made their way through National Guard channels yet, so he wasn't forced to persuade the adjutant general to disregard any previous orders. It would've been troublesome, but he could've done it. The adjutant general wasn't one of *them*—a soldier of the cause—but he had a weakness to please his superiors. A weakness that could be exploited.

Metzger knew he wouldn't be so fortunate when it came to dealing with active duty forces, though. They'd surely received their orders—*lawful* orders—and were hunting down *Air Force One* at this very moment, under the direction of the vice president.

He and the national security advisor had certainly been branded rogue elements by this point. Dangerous people who'd somehow managed to co-opt the president's decision making. Dangerous people who had control over the country's fearsome arsenal of nuclear weapons and had used them against three American cities.

If he were in the vice president's shoes, he'd have immediately ordered fighters to intercept *Air Force One* and force it to land. And if it didn't land—with a president under duress dropping nukes on American soil—he wouldn't hesitate to blow the aircraft out of the sky. Eliminate the threat.

The vice president *was* a Coastie, but he wasn't going to make the mistake of underestimating her again.

They had to get on the ground. Fast.

Given a hurried description of the vice president's coup attempt—spiced with just the right amount of fatalistic urgency—his old friend had offered up the entire resources of the Kentucky National Guard to protect *Air Force One*, and, of course, the president. A call to the governor would have to wait. After all, national security was at stake.

As far as the adjutant general was concerned, he'd just been officially federalized and would answer to no one other than his commander in chief, the lawfully elected president of the United States.

The huge jumbo jet groaned and shook under the stress as it leveled off its decent, g-forces pushing Metzger deeper into the chair cushion as the plane pulled out of its dive. Outside the cabin windows, the landscape screamed by as *Air Force One* hurtled across the green Kentucky farmland a little over one hundred feet above the ground.

Under the radar and toward safety.

CHAPTER 71

"Admiral, we have three confirmed nuclear detonations. High yield."

"Mother of God."

Admiral Grierson stared in disbelief at the three circles glowing on his status board, pulsating blood-red orbs overlaid on a map of the United States.

Minneapolis-St. Paul.

Oklahoma City.

Little Rock.

Gone.

Destroyed.

His command center was absolutely quiet. The people serving with him were dealing with what they were seeing in their own way. Silently.

He'd always figured the day would come when he would see a nuclear detonation of some sort on American soil. Once the Soviet Union imploded, and Moscow's iron-clad control over its nuclear arsenal rusted away, it was only a matter of time before one—or more—of the weapons fell into the wrong hands and made its way to American soil.

Only a matter of time until the terrorists—any one of a multi-tude of radical extremist groups sworn to destroy the Great Satan—would explode a device in his country.

He'd grown to expect that possibility.

But this . . .

The red circles on his status board were supposed to be caused by *them*, not by American bomber crews.

"Admiral, Northeast Air Defense has lost radar contact with *Air Force One*. They think he's flying low to—"

"Where?"

"Over Kentucky, sir. They have fighters inbound to intercept. Two F-15s. The vice president's orders are to escort *Air Force One* back to Andrews and shoot it down if it doesn't respond."

The last few days had seemed like a nightmare, completely unreal, unimaginable.

He'd watched as the reports had rolled in, reports of some kind of mutated things literally devouring cities full of people, reports of mutated birds—*birds*, for Christ's sake—tearing people to shreds where they stood. Doubling their numbers during the day, killing as darkness fell.

And now, he had three nuclear detonations glowing on his sta-tus board.

Three major cities blasted into oblivion.

A rogue president being hunted by American fighter planes.

Orders to shoot down *Air Force One* if it didn't comply.

He wondered what could possibly happen next.

Unfortunately, he didn't have to wait long to get his answer.

"Admiral, this just came into the NMCC."

"What is it?"

"The Brits closed their airspace to all inbound commercial flights from CONUS, and they're directing all CONUS-bound flights to turn back. They're threatening to shoot down any airliner that attempts to land."

"They're what? You've got to be fucking kidding me."

"No, sir. One of their Typhoons fired on a United 767 attempting to land at Heathrow. He's over the Atlantic right now trying to find an alternate field before he runs out of fuel. None of the other European countries are clearing him to land, either."

"What the hell do they think they're doing? I want to know how many airliners we have over the Atlantic right now, and how many are going to have fuel problems if they aren't allowed to land."

"Yes, sir."

The alarm sounding in the background immediately shifted his attention to the worldwide status board. It was an alarm usually heard only during exercises. Combat exercises. "Status!" he shouted.

"Admiral, we have a Mayday from a FedEx 747!"

A green triangle popped up on the status board showing the aircraft's location over the Sea of Japan, just east of Vladivostok, heading south.

"He states he's being fired on by Russian fighters, sir."

"He's nowhere near their sovereign airspace!"

Three red triangles appeared on the status board, tracking with the 747. Right on top of him.

The green triangle suddenly disappeared.

The 747 was gone.

For a second, the command center was quiet.

But only for a second.

"Get me the vice president. Now!"

CHAPTER 72

General Rammes and Colonel Hoffman returned from topside. Carolyn saw a troubled look on the general's face, and Garrett looked as if he'd just witnessed his troops being slaughtered at the airport all over again.

She knew they didn't have good news.

"Carolyn, how long until—"

"About twenty minutes, General. Sundown topside should be in twenty minutes." She walked over to the Plexiglas wall and said, "At the current rate these things are falling apart, they should be completely dissolved at roughly the same time. Have we heard anything about the ground casings? The birds?"

Garrett spoke first. "Things are bad topside, Carolyn."

"What's happened?"

"The president ordered nuclear strikes to destroy the bird casings in Minneapolis, Little Rock, and Oklahoma City." He paused. "They're gone, Carolyn. All three cities are gone."

"Oh my God."

"The president ordered the strikes under duress. The vice president believes the national security advisor and the chairman of the Joint Chiefs are controlling the president's actions. The vice president tried to stop the strikes, but there wasn't enough time."

Carolyn looked at both men in disbelief. The president of the United States, under duress? Nuking his own country?

Insane.

It was all insane!

Rammes continued. "All of our communications have been cut off. I was able to speak to a duty officer at the NMCC for a few minutes, but the call went dead. I don't know if it's an after-effect from the nuclear detonations—the electromagnetic pulse frying our comm systems—or if our lines have been intentionally cut. The NMCC is completely swamped right now trying to figure out who is siding with whom. From what I can tell, we're smack in the middle of a constitutional crisis, with part of the country answering to Andrew Smith, and another part answering to Allison Perez."

"Who's in charge?" Carolyn asked.

"As far as I'm concerned, it's the vice president. This facility will answer to her, and to her alone, until the situation with the president is resolved." He then answered her next question without being asked. "There's no question topside about who's in charge. This base is still taking orders from me. There's no picking sides going on up there. I guarantee it."

"Do we know anything about the other casings?"

He checked the clock and realized that the sun had already set where the ground wave casings were entrenched. "I'm sorry, Carolyn. I didn't get any of that info."

"I guess we'll find out soon enough." She looked at the casings, which had deteriorated enough in the last few minutes to make them appear almost transparent. Through the thin casing walls, the bodies of the two creatures could be seen, curled in what appeared to be fetal positions.

Waiting to be *born again.*

The thought caused a chill to crawl down her back.

She knew they might be witnessing the birth of entirely new species—one humanoid, the other, some sort of rodent.

And the worst part was, she had absolutely no idea what to expect.

"Carolyn, if they're normal again, could this be over? Could the mutations have run their course?" Garrett asked.

"It's not over, Garrett. I don't know how or why any of this happened the way it did today. These two creatures should've mutated into two distinct beings inside those casings. For the life of me, I can't explain it."

"Any explanation for the masses in their brains?"

"Not a clue."

"Well, whatever they are, I think we're going to find out. Right now," Rammes said, pointing at the Plexiglas wall.

THE FOURTH NIGHT

CHAPTER 73

The first F-15 flashed by *Air Force One*'s cockpit with an earsplitting roar, its dual afterburners throwing twin tails of blue flame nearly one hundred feet to the rear of the sleek fighter jet.

Air Force One had been intercepted right before it touched down at Louisville International Airport.

"Come on, almost there!" the pilot yelled, lowering the landing gear and flaps while holding the massive airplane in a fifty-degree bank, turning hard to line up with the runway. The airplane was so low, the left wingtip looked as if it were about to plow a furrow in the ground. His engines were screaming, each one capable of producing nearly fifty-eight thousand pounds of thrust, pushing the gigantic, four-hundred-ton aircraft through the air. "Come on, baby, don't stall on me . . ."

This was definitely not standard Air Force traffic pattern discipline, but when you were trying to save the life of the president, all safety regulations went right out the window.

"*Air Force One*, this is Lobo One. You are instructed to proceed immediately to Andrews AFB, Maryland. Do not, I repeat, do not land at this location. Comply immediately."

The pilot heard the F-15 pilot's warning in his headset—in a matter of seconds, he'd either have the massive jet safely on the runway, or he'd have a Sidewinder missile or two blowing his engines apart.

"Lobo, we have the president of the United States on board! Do not engage! Do *not* engage!" He rolled wings-level, now just a few hundred feet from the end of the runway. He watched as the second F-15 roared by, going vertical as soon as it cleared the 747's nose. He knew both F-15s would quickly move to an attack position to his rear.

"*Air Force One*, do not land at this location! Go around and return to Andrews! This is your last warning!"

"Come on, baby, get us on the ground!" As the massive 747 roared over the runway's threshold, the pilot saw a streak of light off to his left—something he'd seen before.

In combat.

It was a MANPAD—man-portable air defense weapon. A short-range, shoulder-fired surface-to-air missile.

But it wasn't targeting him.

The Kentucky Guard troops were firing at the fighters!

As the 747 touched down on the runway, the pilot watched the missile streak skyward and saw a stream of flares erupt from one of the F-15s as it tried to trick the infrared homing missile into following one of the incredibly bright flares instead of the heat signature of his engines.

But it was too late.

The missile detonated in the tailpipe of one of the F-15's engines, erupting into a huge fireball in the sky as the fighter exploded.

The 747 pilot extended the spoilers, activated the thrust reversers, and stood on the brakes to bring the huge plane to a stop as quickly as he could. The straps dug into his shoulders as he was pushed forward by the force of the rapid deceleration . . . Would it be enough? He had to stop the plane quickly to allow time for the president to get off the aircraft and make it to safety before the second F-15 had a chance to attack.

And it *would* attack.

The warnings had been clear. And, since his wingman had just been blown out of the sky, Colonel Jepperson knew the Eagle Driver would be out for blood.

He keyed his mic. "General Metzger, as soon as the aircraft comes to a stop, you'll need to exit immediately. The crew will configure the escape ramp. You'll need to take the president away from the aircraft as quickly as possible!"

"Copy, Colonel!" came the reply in his headset.

"Come on . . . Stop . . . Stop . . . *Stop!*" The brakes were smoking—just seconds from bursting into flame—as the 747 screeched to a halt. "Egress egress egress! Everybody out! Go go go!"

•   •   •

Jessie was the first down the inflatable ramp, followed immediately by General Metzger, who had his arms wrapped around the president's chest as they both slid down the ramp.

National Guard troops grabbed all three of them and dragged them to the nearest building as 20mm cannon shells from the remaining F-15 stitched *Air Force One* from tail to nose.

A few seconds later, all that remained of *Air Force One* were smoldering pieces of twisted wreckage blown hundreds of feet into the air as a massive explosion lit the nighttime sky.

CHAPTER 74

The rat had chewed its way through the thin casing wall and was sticking its head through the hole it had made. Its nose twitched as it sniffed the air.

It looked completely normal.

Just a rat.

Cautiously, it crawled out of the casing, its body slick with fluid. Its small, beady eyes took in its surroundings, and it nervously eyed the three people in biosuits staring at it through the thick Plexiglas wall.

Carolyn was amazed it was the same creature they'd seen earlier—the snarling beast that had nearly broken out of a locked ammo box, the same beast that had bitten Sergeant Wilson and transformed him into . . . well, a bad dream. It looked so small now. So normal.

The other casing began to deform as the humanoid within it pressed against the thin walls, stretching them past the breaking point.

An arm suddenly protruded from the torn casing, stretching, flexing its fingers.

The rat raised itself on its haunches and watched as its companion slowly emerged from its cocoon.

The being that had once been Sergeant Wilson gripped the edges of the tear it had made in the casing and pulled apart an opening large enough for it to crawl through.

The naked form of a man slowly stood, stretching his arms above his head as a normal person would do after getting out of bed. His body was slick with the greasy fluid now spilling from the inside of the casing and pooling on the floor of the containment room. Facing away from the Plexiglas wall, he held his hands in front of his face, looking at each one, admiring them as if for the first time.

He turned.

What stood before them was Sergeant Wilson—what had *been* Sergeant Wilson. All his features were as they had been before he'd been transformed into a terrible, mutated killing machine. And then it spoke.

"General? General Rammes?"

Rammes didn't respond, dumbfounded by what he was hearing through the overhead speaker.

It couldn't be.

The thing he'd witnessed in the contamination chamber less than twelve hours before was now . . . normal?

"General? What happened? Why am I in . . ." Sergeant Wilson said, suddenly confused.

"Soldier, what's your name?" Rammes asked.

"Sir?"

"What's your *name*, soldier!"

"My name is Randy Wilson, Staff Sergeant, United States Army. Sir, you know who I am! Why am I in here?"

Rammes turned to Carolyn. "Is it him?"

"I . . . I don't know." She honestly wasn't sure what to say, or what to think. She, like General Rammes, couldn't believe what she was seeing. Could it be over, as Garrett had suggested? Could the mutations have run their course?

"Ms. Ridenour? Colonel Hoffman? Can you please tell me what's going on here? Why am I in this room?"

"Sergeant, do you remember anything that happened?" Garrett asked.

"What happened? I was . . . I was trying to . . . The rat. I was trying to see if the rat—" He stopped when he saw the rat sitting on its haunches, looking at him. "Jesus . . . I remember. But it wasn't a rat. It was bigger and—"

"Sergeant, something happened to you when you were in the chamber with the rat," Carolyn said. "It attacked you."

"Yes . . . I remember . . ."

"Do you remember anything that happened after it attacked you?"

"Yes. I remember."

Carolyn continued. "You were changed, Sergeant."

"My God. I remember. But how am I . . ." He glanced at the rat. "It's back to normal! It's okay! I'm okay, too, right?"

"We don't know yet, Sergeant." She turned to the general and switched off her mic so her voice couldn't be heard in the containment chamber. "General, we need to keep him in there. We're not sure what changes have occurred in him, and there's still no explanation for the extra mass in his brain. Or in the rat's brain, for that matter."

"Don't worry, Carolyn. I wasn't about to let him out of there just yet," Rammes said.

"But I want to get out, General."

Carolyn quickly checked her mic switch. It was in the correct position. So was the general's.

"Don't worry about the switches. You have them set correctly," Sergeant Wilson said. He smiled. "I can still hear you."

CHAPTER 75

Admiral Grierson stared at his myriad of status boards, trying to comprehend all he was seeing.

It was unreal.

Even during the most taxing exercises he'd been involved with, he'd never seen anything like *this*.

Three American cities were now radioactive funeral pyres.

American airliners, their fuel tanks dry, unable to land, were dropping into the Atlantic. Shot out of the sky if they tried—by our allies! The Brits!

The Russians had raised their strategic forces to their highest level of alert and were taking potshots at every American aircraft that came anywhere near their coasts.

And now . . .

Israel, in flames.

South Korea and Japan, under attack. The North Koreans had finally made their move.

Taiwan, being obliterated by a massive attack, hundreds of missiles dropping like rain all around the island country. The Chinese had also finally made their move.

It was happening way too fast, as if Satan himself had fired a starter pistol, triggering the mad dash to Armageddon.

And the country was being led by *two* people: the president, holed up in an underground command center in Kentucky, and the vice president, flying somewhere in Canadian airspace.

He would answer to Allison Perez.

But others never would. Their allegiance was to President Andrew Smith. Even in his command center, he could feel the lines of division subtly forming.

The looks on faces.

The tone of voices.

Speed in carrying out orders.

It was happening—his people were picking sides—and Grierson knew he wouldn't be able to stop it.

"Sir?"

"*What!*"

"It's General Metzger, sir . . . on button one."

He stared at the phone for a second, then picked it up.

"Grierson."

"Admiral Grierson. I'm going to say this once and only once. There is a coup in progress, led by the vice president. You are to disregard any further orders from Ms. Perez. You will answer only to your lawfully elected commander in chief."

"No, sir. I will not."

"You fucking, treasonous bastard. Consider yourself relieved."

"When the vice president relieves me, I'll gladly leave my post. You, *sir*, are the treasonous bastard. Release the president, or I'll track you down myself and—"

"I'm in a hardened bunker, Keaton, with the *president* of the United States. He's giving the orders, and I'll carry them out. When this is over, you'll face a firing squad."

"We'll see who ends up wearing the blindfold, Thad, you motherfucker. Grierson out."

CHAPTER 76

"But how can you—"

Sergeant Wilson answered Carolyn's question by tapping the side of his head with his finger. "I can hear you just fine. All of you. And I think you're making a mistake by keeping me in here."

The tone of voice was entirely different. He wasn't confused anymore. He was calm. And cool.

Suddenly, Carolyn was afraid. Very afraid. This wasn't Sergeant Randy Wilson. It looked and talked like him, but it was something else. Something *not* human.

"Don't be afraid, Ms. Ridenour. There's nothing to be afraid of . . . as long as you let me out of here."

"You're not going anywhere, Sergeant," Rammes said.

"Oh, is that right, General? Do you really think you can keep me in here?" The being looked around the containment chamber and laughed.

Garrett had had enough. "I think we've come to the conclusion that you're not Sergeant Wilson, and your furry little friend there isn't just a rat. So—"

"—so, the question is, just what the hell am I, correct? You're right . . . I'm not quite Sergeant Wilson anymore. So much for my little acting job, huh?"

"I'm not going to—"

"—stand there and play twenty questions with some sort of *thing*? Isn't that what you were going to say, Garrett? I'll answer your question. I'm a living, breathing, thinking being that has stepped one rung further up the evolutionary ladder . . . at least I think so. I haven't figured it out entirely yet, but I think it's safe to say that I'm part of a new master race. You like that term, don't you, Garrett?"

"Carolyn, we need to kill this thing right now. Any studies we need to do, we can do on its dead body."

"I can't die, Garrett. You can't kill me. Now, my little furry friend here, he's a little different. Not normal, but darn close. He's here for one purpose now. It was very thoughtful of you to leave him in here with me."

"I can kill you just fine, you son of a bitch. A bullet through your head should shut your goddamned mouth."

"Are you sure? Do you really think a little bullet would be enough? No. I don't think so. And do you know what else? All of those like me, the ones that have been romping around your country on a glorious feeding frenzy—you can't kill them, either." The being smiled. "You really should've let me out of this little box when I asked you the first time."

Suddenly, there was a change.

Carolyn gasped when she saw its eyes.

The thing's eyes had *changed*!

Silver.

Like mirrors.

Two metallic-looking orbs, each with a small black circle at the center, fixed their gaze on her.

They were shining from within, almost luminescent.

And then it smiled as the rat timidly crept closer.

The being knelt down and gently picked up the rodent, stroking its soaked fur, almost as if it were a pet.

Slowly, it walked to the Plexiglas wall and placed one palm against its surface. It slowly ran its hand across the smooth surface and smiled again. It looked at each of the people on the other side of the wall.

The eyes.

Shining.

Carolyn heard it speak.

Yooouuu . . . Caaarrrooolllyyynnn . . .

What? The mouth hadn't moved!

For a second, Carolyn was confused. Had she really heard something?

Riiidddeeennnooouuurrrr . . .

It turned its glance to the general.

Raaammmmmeessss . . .

To Garrett.

Hooofffmmmaaannn . . .

Not once did the mouth move.

She was hearing it speak . . . in her head!

She tried to turn to look at Garrett and the general, to see if they were hearing it as well, but her head was frozen in place.

She wanted to back away, but her legs wouldn't move.

The eyes.

She couldn't look away.

She couldn't *move*!

The being gently placed the rat on its shoulder and opened its mouth.

The rat crawled into the being's mouth, squirming, legs kicking and clawing as it struggled to get inside.

The being tossed its head back and bit the rat's body in two, its neck grotesquely bulging as the front portion of the rat's body slid down its throat.

Carolyn heard its voice in her mind again, as it placed both of its palms against the transparent wall.

Waaannnttt ouuuttt . . .

And then the Plexiglas wall began to crack.

CHAPTER 77

"Ma'am, the secretary of state is on line three."

Allison quickly answered. "Adam, what do you have?"

"Madame Vice President, the Canadians have closed their border. Their airspace is now off-limits to all US-originating traffic. And there've been some skirmishes."

"Firing?"

"Yes, ma'am. At border stations. Dead on both sides."

"What are they thinking?" It dawned on her that *she* was in Canadian airspace.

"The same thing is happening along the Mexican border—all the crossing stations are closed and under armed guard. Their troops are deploying along the entire border. Their airspace is closed, too."

In the matter of a few short hours following the president's nuclear strikes against the three infested cities, it seemed as if war had broken out across the globe.

The Israelis—nuked.

Taiwan—obliterated.

South Korea and Japan—choking under spreading clouds of North Korean chemical and biological weapons.

There were no more allies—America had no friends.

Even the British—at times America's only friend—had killed innocent Americans, blowing airliners out of the sky as they tried to land with empty tanks. Preventing any chance of the mutant horrors across the pond finding their way to England. Saving themselves, out of fear more than anything else.

She'd watched her country torn apart from within, by the horrible creatures. And she knew that if she didn't act quickly to get control of the situation, her country would be torn apart from without, as well.

CHAPTER 78

As the creature stepped through what used to be a thick Plexiglas containment wall—which it had shattered with a touch of its hands—the guards opened fire with their M-16s.

As the bullets slammed into the creature's body, its hold on Carolyn, Garrett, and General Rammes was released—they were able to move! All three of them dove for cover, Garrett protectively covering Carolyn's body with his own.

Through Garrett's arms, Carolyn watched in disbelief as the creature absorbed the rounds from the M-16s. It was just standing there, taking it! As each shell rocketed through its body and spun crazily into the back wall of the containment room, the wounds were closing! She could see holes opening and closing in its flesh with each impact—but that couldn't be! No living thing could absorb that kind of punishment and survive!

But right before her eyes, it was happening. The shots were slamming into it as the guards emptied their magazines—and it wasn't having any effect! The creature just stood there, its body jerking from the incredible amount of kinetic energy pounding into its torso, its arms, legs, neck, and head.

But it wouldn't die.

The wounds were healing almost instantaneously!

The firing abruptly ceased as the ammunition ran out.

The guards quickly grabbed fresh magazines from their belts and slammed them into—

But it was too late.

The creature raised its arms, and the soldiers suddenly froze in place. Unable to move, just as Carolyn, Garrett, and General Rammes had been.

The creature stepped toward the guards, its eyes shining like molten silver.

Carolyn felt it.

It swept through her thoughts like a burst of static in her brain.

The guards began to grimace, their eyes wide and fearful. Trickles of blood began to flow from their nostrils. Their ears. Their eyes.

She could feel the pressure in the room build, the wave of static increasing in intensity. Somehow, she knew the real force of the static was aimed at the guards—she was experiencing only the outer edges of the creature's assault. It was like standing ten feet away from a flamethrower and feeling the indirect heat from its blazing stream.

The humanoid beast was killing them. With its *mind*.

The guards began to scream. Terrible, agonized shrieking.

Carolyn watched as blood poured from the orifices in their heads, spilling into their biosuits. The veins just under their skin began to distend, visibly bulging with each terrified beat of their hearts. Their eyes rolled back into their sockets. One man bit through his tongue.

Through the speakers in her suit, she heard their skulls cracking.

And then, as if their heads could no longer stand the pressure from within, their skulls exploded.

Their bodies dropped to the floor.

The static was gone.

The creature slowly turned toward her.

Caaarrrooolllyyynnn . . .

General Rammes pushed the button.

CHAPTER 79

The call had come in right on schedule.

"President Vladimirov, this is General Thad Metzger."

"I want to speak to your president."

"The president is unavailable at the moment, sir. He was slightly injured during an attack on *Air Force One* and is in the infirmary getting stitches for a wound on his arm."

About ten feet from where Metzger was standing, Andrew was on the floor of the bunker's command center, eyes wide open, nobody home. Jessie was next to him, whispering into his ear.

"Who is in control, General? Is it President Smith, or Vice President Perez?"

"There has been no change in this nation's leadership, Mr. President. Andrew Smith remains the president of the United States. Ms. Perez is the leader of a failed coup attempt and she'll be—"

"Was the attack on the cities successful, General? Were you able to stop the creatures from spreading?"

"Yes, sir. The creatures in those three cities have been destroyed."

"And the others? What is the plan for them, General? Are you going to continue to drop nuclear bombs across your country to destroy them as well?"

"If that's what has to be done to keep the creatures from spreading, then yes. The president hasn't made that decision yet."

"I would like to hear it from him, General. I wish to speak to him now."

Jessie had somehow gotten through to Andrew Smith. He was standing, and she helped him walk to the secure hotline.

"Stand by, President Vladimirov. The president has returned."

Metzger muted the connection.

"Is he good to go?"

"It's as far as I can take him. It has to be quick," Jessie said. "Andrew, you need to speak to the Russian president. You need to tell him his forces' alert status is risking nuclear war. Do you understand, Andrew?"

"Yes. I understand."

Metzger handed Andrew the hotline.

"President Vladimirov, this is Andrew Smith. It's good to hear from you again."

"Mr. President, this is a very dangerous time we find ourselves in, is it not?"

"Yes, it is, Anatoly. A dangerous time." He paused, unsure of what he was supposed to say next.

Metzger quickly muted the connection, and fixed his smallish eyes on Jessie.

"Andrew," Jessie said, "you need to tell him to drop his alert levels or we'll respond in kind."

Andrew slowly nodded his understanding, and Jessie motioned at Metzger to restore the audio.

"We know your forces have entered a heightened state of alert, Anatoly. There's no need for you to—"

"You have dropped nuclear bombs on your own country. Your vice president tried to countermand your orders, did she not? This tells me that the situation in your country is getting out of control."

"No, it's not out of control." He paused again, obviously struggling with his thoughts. Metzger reached for the mute button, but Andrew continued. "She . . . she tried to stop the attack because she didn't think it was the correct course of action."

"I have raised our alert levels as a precaution, Mr. President. The use of nuclear weapons is not a situation Russia takes lightly. Especially when a nuclear-armed country like the United States has a crisis of leadership. You must assure us you are in control of your military forces."

"There is no crisis of leadership, President Vladimirov. I am in charge. The armed forces answer to me."

"That does not seem to be the case, Mr. President."

Jessie muted the connection. "Andrew, he's trying to trick you! Don't you see! You can't show any weakness, not now!"

"Jessie . . . I don't know what to—"

She slapped him. Twice. "Andrew, you will tell President Vladimirov that unless he lowers his alert levels immediately, we'll be forced to raise ours. Tell him, Andrew. Now." She unmuted the call. She noticed his eyes were changing . . . the confusion draining away.

"President Vladimirov. I will be forced to raise our alert levels, unless you lower yours. You are taking us to the brink of a conflict neither country can afford."

"It is not I who is taking us to the brink, Mr. President. You understand that Russia will not allow the creatures in your country to pass beyond your borders."

"What are you implying?"

"You know exactly what I mean, Mr. President. Good luck to you."

The connection went dead.

Jessie gently took the receiver from Andrew's hand. "That was a fine job, Andrew. You did what you had to do."

Andrew said nothing, his gaze fixed at the phone receiver. Jessie watched a scowl form on his face.

"I'll send the order," General Metzger said. "We'll put our forces at DEFCON 1."

They were both shocked to hear Andrew Smith's next words.

"No, General." He gripped the side of the desk and stood. "You will not."

Metzger quickly glanced at Jessie. She looked astounded at what she'd heard.

"Andrew, the general must raise our alert level. The Russians are—"

"It's over, Jessie." Andrew took a step away from both of them. Though he was unsteady on his feet, his eyes were clear now. Piercing.

She walked toward him. "Andrew, please, you know you want to listen to—"

"Get away from me. Get the *fuck* away from me. General Metzger, you will get on the horn to the vice president and—"

He swiftly pulled his sidearm. "No, Mr. President. I will not. You're done giving orders here."

Jessie knew Andrew Smith had been the strongest man she'd ever encountered. After all she'd done to him, he'd *still* been able to fight his way back to the surface. For a moment, he'd been himself again.

His last moment.

The report was unnaturally loud in the small, confined space.

General Metzger holstered his sidearm and picked up the direct line to the bunker's communications center. "This is General Metzger. All forces are to assume DEFCON 1. By order of the president of the United States."

She was sad, in a way.

But it didn't matter.

They wouldn't need him anymore.

Everything was in motion now.

And there was no stopping it.

Alone in a locked command bunker, deep below the fields of Kentucky, Jessie Hruska and Thad Metzger knew their purposes in life had been fulfilled.

After the fires burned out, the dreams of Marx and Lenin could once again be realized.

A utopia on earth.

CHAPTER 80

"Lincoln, this is Grant. I have movement to my front. Over."

Peering through his powerful night vision scope, the Army sniper could see forms emerging from the ground two hundred meters away.

Before the things had gone to ground the night before, he'd been positioned on a hill above the area, picking them off with his M107 long-range sniper rifle—a .50-caliber monster that could put a round through a truck's engine block from over a mile away.

It had worked just as well on the creatures, at a much closer range.

"Lincoln copies. All forces prepare to engage," came the reply over the radio net. Through his headphones, he could hear the muffled thunder of jet aircraft flying overhead in the darkening twilight sky, preparing for their attack runs.

They had blasted the area all day with high-explosive bombs, rockets, and artillery, trying to blow as many of the casings apart as they could before sundown.

The things had gone to ground, but they hadn't gone deep.

Not this time.

They'd killed hundreds of them.

Maybe thousands.

But they were emerging again, and if what the intelligence officer had said was true, there would be two of them for every single casing they'd failed to destroy.

There weren't going to be *as many* of them, but there would still be way too many.

Too many to stop.

But they—*he*—had to try.

His orders this night—as they had been the previous night—were to go after the humanoid creatures, the ones standing on two legs.

It didn't bother him to think the things had once been people.

He'd killed people before, lined them up in his sights and sent a half-inch shell through their skulls at incredible distances.

No sweat.

It was his job.

He'd never enjoyed it, but it was what he'd been trained to do, and he was good at it.

But these things sure as hell weren't people anymore, and he did enjoy killing them. One after the other, after the other, after the other. Ten rounds at a time from his semiauto rifle. Blowing their heads apart as rapidly as he could before having to reload and move back as they advanced.

He drew a bead on one of the glowing green forms . . . and hesitated.

Something was different.

The thing was standing, and around its feet scurried smaller creatures. Both types much smaller than he'd witnessed the night before.

It looks like a person, he thought. "Lincoln, this is Grant. Confirm I have no friendlies to my front. Over?"

"Stand by, Grant."

That's it? Just stand by? Come on, guys . . .

He saw more of the humanoid forms stand up. They were nothing like the long-legged beasts he'd seen the night before. Nothing at all.

It looked like a crowd of people standing in a group.

Milling around.

But he'd seen them emerge, right?

He'd seen them rise up out of the ground, right where the casings had been.

He was *sure* of it.

But what could explain what he was seeing now?

Those are people, he thought. *And the smaller creatures . . . Rats? They're the same size as a normal rat! What the hell is going on?*

He heard a call over the radio net: "This is Lincoln. All forces hold fire. I repeat, hold fire."

A trigger had already been pulled. He watched one of the being's heads violently snap back as another overly eager sniper hit his target. The body dropped to the ground.

The call over the net was immediate. "Hold fire! I repeat, hold your fire!"

The beings closest to the body quickly crouched and huddled together, and then began to . . . wave their arms?

"Jesus Christ! Those are people!" He ripped off his helmet, and heard a sound that chilled him.

Screaming.

Even from two hundred yards away, he could hear it.

It was unmistakable. The sound was human!

"Don't shoot! Please, don't shoot!"

He never saw the dead person stand back up. There was nothing wrong with its head.

If he'd seen it, he'd never have walked toward them.

None of them would have.

But they did.

Lured by the bait. And led to the slaughter.

In a smoldering, bomb-cratered field in the middle of America's heartland, the final battle had begun.

CHAPTER 81

The Navy commander came into her cabin, interrupting the call from the secretary of state. "Ma'am . . . it's the Russian president. He wishes to speak with you immediately. Line one. Translators are on line and ready."

She punched the button.

"Mr. President. This is Allison Perez."

There was a delay as the translator spoke her words in Russian. The Russian leader didn't let him finish.

"There will be no need for a translator. This is President Vladimirov. I will speak English."

"*Spasibo*, sir. What can—"

"There is no time for pleasantries. I will be direct. We have been monitoring your communications. We know you attempted to destroy the bombers President Smith sent to drop nuclear bombs on three of your own cities—an attempt which sadly failed. Are you able to control the rest of your nuclear forces?"

They're nervous. Just as she would be if Russia had nuked some of their own cities. She had to defuse this situation fast. "I am in control of our nuclear forces, Mr. President. Orders have been received—and acknowledged—by all senior commanders. The president cannot, nor will he be allowed to, issue any orders to our nuclear forces. There is no need for you or your country to—"

"I have raised our alert status, as I'm sure you know."

"I am aware of it. I would have done the same. A reasonable precaution on your part, and I understand it." There was something about his voice. She'd met the man on a number of occasions, talked to him at length. But now, he sounded different. "But, I must state in the strongest terms that—"

"You must also know that the world around our two countries is suddenly at war."

"Yes . . . we know what's happening." It suddenly dawned on her. His voice—it sounded like Andrew's voice had sounded!

"Your president is located in your underground command center outside of Louisville, Kentucky, yes?"

It didn't surprise her that the Russians knew about the place. "Yes, that is correct."

"And this command center is designed to withstand a nuclear exchange, yes?"

This isn't going well. "It's a hardened facility. Yes."

"We have monitored communications originating from that bunker, Ms. Perez. Not all of your forces are obeying your orders."

"That is incorrect, sir. The military forces of the United States will answer to me, and me alone, until we are able to rescue the president from—"

"Are you sure he wants to be rescued, Madame Vice President?"

"I don't understand, Mr. President."

"I have spoken to him. He told me he would raise your alert levels if Russia did not lower hers. He, Madame Vice President, believes he is in control of your nuclear forces. I ask you now, who am I to believe?"

"I will state again, Anatoly, the armed forces of the United States will answer to me. My orders, not Andrew Smith's." She paused as she heard a commotion in the background. Her Russian was rusty, but she'd heard enough to know it wasn't good.

"Madame Vice President, if this is so, why have your forces just been ordered to assume DEFCON 1?"

Before she could utter a response, she was thrown from her chair, landing in a heap on the floor as the giant E-4 banked incredibly steeply, its engines screaming. A deafening explosion threw her against the opposite wall, and everything went black.

Around her, the E-4 began to disintegrate as she—and it—fell from the sky.

•   •   •

Two Royal Canadian Air Force CF-18 Hornets circled the flaming debris as it fell to the ground below.

"Unidentified aircraft destroyed. Returning to base . . ."

CHAPTER 82

Admiral Grierson walked from the command center to his office. He had some calls to make. To his wife. And his children. He'd encouraged his people to do the same.

He hoped he'd have enough time to talk to all of them.

In the command center, alarms were blaring.

Computerized voices were announcing event times, threat areas, decision times.

The large status boards were alive with color and motion as the data pumped into the center.

Data from satellites.

Data from radar installations.

Data showing that a massive Russian ballistic missile attack had been launched against the United States of America.

It had finally happened.

His wife answered the phone.

"Honey . . . it's me," he said.

CHAPTER 83

The quick-hardening foam had been developed as a nonlethal weapon for use in riot situations, a form of crowd control, but had quickly been adapted for other uses.

The Vanguard complex employed an enhanced form of the foam as a security measure—if a person was accidentally infected and tried to leave the facility, the foam could be sprayed from jets in the ceiling, completely encasing the person in a thick layer of the substance, instantly rendering them immobile. It was formulated to harden in a matter of seconds. As hard as concrete.

The foam in the Vanguard complex was *not* nonlethal. It was designed to seal a problem away from the outside world, be it a virus, a person, or in this case, a mutated creature.

General Rammes had pressed the emergency button at the last possible moment, trapping the creature in the clean room. Saving their lives.

They'd made it topside right before the last portal automatically slammed shut. The complex would remain in lockdown indefinitely, opened only after the computers determined there was no threat from what was trapped inside.

Garrett and Carolyn stood silently in the night air, taking deep breaths, just glad to be alive.

Carolyn looked up at the stars.

Oddly, there were quite a few falling stars this night.

The few quickly became hundreds.

As the sky to the east of them began to glow, flashing again and again and again with an unnatural brilliance, they knew.

Nothing would ever be the same again.

EPILOGUE

It had been twenty years since the war.

The northern hemisphere of the planet was a desolate, uninhabitable place. Where once-great cities had stood, nothing but twisted, radioactive debris remained. Once-fertile farmland was now a sandy, charred expanse, choked of all life for thousands of years to come.

All the great nations of the Prior Time had passed into history. To the south, however, other great cities were taking their place. In some cases, built by hand. Brick by brick by brick.

The survivors were constructing a new world.

And it looked nothing like it had before.

Peace had settled over the southern hemisphere. National boundaries, some that had lasted for centuries, faded away. Monetary concerns were no more. Starvation, poverty, disease—all had passed into the pages of the history books.

This was the *New* Time.

The survivors had stepped from the fires of a nuclear holocaust and were taking their first steps down the road toward a true utopian existence.

But paradise, it was not.

When the bombs were detonating all those years ago, the animals had scattered. Many had escaped to the four corners of the inhabitable world, found places to hide, and remained there to this day.

They'd been hunted relentlessly, slaughtered by the thousands—by the *millions*—but the pestilence they represented had not yet been scrubbed from the face of the earth.

They'd been breeding, growing in number, plotting in their hiding places.

Striking from the shadows.

And then retreating, to fight another day.

They were smart, cunning. Incredibly resourceful.

They'd learned the secret—the Achilles' heel. And they'd used that knowledge to kill many of his fellow survivors.

He knew there would never be a true peace, not until each and every one of the animals had been found and destroyed. Every last one of them.

But today, that wasn't his concern.

Today was a time for the small one to explore. To learn.

The sky was a brilliant blue dome stretching from horizon to horizon. The peaks of the Andes Mountains—in what had once been called Argentina—stretched toward the sky, scraping the bottoms of the clouds.

"Can we go into the forest?"

They were at the foot of the Andes, on the edge of a huge old-growth forest.

It was safe here.

The animals had been cleared from this area years ago.

They could relax and enjoy the scenery, without having to be on guard.

It was okay.

"Yes. We can go."

"Do you think we'll find some bones? If we do, I want to keep them!"

"If we find some, you can keep a *couple* of them, but no more." The small ones liked to keep the bones as trophies, reminders of a great victory.

The forests here were thick with the remains of the animals. Left to rot where they'd died. Or to be devoured by others of their kind.

He was sure they'd find some. Many had been killed here.

As they walked through the forest, the fallen twigs crunching under their feet, the small one asked, "Tell me again. Tell me about the war."

"It was a long time ago, little one. Far away from here. The beasts fought us, tearing at us, ripping at us, but they couldn't win. They couldn't kill us all."

"Because we were superior, right?"

"That's right. We were—and still are—superior to them."

His senses screamed an alarm. They were being watched.

From the right. From the left. In front. And behind.

Surrounded!

Together, they crouched low to the ground and raised their arms, feeling outward, trying to find them, to hurt them. To kill them.

But it wasn't working.

The animals stepped from the trees. Advancing. Their boldness shocked him—and then, he could see why they'd been able to approach undetected.

They wore the shields. The damned helmets! Crafted from the one substance he couldn't penetrate, the metal that rendered him, and the little one, helpless.

The first dart slid through the small one's skull, piercing the organ that gave him his strength. He dropped to the ground, paralyzed. Still alive, but unable to move.

He watched one of the animals raise its blowgun. Its dart entered his skull right above his left eye, and pierced the organ in the center of his brain—the Achilles' heel of his kind.

As he lay immobile on the forest floor, he could hear them coming for him. He watched the tuft of feathers tied to the end of the long, thin dart wave in the breeze. Above it, he saw the faces of the animals standing over him.

He could do nothing as one of the animals placed the killing herb into his mouth. And into the mouth of the little one.

The effects were immediate.

His vision began to blur.

He felt the little one slip away, their connection abruptly severed by his death.

And then, darkness.

• • •

They were dead.

The animals hacked at the bodies, tore them limb from limb.

They hung the pieces from branches.

It was a warning to any others who dared venture into this forest. This was *their* land now. It would never be taken from them again.

Two of the animals stood on a rock outcropping, looking below at the carnage they'd left in the trees.

Garrett removed his helmet, the hammered lead heavy in his hand.

Carolyn removed hers, as well.

They slipped back into the forest, disappearing like ghosts into the shadows.

They would emerge again, when the time was right.

To kill. And kill again. Until the creatures ruled no more.

Today, their tribe had sent a message.

The war was not over. It was only beginning.

And humanity—what was left of it—was on the prowl.

ACKNOWLEDGMENTS

So . . . who does a writer thank when it comes to producing a novel? As Goose said in *Top Gun*, the list is long and distinguished, but I'll attempt to keep it brief.

First and foremost, many thanks to my wife, Nessa, without whom I'd have surely ended up living in a van down by the river. She's my common sense, my gut check, my swift kick, my most honest critic and most fervent supporter, and the mother of our three kiddos—two beautiful daughters and an amazing son, whose hearts are all in the right place because she made sure of it. Most of all, though, she's been my candle in the window since 1984 . . . and it's never dimmed.

To my mom, Jackie, who I'll always remember sitting in front of an electric Royal in her cluttered writing room, clacking away at the keys and stamping her unique wisdom down on heavy bond paper. Every time I see a yellow rose or stand in a silent swirl of snowflakes on a quiet February night, I'll know you're near.

To my dad, Lieutenant Colonel James J. Grossart, USAF, for every single cherished moment. I wish there'd been more time.

To Bruce Allen, my creative writing teacher at Northglenn High, who was one of the first to open my eyes to the power and joy of the written word. I hope you get to read this and understand the impact you had.

To the team at 47North, what can I say? You picked *The Gemini Effect* over so many others as the winner of the 2014 Amazon Breakthrough Novel Award for Science Fiction/Fantasy/Horror, and for that I'm eternally grateful. I count myself fortunate as well to have had my book land in the expert hands of Jason Kirk, my editor, who helped craft my self-published novel into what it is today. He taught me the meaning of "split infinitive" (apparently, it's not some kind of spicy soup . . . who'da thunk it?), and I taught him the word *Missileer*. Thank you for your patience, Jason. To Ben Grossblatt, my copyeditor, who ensured each comma was in its proper place and called out every single instance where my "words by phonics" spelling style made an appearance, I say thank you, and I hope I didn't make your eyes bleed too badly. Any guy with "Gross" in his last name is okay by me! To Scott Barrie of Cyanotype Book Architects, thank you for producing a cover that captures the story so well; the blending of the biohazard symbol, the DNA helix, and the Gemini symbol is simply amazing.

Finally, I want to thank you, my reader. May this novel be the start of a long and enjoyable relationship. You bring the popcorn, and I'll bring the pages.

Chuck Grossart
Bellevue, Nebraska
March 1, 2015

ABOUT THE AUTHOR

2013 Ashley Crawford

Chuck Grossart lives in Bellevue, Nebraska, with his wife, kids, and usually too many dogs.